NETWORK
OF
EVIL

BILL KITSON

Joffe Books, London
www.joffebooks.com

First published in Great Britain in 2025

© Bill Kitson 2025

Cover art by Nick Castle

ISBN: 978-1-80573-172-6

Network of Evil

ALSO BY BILL KITSON

To my darling Val,

my rock and inspiration

PROLOGUE

The room was almost silent, the lighting subdued. The only sound was the regular gentle hiss of the ventilator as it performed the breathing function on behalf of the patient. A nurse was seated alongside a bank of electronic equipment, her sole purpose being the regular monitoring and recording of their displays.

Between those tasks, she whiled away her time by reading. This was not from choice. Her preference would have been to watch the state-of-the-art television set on the wall opposite her chair, but that was strictly forbidden.

The patient's next of kin had placed an embargo on all extraneous sounds that could possibly cause distress to their loved one, even though the patient was in a comatose state. Any protest the nurse might have considered making against this ban went unsaid, her objections overruled by the amount of money she was being paid for a task she regarded as a sinecure.

The arrangement had been going on for over two months and the extra salary she had received was already sufficient for her to reduce the mortgage on her house. Although she could not see this job being long-term, the benefits outweighed any doubts about the future. She had just completed the task of

1

entering a new set of statistics on the patient's chart when the door opened.

The man who entered the room looked at the nurse, who anticipated the inevitable question by telling him, 'Still no change, I'm afraid.' In fact, the longer this situation dragged on, the more 'no change' represented bad news rather than good. The nurse, her colleagues, and the renowned specialist who had been brought in specifically to treat this patient were all convinced that there could be only one possible outcome — and that would not be a happy one. In fact, but for the patient's next of kin having the resources to fund private care, the issue would already have been resolved, and life support would have been withdrawn long ago at the hospital.

The steps taken to maintain the patient's status quo had already reached their limit. In addition to the ventilator, the patient was connected to a battery of devices whose sole purpose was to support the subject's life force by substituting their mechanical functions for the natural ones.

All this was to combat what the specialists saw as inevitable. The final act would be to turn off the machines. The resulting multi-organ failure would in turn cause the patient to stop breathing, triggering the apnoea alarm which would signal the end.

Following the routine that had been established on the day the patient had been moved to the family home, the nurse initialled the duty roster to signify her absence from the room. Before leaving, she paused in the doorway and glanced back. The visitor was already sitting, as always, alongside the comatose patient.

As the man took the hand of the child and spoke quiet, comforting platitudes, the nurse, a hardened professional, felt a lump in her throat and tears pricking at the corners of her eyes. The image she had just witnessed, the dreadful tragedy that had brought patient and parent to this room, would remain with the nurse for a long, long time.

Even more heart-wrenching was the knowledge that the child's mother was in a private room at the local hospital.

Although the outcome for her was not without a degree of hope, the catastrophic injuries she had suffered would be life-changing — and even that gloomy diagnosis was the best-case scenario.

Despite the nurse's in-depth familiarity with the case, there was no way she could ever have guessed the terrible consequences that would follow as retaliation and revenge were sought.

When the inevitable happened six weeks later, the child's death was recorded in the local press, and reported on regional radio and television, but events on the world stage swiftly pushed the tragedy to one side. Not for those close to the victim, however. For them, it was merely another instalment in the distress that would last a lifetime. That distress could not be diluted, even by the passage of days, months or years, but as the family of the deceased mourned their loss, they vowed that the agony they were suffering would one day be shared by the person who had caused it, and that pain would be extended to others of a similar perverted nature.

* * *

Philip's life had been changed forever. The events had been traumatic, especially for the adults concerned, but to him they had become a constant horror that dogged his every waking moment and haunted his dreams, turning them into nightmares.

At the funeral, he'd stood alongside his father, trying to remain calm. He remembered the pain as he'd bitten his lip to disguise his distress from the many onlookers.

The place had been crowded. Friends of his parents, neighbours, police officers, reporters and general nosey parkers, all there to witness the last rites. Philip had ignored them all, his attention fixed firmly on that box. The box that contained the body of his sister.

Although his parents had tried to shield him by not revealing what had been done to her, his mates were less protective, revelling in telling him every gory detail.

After the person responsible was arrested, he vowed that one day he would seek vengeance for her ordeal. One day, somehow, somewhere, he would find John Penney and punish him.

Until then, Philip would continue to be tormented.

CHAPTER ONE

The owner of Ramsdale Holiday Village was staring ruefully at the figures compiled by his wife, who acted as his secretary, accounts clerk, receptionist and office cleaner. It was the end of the season and he'd known that the year's trading had been poor, but he hadn't realized quite how bad it was. The poor weather over the summer months, allied to the cheap overseas holiday trips advertised during every programme break on TV, had dramatically reduced the number of people utilizing their luxury lodges.

The choice between risking the British climate to stay in the Yorkshire countryside, or to chance sunstroke on one of the Spanish Costas, was a no-brainer for many people.

He was distracted from his gloomy scrutiny by the sound of the phone on the reception desk. He hastened to answer, keen to see if this might be a potential booking for next season. Even a weekend stopover would be welcome as things were.

'Good evening, are you the park owner?' the caller asked.

'I am. How can I help?'

'I wanted to ask if it would be possible to rent a lodge. I'm in need of one with disabled facilities such as you advertise on your website. My wife is restricted to a wheelchair.

The problem I've been up against is finding somewhere quiet and peaceful. And comfortable, of course. Somewhere she can stay and work over a long period of time. She's an author, you see, which is why she needs the peace and quiet, so she can concentrate.'

'How long are you thinking?'

'Six months, a year perhaps, it all depends on how the plot comes together, or how much of what she's written ends up in the shredder.'

'I'm sorry, there's a problem with that, I'm afraid. There are limitations. The maximum length of stay is set at twenty-eight days. That's not just here, it's a general rule set down by the local authority. And we're only open from March to the end of September. We're already closed for the winter. The rules are to prevent us taking permanent tenants.'

As he was speaking, he remembered the figures he'd just been reading and cursed silently. A long-term let would have been ideal, but for what he considered to be no more than pettifogging regulations. He was surprised when the prospective occupant asked, 'I take it you've never heard of the Ways and Means Act?'

The owner was baffled, but listened carefully as the man explained. 'It's the method used to achieve your objective, by surmounting seemingly impossible obstructions.'

'Sorry?'

'OK, here's another thought for you. Say, for example, Mr and Mrs Smith rent one of your delightful lodges for a month, having paid cash in advance. At the end of that period, you then lease the same lodge to Mr and Mrs Jones, who also pay cash in advance for their month's stay. Then, when it's their turn to move on, lo and behold, Mr and Mrs Brown, who are also cash customers, arrive and move into the same lodge. On the face of it, no regulations have been broken, and you have received three months' rental, all paid in cash. Who, apart from you, would know that Mr and Mrs Brown, alias Smith and Jones, are one and the same people? I'm sure there would be many others willing to take a monthly lease. And who knows? It could even last for a year. If you have a secluded lodge, you would hardly know they were there — except when it was rent day, of course.'

Adhering strictly to regulations warred with the parlous state of the park's finances — in the end it was no contest. 'If you'd like to call and check out the facilities we offer, I'm sure we could manage to come to some arrangement.'

'I'll see you tomorrow.'

'And your name, sir?'

'Berry, Mr Berry.'

* * *

The following morning, the site owner was showing Mr Berry the facilities, and the deal was done. The occupancy would commence the beginning of December.

'My wife will need her computer, so I'll bring that the day before we move in and get it set up for her. Along with the shredder,' he joked. 'We won't need the lodge servicing, I can see to all that. My wife doesn't like to be disturbed when she's working.'

'Of course.' The owner was only too happy to assist where he could. 'And may I ask for a little discretion on your part? Should anyone, such as staff members, enquire as to why you're on-site once the season starts, tell them you're family, or some such line. Make some excuse. Say our home can't accommodate your wife.'

'Good point. And I don't think we need a formal agreement, do we?' the guest asked as he took his wallet from his pocket.

'Not specifically. This is just an entry to record a booking for next season, you understand?' We wouldn't want to double-book the lodge. What name should I say? I assume it isn't Brown, Smith or Jones.'

He smiled at his little joke as the man told him, 'Use my wife's name, Mary. Mary Berry.'

He looked up, startled, and saw the man laughing.

'No, not that Mary Berry. She's a pretty good cook, but I certainly wouldn't put her in that category. She's also about forty years younger.'

'Shall I assume you'd like me to reserve the lodge for the summer season?'

'Yes, please do. Of course, should she finish her writing sooner, I will recompense you for any loss incurred.'

Carrying the key to the Bramhope, the two-bedroom luxury lodge at the furthest, quietest area of the park, and a key for the site gate, the visitor departed.

The owner returned to his office. He opened the safe and placed three thousand, six hundred pounds inside, reflecting that this was probably the biggest cash payment that had been lodged in there for a long time, if not ever. He thought the gentleman looked vaguely familiar, but couldn't recall. Besides, he thought, looking at the cash, who cares?

An hour later, the new tenant of Bramhope Lodge reported his successful negotiation. In reply, his partner told him, 'And now the work starts.'

* * *

The January weather had deteriorated quickly over the previous twenty-four hours. A strong north-easterly wind was bringing rain sweeping across the most remote area of woodland near the top of Stark Ghyll, the highest peak in the region. The forecast was for snow. There was only one vehicle in the parking area, and as the man walked towards his car, he hardly noticed the weather, or the rain that was driving almost horizontally. The event that had just occurred brought a sense of great satisfaction. But this was merely a beginning. Hopefully, it would be the first of many.

It had taken over a week to achieve the objective. It had been meticulously planned, a necessary precaution.

First, the victim's abduction — that was the easy bit. As the target was getting into his car in the multi-storey car park, the administration of a sedative via a needle in his neck had rendered him unconscious. Pushing him across to the passenger seat had been a little trickier.

Once that was done, the attention to detail was evident as the kidnapper fastened a seat belt round him. Being stopped by an eagle-eyed traffic cop for failing to obey a minor traffic regulation would have led to some unanswerable questions. Having secured the victim, he climbed into the victim's car and drove away.

That was technically vehicle theft, but the crime paled into insignificance compared to the offence that was about to be committed.

The car was driven to the place selected for the endgame. If anyone was observing the tableau, it would appear a kind person was assisting a friend who had overindulged at some local watering hole. In effect, the victim was being led to an isolated area where he would be hanged from a tree. Before that happened, there remained only the final questions.

Leading the barely conscious man to the site, a small wooded area close to the summit, he asked, 'Do you know what day it is?'

The prisoner shook his head, but when his companion told him the day and the month he realized their significance. Any doubt that remained ended with the follow-up question. 'And do you know where you are? Take a good look round, listen carefully and you'll know.'

He was just able to make out the sound of running water above the near gale-force wind. As he recognized the location, he wondered how his abductor had become aware of its importance. He also feared that he was about to die.

'Who are you?' the captive gasped, as a noose was placed around his neck.

'I'm the person who holds your life in their hands.' By way of explanation, there was a sharp tug on the rope. 'Now, you're going to answer some questions. You have two choices. You can tell me what I want to know or I will hang you — right now!'

The prisoner nodded vigorously. 'What do you want to know?'

'You will tell me who your contact is, and how I find him.'

Having answered more questions, the target was sure he had given as much information as he could. He had done as he was asked. All he needed now was to be released.

'I don't know anything more. Can you let me go now?'

The man, who had been leaning, arms folded, against a tree while he asked the questions, had all he needed and walked towards his prisoner.

The terrified man shuffled backwards, as far as he could. He saw the look of malevolence in his captor's eyes.

'Yes,' he was told, 'I'm going to let you go — to hell!'

The fear escalated to terror when the kidnapper whispered in his ear, 'This is for Emily.'

Seconds later, the prisoner jerked as a pull on the rope lifted his feet off the ground by a few inches. His hands were tied, his legs flailing as he tried to fight the inevitable. He let out a long, piercing scream before the killer anchored the rope around an adjacent tree.

The killer stared at the victim, struggling before him, and delivered a fitting epitaph. The words 'Rot in Hell, scumbag' were accompanied by a vicious kick to the dying man's testicles. The murderer added, 'Don't worry, you're only the first. We've several more of your kind to deal with now — thanks to you.'

The thought of the murders they were planning to commit made the killer smile. Strolling away from the secluded crime scene without a backward glance at the man who had just been left to die reflected the murderer's confidence that it could be months before the remains were found — if ever. But that was not in line with the plan. If the corpse was not discovered soon, he might have to force the issue. Most killers abhor the thought of their deeds becoming known. In this case, the opposite was both necessary and desirable.

Having reached the victim's car and driven to the main road, there remained only the task of returning the vehicle to the car park without leaving any trace of the crime committed. Only then could the text message, that read simply '*One down, info received, your turn now*', be sent.

CHAPTER TWO

A week later, the police received an anonymous phone call from, as they later discovered, a pay-as-you go mobile. The message was simple, the meaning horrific. 'If you send officers to the woods on Stark Ghyll, they'll find a man hanging from a tree. He's dead, and in hell where he belongs.'

Uniform were summoned. It took some time before they located the scene. The victim had obviously been there a considerable length of time, judging by the amount of predation. This was clearly a job for CID. The phrase 'passing the buck' never crossed their minds, even as they waited for Detective Inspector Mike Nash, along with his second in command, Detective Sergeant Clara Mironova, to respond.

They were the only detectives available. Viv Pearce, the tall Antiguan detective constable, was giving evidence in court. DC Adil Hassan, recently transferred from Manchester to be nearer family, was on holiday and DC Lisa Andrews was on maternity leave.

Nash had only recently returned from France. On this occasion, the visit was not a holiday. His fifteen-year-old son Daniel owned the family home which had belonged to his late mother, Monique. They visited as often as time allowed to see his elderly Aunt Mirabelle, who acted as caretaker.

Following his mother's death, she had raised Daniel up to the age of six before she brought him to England to meet and live with the father who'd had no knowledge of him.

Sadly, Tante Mirabelle, as Daniel called her, had succumbed to old age, and Nash had taken the family to her funeral. Whilst in France he had employed a notary, to sort out both hers and Daniel's affairs.

Now, as he drove towards the towering peak of Stark Ghyll, Nash told Clara, 'It seems like every time I return from leave there's a body found.'

'I shouldn't worry about that, Mike,' Clara replied. 'There are plenty of such incidents even when you haven't been away.' Little did they know how prophetic her words would be.

They arrived at the parking area and set off to find the uniformed officers.

They looked at the body, keeping their distance for fear of contaminating the scene. Then they checked the surrounding area, but their inspection yielded little of value.

'About the only point of interest from all that,' Nash told her as he called a halt to proceedings, 'is that we can't see any indication of other people having visited this area. That surprises me a little, because the view from up here is spectacular. However, I suppose it explains how the body has remained undiscovered.'

'Perhaps that's because it's so damn cold up here.' She shivered and pushed her hands deeper into her pockets.

* * *

'I should have known you were back, the minute I got the call,' Professor Ramirez greeted Nash. The pathologist and his assistants had abandoned the mortuary vans in favour of two Land Rovers, borrowed, as was plain from their logos, from the local mountain rescue service. 'Nobody else would drag me out to the back of beyond within hours of their return to examine a body in a wilderness.'

'It's good to see you too, Professor,' Nash retorted, adding with a straight face, 'I didn't realize you'd missed me so much. Your customer awaits you in that clearing.'

As Nash was speaking, two further vehicles pulled up, each bearing the CSI logo. Nash walked across to seek out their leader. 'I think about all you can do here is a search. We've had a preliminary look, can't see anything other than the rope.'

They turned the scene over to the scientific team and retraced their tracks towards the main road. As they were nearing the Helmsdale turning, Nash told Clara, 'We need to find out who owns the land where the body was found. They might be able to cast light on why someone was in so remote a spot, and why they were murdered.'

'It sounds a bit of a long shot, Mike. I believe it belongs to the National Parks.'

'Fair enough.'

'Do you want me to attend the post-mortem?'

Nash glanced sideways, taken aback by Clara's offer. 'Why the sudden rush to volunteer?'

'I thought you might want to ease your way back into things after your, erm, time off, that's all.'

'I'll be fine, don't worry. I need to settle back into my old routine. Teal has to be walked first thing and I'll be out of the house early anyway. Alondra's starting work on a new canvas and warned me to keep my distance. She says Lucy is less of a distraction when she's painting than I am.'

'How's Daniel coping? He and his aunt were very close.'

'I found him staring into space a few times while we were away, and Alondra assures me he's shed a few tears. But he seemed to accept everything. Mirabelle had been like a mother to him, but had warned Daniel she wouldn't be around forever. It will be half-term in a few weeks, and for the first time in years I won't have to take him to France. He's back at school.'

Clara looked surprised.

'Exam season is looming and he wants to do well.'

* * *

The only useful pieces of information to come from the post-mortem, as Nash told Clara and the other team members late the following morning, were that the victim was male, and believed by the pathologist to be in his thirties or forties. He had been hanging for approximately a week and also had traces of strong sedatives in his blood.

'Suicide then,' Viv Pearce stated. 'An addict. Just need an ID and case closed.'

'Really? You do surprise me, Viv. And how many suicides do you know of where the person managed to kill themselves with their hands tied behind their back and the rope secured to a tree?'

'Sorry, Mike, I haven't looked at the scene photos.'

'Obviously.' Nash continued, 'The professor is checking fingerprints and, failing that, will try DNA. Of course, that would only be useful if he or a family member happens to be recorded in our database. So we have to keep our fingers crossed that, if necessary, he's part of a big criminal clan.'

Later that day, the fingerprint identity came through. Nash told the team, 'The body hanging on Stark Ghyll has been identified. His name was Andrew Bainbridge, commonly known as Drew. He's in our system because he was convicted of online fraud and embezzlement. Bainbridge used his skills as a computer programmer to swindle people out of a lot of money, including his employers. He was sentenced to seven years' imprisonment and was released approximately two and a half years ago.'

'Shall I notify next of kin?' Clara asked.

'Yes, arrange that while we all start working on this. You all know the drill. Someone disliked this man and we need to find out who.'

* * *

A week later, two men were standing at the top of Black Fell. To any observer, they would appear to be admiring the view.

But one man was blindfolded and shivering with fear; all he knew was his abductor was male by the aftershave he was wearing.

Standing directly behind him, his abductor leaned forward and whispered gently in his ear. '*Nasvidenje*, Janez.' As he heard the Slovenian for 'goodbye' coupled with his first name, his blindfold was ripped away. Janez Vidmar's eyes opened wide with fear. Fear that was justified seconds later, when he was pushed violently in the middle of his back.

The second man watched the body tumbling over and over in its fall from the sheer face of the cliff, noting with satisfaction that it struck several outcrops of rock violently, before coming to rest at the base of the precipice.

Back at the car park, he took out his mobile and sent a text. The message simply read, '*Two down — back to you.*'

* * *

It had been a really good day so far. Arthur had been an enthusiastic angler for many years, and the River Helm was his favourite local playground. His passion bordered on an obsession, and it was to feed this addiction that he had deserted his wife for the day. Not that she minded his absconding.

Once he'd bidden his wife farewell, he drove up Helmsdale valley, heading for the rift between Stark Ghyll and Black Fell that had been gouged out during the Ice Age. The cleft between the two peaks was the site of one of several spectacular waterfalls. The wide pool below the cascade was Arthur's target area. There, he knew he'd have a good chance to land some rainbow trout, and possibly even carp, thereby restocking the freezer at home. Alternatively, he might return home with an empty game bag. Such was the uncertainty of his chosen hobby.

Having parked up, and suitably equipped, he set off for his first casting site.

By mid-afternoon, he had changed position three times. His final location gave him an excellent view of the lower reaches of Black Fell, where the near-vertical upper slopes flattened out slightly towards the base. He settled in, devouring his second chocolate bar, his eyes constantly watching the tip of his rod for the slightest movement.

After a while, he saw something strange near the base of the cliff. He rammed the chocolate in his mouth and snatched up his binoculars to focus on the area. Suddenly, all thoughts of fishing vanished, blown away by the horror of what he could see. His initial instinct had been totally correct. 'Oh, dear Lord, this is awful,' he muttered.

Nestling at the base of Black Fell, only metres below the line he'd cast, was a body. It was undoubtedly human — and most probably dead.

CHAPTER THREE

At Helmsdale Police Station, Nash's phone rang.

'Netherdale Control has just received a call from an angler,' the desk sergeant, Steve Meadows, told him. 'He reckons he's found a body at the foot of Black Fell.'

'Sorry, did you say an angler, Steve?'

'That's correct, Mike. He was fishing in the Helm River below the Stark Ghyll Spout waterfall when he spotted a corpse on the rocks. Netherdale sent a couple of uniforms, and they confirm there's a dead man lying there. They think it could be the result of an accidental fall, but they thought it best to be sure.'

'OK, we'll take a look. Have you informed Mexican Pete?'

'I have. And as usual Professor Ramirez' reply was probably unrepeatable, but luckily I don't speak Spanish.'

Although Ramirez was a Spaniard, the title Mexican Pete, based on *The Ballard of Eskimo Nell*, had been a long-standing joke at the station.

Nash put the receiver down. 'Another body. This time at the foot of Black Fell,' he told Clara. 'We'll go take a look and leave Viv and Adil to hold the fort here. Better tell David you'll be late home. I'll speak to Alondra while we're en route.'

* * *

Having left the Range Rover in the car park, deserted apart from the gaudily-painted patrol car, they took the long, winding path that transversed the precipitous cliff in a series of zigzags. When they reached the base they found the two uniformed officers, who were looking extremely cold and bored. 'Anything strike you about this scene?' Nash asked.

One of them shrugged. 'It could be accidental or possibly suicide, it's difficult to tell.'

Clara listened as Nash asked, 'Where's the person who rang it in?'

'He was on the far bank fishing. Control has his details, so we told him he could leave.'

'Fair enough. Will you wait here until the pathologist and a CSI team arrives? I've ordered them to ensure we cover all eventualities.'

'They'd better hurry,' the officer replied, 'there's not much daylight left.'

Having carried out their preliminary examination of the mangled remains, Nash looked at Clara and asked, 'I wonder what the killer's motive was?'

She blinked in surprise. 'What makes you think it was murder? I haven't seen anything to suggest foul play.'

Nash smiled. 'That's the point. It isn't what we can see, more what we can't see.' Seeing Clara's tortured expression, he explained. She thought about it for a few seconds, and then realized he was absolutely correct. He'd noticed what neither she nor the uniformed officers had picked up on.

It was almost half an hour later when they heard the sound of multiple footsteps tramping through the dead bracken, signalling the arrival of the pathologist and CSI crew.

'*Buenos tardes*, Don Pedro,' Nash greeted Ramirez using his private nickname.

The pathologist grunted something that might have been good afternoon, although Clara doubted it.

His opening words confirmed that her suspicion was correct. 'Can't you confine your relentless pursuit of the macabre to more accessible sites, Nash? You've dragged me to some godforsaken places in the past, but this one, and the previous site, takes some beating.'

'And there I was, thinking how bored you might be and desperate for some excitement to liven up your dull day.'

This time there was no mistaking the response, and even Clara didn't need a translation.

Before Nash had chance to say anything, Ramirez continued, 'I assume by your very presence that I should treat this as a murder victim. I'm surprised you haven't identified the body, conducted the post-mortem, arrested the killer and sent the paperwork to the CPS ready for trial.'

Nash smiled sweetly, deflecting the withering sarcasm as he replied, 'I'm shocked that you would even suggest such a thing, Professor. I wouldn't want to deprive you of the task, knowing how much you enjoy your work.'

Clara rarely heard Ramirez laugh out loud — it wasn't something pathologists were prone to doing. But he did so, and it was several seconds before he was able to ask, 'What leads you to believe this was murder rather than a sad accident or suicide?'

'This is an extremely remote location. The only place to leave a vehicle is the car park back up there.' Nash gestured towards the small top of the cliff. 'And, as it takes twenty-five or thirty minutes to drive from the nearest village, I wondered how the dead man got here. He certainly isn't dressed for hiking, and there are no vehicles other than ours in the car park. That means he was brought here, presumably by the person who pushed him over the cliff.'

Nash smiled before adding, 'We'll leave the crime scene to you, Professor. I know I can rely on you to come up with an accurate time of death, despite the smoke and mirrors the killer has used to try and fool us.'

'*Muy bueno*, Miguel,' Ramirez responded, using his nickname for Nash. 'I think we might make a detective of you yet.'

As they walked away, Clara was puzzled and asked, 'What did he say?'

'Only "very good".'

* * *

The post-mortem on the as-yet-unidentified body found on Black Fell provided no surprises. During the course of his examination of the remains, Professor Ramirez confirmed the time of death, which was, he said, somewhere in the region of two days ago. 'Probably at twelve thirty-six,' he said.

'Pardon? How—?'

Ramirez grinned and picked up an evidence bag containing a broken wristwatch with a cracked face.

The only other significant item the physical examination of the body revealed was that the deceased had been injected with sedatives before his death, similar to Bainbridge, the man hanging at Stark Ghyll.

Next morning, however, that all changed dramatically. Nash had been contemplating yet another fruitless, frustrating day. Two murders committed within one week meant a heavy workload for the team. Sometimes the public perception of a detective's work, fuelled no doubt by film and TV drama, is vastly different to reality. However, if producers of cop shows were to portray the amount of paperwork and long periods of enforced inactivity, they would attract very few viewers.

'I have news for you.'

Professor Ramirez' statement and the information that followed ended the tedium and enforced stalemate abruptly. Nash listened, scribbling notes on his pad and at one point requesting a spelling check. At the end, Nash thanked him.

Ramirez' final words were a fitting — if damning — epitaph. 'I will not be losing any sleep over the demise of these men, and when you have read their files, I doubt whether you will.'

Nash replaced the receiver and went into the main office in time to intercept a makeshift tennis ball of screwed-up paper. His detective constables, Adil and Viv, were using it for an impromptu game of catch.

Having disposed of the low-flying article, Nash told them, 'Sorry to interrupt your fielding practice, gentlemen, but our worthy pathologist has given us some more work to do. Viv, I'd like you to download these files.' He handed him the details.

'He's identified the second victim? That's good news,' Adil said.

'Even though it interrupts playtime?' Nash asked.

Viv grinned at Adil, then turned to Nash. 'I assume you'd like them printed?' The team knew Nash believed important facts could be missed when staring at a screen.

'Why do you want the first file?' Pearce asked, as he downloaded the files and sent them to the printer.

'I'll tell you in a moment.' Nash claimed one of the files, handing the other to Mironova, and after studying it for a while, he read the details to his colleagues.

* * *

'I'm paraphrasing this because it goes on for about a week. Normally I'd ask Viv to print a copy each, but that would probably use up our stationery budget for the next two years. You young computer wizards can read them onscreen.'

'Er, it's *online*, Mike,' Adil corrected him, only to receive a blank look in return.

Nash turned the page, and his expression darkened as he continued to explain. 'We know about Bainbridge, but what we weren't aware of is something Mexican Pete unearthed when he was attempting to identify the Black Fell victim. The second part of Bainbridge's file refers to the death of his stepdaughter, Emily. She was thirteen years of age when she committed suicide. After her death, they found a suicide note, in which she alleges that Bainbridge had been having USI with her.'

'USI, as in unlawful sexual intercourse?' Viv was clearly revolted.

'That's correct, and although police in Wakefield, where they lived, investigated at the time, there was no evidence and no witnesses to warrant bringing charges against Bainbridge.'

'How did she kill herself?'

Nash didn't answer Pearce's question directly. 'She disappeared from home and although they searched, it was a couple of weeks later that a gamekeeper found her body. It was close to what was the family's favourite picnic site, one they'd visited many times. Emily had hanged herself.' Nash paused. 'Her body was found in the woodland where Bainbridge was killed.'

Eventually, Pearce stated, 'That has to be a revenge killing if ever I heard one.'

As they thought about this, Nash prompted Clara to reveal what the second file contained.

She took a deep breath and began. 'The man who we believe was either thrown or pushed off Black Fell was actually a fugitive from justice, although not in this country. His name is Janez Vidmar, and he is, or rather was, wanted in his native Slovenia for several crimes which are even more revolting than Bainbridge's.

'Vidmar was a wholesale merchant who the authorities believe was also an arms dealer and drugs supplier. However, the crimes for which he was about to be arrested in Slovenia were even more serious. They involved the trafficking of young girls and boys for sex. Two of Vidmar's victims also accused him of rape, but before he could be brought to trial, Vidmar did a runner. Although Interpol organized a Europe-wide manhunt, he's never been traced — until now. Fortunately for us, Slovenian police recovered fingerprints from Vidmar's apartment in Ljubljana, and also DNA. It was from those that Mexican Pete was able to make the identification.'

Nash gestured to the files and Clara noted the contempt in his voice as he spoke. 'The professor told me he wasn't about to lose any sleep over these two. Now that I've heard the atrocious things they've done, I don't blame our worthy professor one iota. However, much as we detest them, and the evil crimes they've committed, the plain fact is that both of these men were murdered, and it's our job to bring their killers to justice.'

'That's a good point, Mike, but there is one possible explanation. What if Vidmar was up to his old tricks? That sort of behaviour would certainly create an extremely strong motive for murder.' Clara looked at the file again. 'I'm not certain if it's significant or not, but one of Vidmar's suspected victims in Slovenia, a thirteen-year-old girl, committed suicide by jumping off a high cliff, which bears close resemblance to the way he was killed.'

'That could be more than significant, Clara, well spotted. Will you sort out someone to notify the families when you've a minute?'

CHAPTER FOUR

Jenny Rhodes muttered angrily to herself. Not that it would have mattered if she had sworn aloud. Her next-door neighbour was cutting his hedge, and the sound of the trimmer would have drowned her curses. There is never a good time to get a flat tyre, but just as you are about to set off to collect your daughter from her gymnastics training is about as bad as timing can get.

Sammy Rhodes was more than promising — she was an exceptionally talented gymnast. Local competitions had long been a foregone conclusion, and the thirteen-year-old had won national events for her age group for the past two years. Jenny tried her daughter's phone, but got no response. She sent Sammy a text explaining that she would be late, and why.

Waiting for the local garage to come to her aid seemed to take forever, although the wheel change took the mechanic only minutes.

Jenny finally set off for Netherdale Grammar School. As there was a national competition looming, an extra session was being held on-site, even though the school had closed that day for the start of the Easter holidays. The time when she should have collected Sammy was already long past.

Jenny reached the school gates and experienced her first twinge of alarm when she saw that they were closed. She got out of the car and glanced along the road in both directions, but there was no sign of Sammy. Jenny's text had been explicit. Sammy was to wait outside the school. On no account was she to set off walking home. Had she ignored these instructions? If so, why? And if so, where was she?

The journey from their house to the school was two miles. The traffic was light, and Jenny's distinctive yellow car would have been visible to anyone along that road. If she had been walking home, Sammy would have been certain to have flagged her mother down. Equally, Jenny was sure she hadn't noticed any pedestrians along the route. Her alarm escalated. She tried the gates, and when she found that they were locked, her feeling of anxiety deepened.

She pressed the bell to call the caretaker from his bungalow alongside the school. Perhaps Sammy had opted to wait with him until her mother arrived. The caretaker was some time answering the summons, and when he did so, the news he conveyed was bad.

'No, there was nobody left in the gymnasium when I locked up. I even checked the changing rooms, toilets and showers. Normally, I leave that to the instructor, but she had to leave straight after the class. It's her wedding anniversary and her husband was taking her out to dinner,' he added inconsequentially. 'Are you sure your daughter didn't decide to walk home?'

The problem was, Jenny couldn't be sure, not completely, and that delayed matters even further. She tried her daughter's phone again, but it went straight to voicemail. In desperation, Jenny tried their landline at home, but after a frustrating wait, that too went to the answer machine. 'I'll have to drive home and see if she's waiting for me. Will you phone me if she turns up here?'

'Of course I will. You'd better give me your mobile number to be on the safe side.'

On her return journey, Jenny scanned the pavements and the entrances to all the side roads en route, but to no avail. She reached home and went indoors, although she was already convinced that Sammy wasn't inside. It was almost dusk, and Sammy would have been certain to have switched some lights on.

Jenny checked with the neighbours on both sides of their house, but neither of them could recall having seen Sammy. She knew her daughter's best friend, who lived on the other side of Netherdale. Jenny looked up the girl's number and spoke to both the girl and her mother. The child hadn't spoken to Sammy today, but she knew she had been looking forward to the training. She was hoping to perfect part of her routine that she knew was preventing her getting higher scores. Other than that, Jenny learned nothing from the phone call. And every delay, every minute Sammy was missing, deepened the feeling that something was terribly wrong. Jenny thanked the girl and rang off.

Panic was setting in. She phoned the local hospital, praying there hadn't been an accident, knowing she could at least find her, but had no success.

She took a deep breath and dialled 999. The emergency operator answered immediately.

'Police, please.'

* * *

Her call was directed to Netherdale police Control, and Jenny fought to keep her voice calm as she told the officer, 'I want to report a missing child. My daughter Sammy has disappeared.'

The officer recognized the note of hysteria in the caller's voice, and calmly asked for her name, address and telephone number.

He promised to have officers at the house immediately, and once he had all the details, he rang off, pointing out that it was important that she kept the line free in case her daughter rang. All his subsequent actions were the right ones, but he doubted that any of them would have the slightest effect.

26

No amount of training, role playing or courses can prepare officers adequately for a phone call from a hysterical parent whose child has gone missing. The sergeant on duty at Netherdale did his best, but when the call was over he was painfully aware that nothing he could have said in response to Jenny Rhodes' plea for help would have lessened her anxiety in any way.

Having dispatched a patrol car to the house of the missing teenager, the sergeant waited for a response from his officers.

Getting the confirmation that the house had been checked over and having taken the facts he needed — the girl's description et cetera — he followed protocol and phoned Detective Superintendent Fleming. She instructed him to have a message put out to all patrolling officers, and to await further instructions either from her or Detective Inspector Nash. She would get in touch with CID.

Knowing senior officers were involved, the sergeant relaxed marginally. Given time to reflect on what had just happened, he wondered what his reaction would have been had it been his daughter who had gone missing. Pretty much the same as that of Mrs Rhodes, he thought. He didn't dwell on how his wife might have reacted, but it brought home to him how terrible an ordeal this was for the girl's mother, and how little help or comfort the police could be. It was highly unlikely that they could do anything other than respond to events as they happened. Now he could understand the frustration expressed by officers from other forces who had spoken or written of their helplessness when placed in a similar position. Appreciating that didn't make it any easier to live with.

* * *

The car that pulled up outside the block of flats on the outskirts of Netherdale contained only one occupant. The driver looked towards the building and noted a light on in the flat that was to be the target. The driver waited for a moment, considering once more the plan that had been carefully put together. This would be the first stage of the operation.

The need to operate quickly was a crucial factor, because timing was essential. One slip, a few minutes' delay, could alert the man he was after to the danger. Once out of the car, the driver removed a small rucksack packed with everything he needed and moved towards the building's entrance. Behind him, the hazard lights on the car flashed briefly in response to the signal from the ignition key. It was the action of a careful person, and the driver was renowned for leaving nothing to chance.

At the front door, the intruder selected an item from among his tools. Once inside, the door closed silently behind him. He moved towards the stairs leading to the first floor. The fifth stair creaked; a previous inspection of the building and the flat had revealed that. Avoiding the noisy step, he reached the landing, where the flat door presented less of a challenge.

Seconds later, he was inside and about to open the lounge door when the flat owner appeared from the bathroom. 'What the hell?'

The trespasser struck hard, the weapon making solid contact with the man's skull. The victim slumped to the floor and the assailant went to work, quickly binding ankles and wrists with duct tape, before covering the unconscious man's mouth with the stifling gag. The attacker dragged the man towards the bedroom, certain of the way. It was only when the door was opened that he saw the room was already occupied. This was something that he hadn't bargained for. Nothing in the careful planning could have prepared him for this. The attacker let go of the victim and stood looking at the girl on the bed, who stared back, her eyes wide with terror.

'What on earth are you doing here? And what am I going to do with you?' the intruder wondered aloud. But although the girl heard, she was unable to reply, for she, like her captor, was bound and gagged. In any event, the intruder hadn't meant the question for her — it was a purely rhetorical one.

One thing for sure, she couldn't be left here. Not in view of what was planned. Luckily, the child hadn't seen his face. The ideal solution would be to get her out and then return here to finish his task. But then he risked being seen. And what if she had already been reported missing? It would be ironic to be arrested for abduction in the process of rescuing her. Alternatively, keeping her tied up and removing her once his mission was completed was totally impractical.

Hiding her in the car and getting her away was an option, but that would need her cooperation. In view of what the girl had already gone through, that might be too much to ask. He thought for a moment. No, releasing her was his only option, but even that would have to be planned carefully. If she was asked, maybe she would develop temporary amnesia about how she got to safety.

The girl was still staring at the sudden apparition, her fear evident. That was hardly surprising in the circumstances. Already terrified as to what her abductor was about to do to her, then to be confronted by another seemingly more sinister figure, dressed from head to toe in black with their face covered in a balaclava, must have pushed her close to the edge.

The girl would be about thirteen or fourteen, the intruder guessed, old enough to try and reason with. 'I'm not going to hurt you.' The words were delivered slowly and clearly. 'I'm here to rescue you. Has he harmed you? Has he done anything bad to you? Just nod or shake your head.'

After a few seconds, the girl gave a shake of her head. That was a relief. The intrusion had been just in time. 'If I take your gag off, will you promise not to scream?'

She looked at the speaker for a long moment, then glanced down at the man on the floor, who was beginning to regain consciousness. Sammy nodded frantically.

'Good girl. Now, I'm going to free you. Sorry, there's no way of doing this without it hurting.' Sammy winced as the strip of tape over her mouth was removed. 'Now, I want to make a bargain with you. Here's what I have in mind . . .'

* * *

It was Daniel's half-term break, and Mike Nash had taken the Friday off for a long weekend. He hoped to spend time with his son, his wife Alondra, and six-month-old Lucy. After some family time spent playing soccer on the back lawn and going for a long cycle ride, Nash was watching Daniel feeding his little sister, seated in the highchair for her supper. She seemed to be enjoying grabbing the spoon from Daniel's grasp in an attempt to feed herself. It appeared to Nash there was more food on the tray than in his daughter's mouth.

The entertainment was interrupted when his mobile rang. He glanced at the screen and frowned. The display was showing Superintendent Fleming's name. For Jackie to call him on his day off could only mean trouble. 'Yes, Jackie, what's the problem?'

He listened as Fleming outlined the situation, his mind racing as he considered possibilities, filing some for action, discarding others.

'How should we play it, Mike?'

It would have surprised many that Fleming should ask that question, but theirs was an unusual situation. Although she was the senior officer, hers was primarily an administrative role, whereas Nash was a far more experienced detective, making him the more natural choice to lead the hands-on side of an investigation.

Fleming said, 'I'd suggest it would be better for you and a policewoman to go to the mother's house. Clara's on late cover and already out on a job, or I wouldn't have rung you. I think the girl's mother will be far more comfortable with a female officer present at this stage. Leave the officer at the house with her. Mum had already contacted as many school friends as possible by the time our officers reached the house. And from what I've been told, this girl is not to be classed as a likely runaway. Good home environment and good family — completely out of character. If you agree, then I'll go straight to Netherdale and take charge of things from HQ. We need to know if the girl did attend the gymnastics class. I'll get the details from the school caretaker and try to contact the teacher. Then I think I should begin appealing for witnesses and announcements on local radio and the press. I'll have Steve Meadows and his oppo at Netherdale put every available officer on standby. Only then will I organize a search, if she's not found.'

'You're proposing to go at it mob-handed? Isn't it a bit early to be doing that?'

'I don't think so. There's an expression in medical circles to describe the time immediately following a traumatic injury. They refer to it as "the golden hour", and I think we have pretty much the same situation here.'

'Give me the address.'

CHAPTER FIVE

Sammy's eyes opened wide when she saw the big blade of the weapon in the intruder's hand.

'I'm going to cut you free. Stay perfectly still, because this knife is very sharp.'

She obeyed. Once the tape had been cut, the intruder helped her remove it. 'Now stand up.'

The sudden movement caused her head to swim, and for a second Sammy had to lean on her rescuer for support. Once she recovered, and was able to stand unaided, she was told, 'Go into the kitchen, have a drink of water, and then wait. I'll be a few minutes. And close both doors behind you.'

Sammy did as she was told without question, glad to be able to put a solid wall between her and the man who had abducted her. Should she try and get outside? Should she run? But she had no idea where she was. What if she was nowhere near home? She knew she had to trust her rescuer. If she'd been unsure earlier, that uncertainty was gone. As she was closing the bedroom door, she saw the intruder bending over the bound man and noticed for the first time that her saviour was wearing surgical gloves. What she didn't see was the protective coverall he was putting on.

As she waited, Sammy looked out of the window. It was dark, far too dark for her to see anything at the rear of the property. And she wasn't certain what was going to happen behind that door — wasn't sure she wanted to know. Even if the intruder was going to do something bad to the man who had snatched her from outside the school gates, Sammy didn't care. Her head was aching from the blow he had given her before stuffing her into the back of his van.

She remembered nothing of the journey, and little of what had happened when they arrived at this place. What she did remember was coming round to find herself tied up in that room with that man standing over her, staring at her in a very nasty way. Then he'd told her what he intended to do to her. His language was horrible — explicit and brutal. Sammy knew that had it not been for her mysterious rescuer, she would have been subjected to a terrible ordeal.

Reaction to what she had been through started to set in, and Sammy leaned against the kitchen unit for support, afraid she would faint. Her legs were shaking. She slid down to the floor and began to weep, quietly but copiously. She took deep breaths, telling herself over and over that she was going to be safe. Whatever her rescuer was doing to that filthy pervert didn't matter. Sammy just wanted to go home. She needed her mother.

She waited, her fear subsiding as time passed. She wasn't sure how long it was before she heard a door close and the masked figure entered the kitchen. There was no sign of the knife. Maybe it was in the bag the intruder was carrying. Or perhaps it was . . . Sammy didn't want to think where else it might be.

'Do you know this place? Did you see where he brought you?' he asked.

Sammy shook her head. What did it matter? All she wanted was to be out of here — to go home.

'Good, in that case, before we go outside I'm going to have to blindfold you.' He picked up a tea towel. 'Then I shall drive you into town and leave you there. I can't take you home. Your mother will have called the police, I guess, and it won't be safe for me. Before then I want you to promise me you'll remember what we agreed. It will be a solemn and binding promise, OK?'

* * *

Having spoken to Jenny Rhodes, Nash reached Netherdale police station and found DCs Pearce, Hassan and their civilian support officer, Tom Pratt, already there, helping to phone officers to enlist their help in trying to find the missing girl. Nash signalled to Steve Meadows, who, on ending a call, walked over to update Nash on their progress. 'We've contacted almost all available officers. There are already enough here to form a search party if you want to make a start. They're waiting in the canteen, supping tea and ready for a briefing. More of our men are on their way in. The problem is we can't do much without a photo of the missing girl and a description of the clothes she was wearing.'

'I took a copy at the house on my mobile. We can print it off and distribute copies to all the officers.'

Meadows smiled. 'My, you are getting high-tech, aren't you?'

Nash stared at Meadows. 'You're getting more like Jack Binns every day,' he retorted, referring to Meadows' retired predecessor. 'What I meant was, I'll hand my mobile to Viv and he can print the photo.'

Nash waited close to the printer, where he had summoned Pearce to come and complete the technical part.

The office door opened. He looked up, expecting nothing more than further recruits for the search. He stared at the newcomer in shock.

He glanced down at the photo, then back to the wide-eyed young girl standing in the doorway. She was supported by a female officer who was carrying an evidence bag containing what looked to be a tea towel. He noticed the bruise beginning

34

to form alongside the girl's eye, the red marks across her lower face and wrists, realizing she had been gagged and bound.

'Sammy? Sammy Rhodes?'

She nodded. 'I want my mum. I want to go home.' She began to sob. The officer led her to a chair and put her arms around her.

Nash looked at the youngster, and was shocked to see the tears rolling down her cheeks. 'Hey, steady on, Sammy. It's OK, you're safe, that's all that matters. OK, let's call your mum, shall we? Then we can see about getting you home. She's been very worried.'

His call was answered immediately. 'Mrs Rhodes, I have someone here who very much wants to speak to you.'

Nash held the phone out to Sammy. 'Talk to your mum, and then we'll take you to the hospital and get that bump on your head checked out. We can meet Mum there.'

Moments later, he turned to Viv Pearce. 'Call upstairs to Jackie to cancel the search, will you? And ask her to meet me at Netherdale General.'

* * *

It was approaching 2 a.m. when Nash returned home. The joyful reunion between mother and daughter at the hospital had been heart-warming to see. Thankfully, Sammy's injuries were only superficial. A darker, far more sombre mood prevailed soon afterwards, when they heard Sammy's account of what had happened to her. Nash had listened to the story in Jenny Rhodes' lounge, along with Superintendent Fleming. Sammy's reassurance that her abductor hadn't touched her improperly was more than balanced by the threats he had made of what he intended to do.

She was reluctant to utter the specific words the man had used with Nash present, so he made his excuses and left the room. He returned once Jackie Fleming called him, and saw the girl had recovered from her embarrassment. It was abundantly clear to both officers that had it not been for the timely intervention of the mystery intruder, the outcome for Sammy would have been far worse. The fright she had received and the blow on the head the man had given her to subdue her, was her only injury. The question in all their minds was who was Sammy's rescuer? And what had been his motive in entering the abductor's flat?

When asked to be specific about her abduction and where she was held prisoner, Sammy could tell them little.

'I was waiting at the gates after training and a man pulled up in a van. It had sliding doors on the side. He got out and looked at a parcel in the back, then asked me if I knew where this address was. I went to look at the label, and he hit me and pushed me inside. When I woke up I was laid on a bed, gagged and tied up.' She began to cry.

The only significant fact that emerged came when Jackie asked about his appearance and the way he spoke. 'He was just ordinary, with a hi-vis jacket and a beanie hat, and he had a funny accent — not from round here.'

Fleming zeroed in on this fact immediately. 'When you say a funny accent, do you mean he was foreign?'

Sammy shook her head. She looked at her mother. 'It was like when we were on holiday last summer.'

Jenny Rhodes looked puzzled for a second, then explained, 'I think Sammy's trying to say that the man who attacked her was from the West Country. We went to Devon and Cornwall last year.'

'How did you escape?'

'I didn't. I was rescued by the second man.'

'You mean there were two men?'

'No. He came later, got me out and took me to the police station.'

Fleming asked Sammy for a description of the man who saved her. She hesitated. Her response was such a vague one that, apart from stating that her rescuer was Scottish and of medium build, she revealed nothing about her saviour.

* * *

Nash, who was watching Sammy during the question-and-answer session, felt sure that the tearful girl was holding something back. They extracted a promise from Jenny that she would bring Sammy to the police station later that day to complete a formal statement, and after leaving the house, the officers held a short debriefing session at Netherdale HQ.

Although there was overall satisfaction as to how things had turned out, they all had reservations that Sammy's abductor might strike again, this time with less happy results.

Fleming noted that Nash had contributed nothing to the early part of the debate. 'What are your thoughts, Mike?' she asked.

'I'm a little confused, to be honest. I think there's something Sammy isn't telling us. I'm not sure if it's about the man who abducted her, the place she was kept, or the man who rescued her. I think she's telling the truth when she says the kidnapper didn't harm her, which is a real blessing. But that seems to have been more down to luck than anything. Had it not been for the appearance of her knight in shining armour, it could have been a very different story.

'It's a shame Sammy wasn't able to tell us where she was being held, because we really need to locate the place quickly. I'm more than a bit interested to find out what happened inside that room once Sammy left. We could very well be looking at a crime scene. Whether we like it or not, we might have to investigate the aftermath of what Sammy's rescuer might have done to that pervert, because it sounded to me as if he entered that flat with the sole intention of harming the occupant, or worse.'

'What about her description of her abductor? Might that help us?' Pearce asked.

'Hardly.' Nash's tone was dry. 'Apart from the West Country accent, it was vague enough to fit hundreds of men in this town alone.' He frowned, changing the subject. 'One thing that struck me is this business of the mother's flat tyre. Unless we believe that this was a chance abduction by a predator on the prowl, it seems far too convenient to be pure coincidence. That means the abductor had already targeted Sammy. If we do find Jenny Rhodes' car had been tampered with, that would suggest that the abductor is either known to the family, or was stalking her.'

'Why is that so important?' Fleming asked.

'Because it suggests a level of planning and expertise that in turn points to someone who has probably done this sort of thing before.'

'You said we need to find where she was kept prisoner,' Adil spoke slowly, as if uncertain as to how his idea would be greeted. 'I think I might know of a way.'

'Tell us,' Fleming encouraged him, 'because if you have an idea, I think you're one up on the rest of us.'

'Was Sammy's bag and mobile recovered?'

'No, she wasn't able to get it from the room,' Fleming said.

'Then, if her phone wasn't switched off, we could enlist the help of her service provider to try and get a fix on it. I guess they'd be accurate to within a street or so.'

'I think that's worth a shot,' Fleming agreed. 'Will you get onto it first thing in the morning?' She looked at her watch. 'I should say later. If you need any help convincing them, tell them to talk to me.' She glanced at Nash. 'Is there anything else we should be doing?'

'We ought to question Sammy again, because I'm sure there's more she could tell us. But not when she comes in to make her statement. Leave it until DC Andrews is back on Monday, and I believe that any in-depth interview ought to be conducted by Clara and Lisa. They don't represent as powerful an authority figure as someone with your grandiose title.' Nash grinned at Fleming's wide-eyed expression. 'And also, though it's difficult to believe at times, to the best of my knowledge they're both females. Given the ordeal she's been through, I don't think Sammy will be happy talking to a man.'

'Before we try and get a few hours' sleep, would you like to insult Viv and Adil now?' Jackie asked sarcastically. 'Why leave them out when you've been rude to the rest of us?'

CHAPTER SIX

When DC Lisa Andrews returned to duty, she was greeted with enthusiasm by her colleagues. For the first few minutes in the CID suite, she was busy answering questions about her son. 'Even though he was christened Alan Thomas Marshall, we call him Tommy. We couldn't refer to him as Alan, because that would confuse everyone with Alan, his father. Tommy started at day care last month, and he's settled in very nicely, so I was happy to come back to work. Now, tell me what I've missed?'

That took some time, but eventually Nash was able to guide the conversation to current events, and briefed her as to what her first assignment would be. 'All I have to do first is contact Sammy Rhodes' mother and arrange for the girl to be brought here.'

Jenny Rhodes agreed to bring Sammy into Helmsdale for them to try and gather more information. She told Nash that Sammy had missed the gymnastics competition and was glad to be having the school holiday until her black eye had healed. She didn't want her friends to know what had happened.

During their brief conversation, Nash told her the interview should be conducted by Clara and Lisa. 'I'm sure

Sammy will feel more comfortable in the presence of ladies, and they're very kind-natured. The last thing I want is for your daughter to feel stressed or under pressure.'

Nash gave the interviewers instructions on specific points he wanted them to bring into the conversation. 'Don't make a song and dance about it, though, I'd rather she believes it to be nothing more than a throwaway line, if you get my meaning.' He turned to Lisa and added, 'I'd like Clara to put the questions to Sammy, with you as onlooker. Don't get me wrong; your job will be equally important, if not more so. I want you to act as observer, noting changes of expression and body language. That can tell us as much about what she's saying as the words themselves.'

* * *

Once they were settled in Nash's office, which Nash had suggested would be less intimidating than the interview room, Clara began. The extent of Mike's preparation had even extended to ensuring that he and the other DCs were out of the room before Sammy and her mother appeared.

'I guess you don't want to talk about what happened to you again, Sammy, and I can quite understand that, but there are one or two things we need to clarify from your statement, so please forgive me for bringing the subject up again.' Having taken Sammy through the details of her abduction, her description of the man who had kidnapped her, and the room in which she was held captive, Clara relaxed, sitting back in her chair as she asked, 'Was it a house where you were?'

'No, it was a flat.'

'And did you see the street at all?'

'No, it was dark, so I couldn't see anything out the back when I was in the kitchen.'

'What about the route your rescuer brought you to town? Anything that would help us find the man that took you?'

'When I came outside, I was blindfolded.'

'And how did you get to the police station?'

'I was under a blanket on the back seat of the car.'

'Didn't you think that was a little strange?'

'No.' Sammy almost smiled. 'He didn't want to be seen with me, in case people thought he was the man that took me. He said so.'

'So why did you need a blindfold?'

'Erm, I'm not sure.' Sammy looked confused.

But Clara was sure. He didn't want her to see the vehicle or to identify him.

'You see, Sammy, what I really need is a description of the person who rescued you from that horrible man.'

Up to that point Sammy had been settled, almost at ease, but as Clara asked the question, Lisa saw the young girl's expression change, become guarded. She fidgeted in her seat. 'I didn't see his face. I told you, he was wearing a mask.'

Clara continued, seemingly accepting Sammy's statement at face value. 'And you also said he spoke with a Scottish accent. Is that correct?'

Once again, Lisa was intrigued by Sammy's reaction. She had been looking directly at Clara, but as she replied the youngster's eyes dropped and her glance went to her left. Her hands were clenched tight. She's lying, Lisa thought.

'Yeah, that's right.' She looked worried and began to bite her bottom lip.

This time, it was Clara who was economical with the truth. 'When DI Nash and Superintendent Fleming were at your house, you told them the person who came to your rescue was "sort of medium build".' Clara shrugged. 'Does that mean he was around your height?'

'Oh no, he was much taller than me.' Sammy relaxed again.

'But our pathologist says the stab wounds on the body suggest someone of short stature, possibly no taller than you, Sammy.' Clara paused for emphasis. 'Is that true, or has he got it wrong?'

Jenny Rhodes sat forward. 'Sammy wouldn't do anything like that!'

Lisa signalled for her to sit back.

The implication that she might have killed someone appalled Sammy. 'I didn't do it,' she said, her eyes wide as she shook her head, a look of panic on her face. She looked at her mother. 'It wasn't me! But I promised I wouldn't tell.'

'Wouldn't tell what, Sammy? What was it you promised not to tell us?' Clara asked.

Sammy's complexion was bright red as she admitted, her voice little louder than a whisper, 'I don't want to say.'

'Say what? He can't hurt you. He doesn't know who you are or where you live.'

The girl looked from one to the other, then at her mother again.

'Sammy,' Jenny said, firmly, 'you have to tell them.'

Sammy looked scared. She shook her head.

'Sammy, tell them,' her mother insisted.

She covered her face and began to cry. 'He's not Scottish,' she muttered. 'He sounded Yorkshire. And he's very tall.'

'So why did you lie?'

'He made me promise to say that.'

Clara's phone rang at that moment, startling everyone. Meadows had been instructed not to put any calls through.

'Excuse me,' Clara said, as she picked up the receiver. 'What is it?' she demanded.

'That's enough. You can let Sammy and her mother leave now.'

'Very well, if that's what you want.'

In the room where Nash and Pearce had been watching the interview on a link, Nash replaced the phone.

Pearce turned to him and said, 'It was damned clever of Clara to infer that we'd found a body and that the person had been stabbed.'

'It was absolutely brilliant. Just don't tell her I said so,' Nash agreed.

* * *

On the outskirts of Leeds, the click of the letter box made the man put his newspaper down. He left the small sitting room and walked slowly down the hallway. He had learned to be cautious — knowing from experience that what came through the small aperture was not always welcome. On this occasion, however, there was nothing unpleasant. No lumps of faeces, no pungent smell of petrol that would be followed by a lighted match or spill of paper. Both had happened to him in the past, although not at this address. He was hopeful that his new identity would prevent that sort of thing, but could never be certain that it had not been revealed. He had been forced to move on three occasions. It was getting to be tiresome.

There was only one item of mail on the mat. As he bent to pick it up, the size and shape of the padded envelope intrigued him. Could this be what he was waiting for? He tore open the end of the packet, which had been secured with parcel tape, and tipped the contents into his hand. It was a DVD case. His excitement grew as he pondered what the film might contain. If it was as good as he'd been promised, it was a treat worth waiting for. But it would have to wait, for a couple of hours at least.

He didn't relish the task he had to perform, even though it was necessary. Going out meant the danger of being recognized, and that he could well do without. Sometimes, however, the risk had to be taken. He normally ensured his groceries were delivered, but on this occasion, he had been too preoccupied to notice he had run short of a few essentials. Once he had returned from the supermarket, however, watching the DVD would be his main priority — in fact, his only priority.

CHAPTER SEVEN

The property on the Leeds industrial estate was best described as down at heel. It had obviously seen better days, and those days had been a long time ago. Constructed on two storeys, it was purely functional. No large logos or sign boards adorned the facade to break up the drab exterior, which was hardly enhanced by the peeling paint on the steel-framed windows. There was nothing to announce the activity of the building's occupants, save a small piece of plastic above the letter box, which had faded white lettering, barely legible against the black background.

Inside, the decor was as uninviting as the exterior. The set of worn steps leading to the first floor had a skeletal hand-rail alongside them. A man in his late thirties, whose walk and appearance suggested someone older, climbed the stair-case towards his boss's office. The room matched the rest of the building, discouraging anyone from remaining there one second longer than was absolutely necessary. This might have been unintentional, but in view of the users' profession, possibly not. The sole occupant of the office looked up from the papers he was studying and greeted his deputy with a faint smile.

'How did the home visit go?'

The probation officer grimaced at his superior's question. 'About as well as any visit to James Weston could go, I reckon.'

'Is he all right? Any specific problems?'

'Of course he isn't all right. I don't believe for one minute he'll ever be *all right* as long as he's breathing. Not up here, I mean.' He touched his temple. 'Having said that, I suppose he's no worse than the last time I had the misfortune to see him.'

'He hasn't been recognized, I hope? That would mean we'd have to move him.'

'No, he hasn't been recognized, but that's because he rarely leaves the house.' The probation officer smiled, but without much evidence of humour. 'I have to admit there have been times when he's been difficult. I've been tempted to run out into the street and stop the first person I see and tell them who they've got living alongside them. Especially women with small children. That way he'd have to be moved and he'd become someone else's problem.'

He saw the look of alarm on his boss's face. 'Don't worry, I'd never do it, you know that. I'm just sounding off.'

'How does he go on for shopping, if he never goes out?'

'He orders by phone from a local supermarket and they deliver. Luckily, he told me the driver is ancient. He just dumps the order and ignores him, so there's next to no chance of recognition.'

'That's no bad thing. It doesn't help our work when the tabloid press reprints those old photos of him whenever they want to start a crusade about teenage evil. I suppose never leaving the house is one sure way of avoiding recognition. The other advantage is that nobody on the outside has seen him since he acquired those scars, so that makes the chance even more remote. So what does he do all day? Has he got a hobby of some sort to occupy his time? If not, it can't be much of an existence, being cooped up for twenty-four hours on end, seven days a week. It must seem as if he's swapped one prison cell for another.'

'The sentence was supposed to be life imprisonment, remember,' the probation officer pointed out. 'Maybe there is some justice in him being so restricted. As to what he does all day' — the officer gave a look of disgust — 'he spends most of the time watching hardcore pornography, probably wanking himself off. God knows where he gets the stuff from. Last time I was there, I walked into the sitting room before he had chance to switch the TV off. I couldn't believe what I saw on the screen. It was absolutely revolting.'

He shook his head in bewilderment. 'And the psychiatrists reckon he's cured, and no longer represents a danger. If I had my way, I'd sling him back inside, where he's no threat to any children.'

'Yes, well, we've all heard the psychiatrists say things like that before, then wash their hands of the case when it goes tits up. Our problem is we have to live with the situation as it is, not as we'd like it to be. Our hands are tied by the decisions of others.'

'Is there anything else I should know about?' the boss asked.

'No, that's about it.'

The probation officer turned to leave. 'Oh, hang on. There is one other thing to deal with. He's asked me if he can go on holiday. I said yes, subject to your approval. I've got him to put the request in writing for you.' He passed him a badly written note, the best they could expect.

'He's found a holiday cottage in North Yorkshire that's available to rent for a couple of weeks. It's in a small village. The chance of anyone recognizing him so far away, and in so remote a location, is infinitesimal.'

He saw what his boss was about to say, guessed the subject matter, and forestalled him. 'Yes, I know there were those images of him that mysteriously appeared in the papers, but that was a long time ago. I don't think he bears much resemblance to them now. For one thing, he's almost bald, and for another, those photos appeared before that gang of prisoners carved him up and put all those scars on his face. He seems oblivious of the fact that he looks nothing like the images of him that were published. He's tried to grow a beard too, and that helps add to the disguise. And who am I to encourage him to think differently? I'm not sure he ever looks in a mirror. I can't say I blame him if he doesn't look at himself. If I had a face like his, I'd risk the years of bad luck and smash every mirror in the house.'

'OK, you can phone him and tell him it's OK, but don't forget to inform the local police force to let them know they have the dubious distinction of James Weston's company for the time being. Tell them the address he'll be living at, and the dates of his visit.'

'I'll do that, boss, and that's everything, I think. I've just got to write up the report from this visit and then I'm done.'

'Yes, you can forget about him for a couple of weeks now. You're off on holiday from tomorrow, aren't you?' the boss continued. 'Where is it you're going?'

'I'm taking the wife and kids to Majorca at the weekend, to celebrate the fact that I'm rid of Weston for a while.'

'It's a good job Weston's not going to Majorca.' His boss laughed.

'Don't say that, even as a joke. They'd never let him into the country, even if he could get a passport.'

'OK, you have a good holiday, and try to forget work.'

'I can't see that being a problem.'

* * *

The saying that there's many a true word spoken in jest was proved true in fairly dramatic fashion soon after the probation officer left his superior's office for his own, even humbler room. He phoned Weston to convey their acceptance of his holiday request, and was about to switch his computer on to send the requisite email to the local police force near where he would be staying. Before he had chance to do that, his mobile rang. The distinctive tones of *Take That* echoed around the sparsely furnished office. The ringtone had been uploaded by his elder daughter, to make it easy to distinguish his phone in crowded places. He pulled the phone from his jacket pocket. The word on the screen was 'Home'.

'Hi, darling. Have you finished the packing yet?'

His wife's answer and the alarm in her voice caused him to stand up, listening intently. 'You're where? The hospital? Why, what's happened?'

The news was potentially calamitous. Their son had been rushed to hospital having fallen from a swing in the play park. He had been knocked unconscious and suffered a cut on the side of his head. The paramedics were concerned about the possibility of a fractured skull or at least the boy suffering from concussion. If that was the case, Majorca would be out of the question. Even if they were prepared to take the risk, the airline and their travel insurance would not allow the boy to travel. With their holiday in jeopardy and the possibility that his son might be seriously hurt, all other considerations were pushed aside. 'I'll be there as fast as I can,' he told his wife.

In the event, they were lucky. Having received the all-clear from the doctors, much to the relief of the whole family, they made the flight and enjoyed a relaxing time on the Spanish island.

It wouldn't be until they queued at the check-in desk at Palma airport for their return flight that the probation officer's thoughts would return to work. That would prompt him to remember he had omitted to send the email informing the North Yorkshire Police of James Weston's whereabouts during his stay in their territory. Whatever the outcome, there was nothing he could do about it.

* * *

The minute James Weston received the phone call from the probation officer, granting permission for his holiday in North Yorkshire, he left the sitting room and opened a door beneath the stairs to the cellar.

The space had been converted with great skill into a studio-cum-office. Weston had taken a course on carpentry whilst in prison and had proved to be a talented pupil. The skills he had gained enabled him to disguise the entry door to his sanctuary. The other skill he had acquired during his confinement had been in computing, though he continued to give people the impression of illiteracy. The workstation on one wall of the room housed a state-of-the-art PC. He logged on, opened his email folder and began to type. '*Holiday is OK*'. He completed the message and waited, hoping that his friend would be online and able to reply. His excitement and anticipation mounted. He glanced across the room at the opposite wall, where a montage of photos took pride of place. The subjects were young girls, whose faces would be familiar to anyone who read newspapers or watched television news broadcasts.

Weston shifted slightly in his chair. His excitement was becoming uncomfortable. It was heightened further when he saw his contact had replied, giving him his instructions. He read the content and immediately deleted the message, knowing the sender would do the same. It was part of the agreement he shared with the men he was in touch with. Although they had never met, they all shared an interest that had to remain strictly private.

Others would never understand. The names they used to describe Weston and those like him showed the revulsion they felt. He didn't care what they thought. His only reason for keeping the room and its contents secure was to avoid discovery. If the room was found, he would be returned to prison.

He switched off the computer and stood up. He looked once more at the photos. There was space for several more on the board. One of the vacancies would soon be filled.

He went to find his suitcase.

CHAPTER EIGHT

Earlier that morning, Adil had reported a frustrating delay in tracking Sammy Rhodes' mobile, owing to the lack of cooperation from the service provider. They wouldn't take any action without the written consent of Mrs Rhodes. Even Superintendent Fleming had spoken to them, but it did no good. They said it was to do with child protection, and it was difficult to argue with that. 'Computers are more my area of expertise than mobiles. I'm going to see Mrs Rhodes, and try and get her to contact the network provider.'

Within the hour he was back. Adil entered Nash's office and flourished a piece of paper. 'At last, I've managed to get an approximate location for the girl's phone,' he told Nash and Mironova.

'How did you manage that?'

'Mrs Rhodes was a great help.' Adil shook his head. 'I feel sorry for that poor woman. It transpires Sammy's phone has a GPS tracker on it her mother had installed. She never thought about it at the time as she was so distressed.'

'So whereabouts is it?'

'Somewhere on the outskirts of Netherdale, between the ring road and Longlands Avenue, is about as precise as they can be. As I remember it, that area is almost all bungalows, which should make spotting likely properties a bit easier.'

'That's true, there can't be many flats around there, and Sammy Rhodes was adamant she was in a first-floor flat. She went down a dark flight of steps before she was blindfolded by her rescuer when they left the building.'

'Do you want me to drive around the area and take a look on the off-chance?'

'Yes, but take Lisa with you, so she can act as spotter whilst you concentrate on driving — don't use a patrol car. We don't want to spook the natives, or scare the abductor away if you find him.'

Adil called to Lisa, 'Come on, we're going sightseeing.'

* * *

After a boring time finding nothing of interest, Lisa said, 'That house looks promising.' She pointed over to Adil's right.

'Any building with an upstairs would look promising after an hour staring at row upon row of bungalows. I was beginning to wonder if the builder suffered from vertigo,' Adil grumbled.

'Acrophobia,' Lisa corrected him.

'What?'

'Vertigo is dizziness. Acrophobia is fear of heights.'

'I think you've swallowed a dictionary.' As he was speaking, he slowed the car to a halt at the kerbside.

'Look there, alongside the front door there are half a dozen nameplates with doorbells next to them. That must mean the building is divided up into flats. It's the most likely looking property we've seen.'

'You mean it's the only likely property we've seen,' Adil retorted. He pointed along the road, beyond the house that had caught Lisa's attention. 'However, there are at least three similar along this road, so maybe we've left bungalow-land.'

'I have to admit that although I've worked Netherdale for a few years, this is a road I've not been down before,' Lisa told him.

'It's hardly surprising, tucked away back here. The road end is concealed too — I almost missed it. If I hadn't been desperate, I might not have bothered checking it, having seen the cul-de-sac sign at the corner. Let's walk over and take a closer look.'

'How will we know which flat we're looking for?' Lisa asked. 'We don't even know if it's the right building.'

'Good question.' Adil thought about it for a moment. 'I suppose I could call Tom Pratt and give him the details off the nameplates. He could check them out against the PNC. If our man has been arrested before, he'll be on there.'

'If he's been arrested for the sort of crime we're investigating, he must be on the Sex Offenders' Register. And that has to be kept up to date with offenders' current addresses, doesn't it?'

'You're dead right, and that's an even better idea, because I'll bet you any money half of the names will be missing from those plates. Either because the occupants don't want to be found, or don't want nuisance callers to know their name.'

'Or they're simply too lazy to write their name on a piece of card and slide it into the slot,' Lisa added. 'It's a shame we don't have an ANPR reader with us. If the pervert's car is outside one of these buildings, we could run a number plate check. That would link to any offences the registered keeper has committed and cross-reference it with the SOR.'

'Tut-tut, Lisa, issuing detective constables with anything as useful as an ANPR reader would be a waste of valuable resources. That's an expense that couldn't be justified when the watchword is economy. Don't you know there's a recession when it comes to police budgets?'

'If this fashion for economizing gets any worse, they'll have us back on bicycles next.'

'You mean you haven't had the memo?'

* * *

The detectives reached the other side of the road and Adil rang Tom Pratt. After explaining the situation, he waited for Pratt to check the SOR on his computer. A few minutes passed before Tom said, 'Adil, are you still there? I've found a Leonard Wright on the register who sounds like he could be the guy you're after. Wright is originally from Exeter where he was convicted of the kidnap and rape of a young girl, plus two more for the possession and distribution of pornographic images of children. He was released from prison six months ago. Wright is listed at flat 4A, number seventeen, Longlands Close, going under the name George Grey. Is that near where you are?'

'The house is two buildings down. What's more, Wright's background tallies with what Sammy Rhodes told us. She said the man who abducted her had a West Country accent. Stay on the line, Tom. We may need an ANPR check.'

They reached number seventeen. The building, a stone-built Victorian detached house, was on three storeys. The tarmac drive in front of the property had been broadened out, at the expense of a large section of the garden, to allow parking for the residents' vehicles. There was only one vehicle parked there, a white Transit. Adil gave the details to Pratt and they waited.

'That's Wright's vehicle — or at least it's registered to George Grey,' Pratt confirmed.

'If we'd had our wits about us, we'd have checked the SOR earlier and saved ourselves all this hassle,' Lisa commented after Adil ended the call. 'Mind you, even Mike and the super missed that trick.'

'Easy to do, I suppose. Seeing how the girl was safe.'

'What do we do now? Check to see if Leonard Wright is in residence?'

'Maybe we should report in to Mike first, see what he wants us to do, although I have to admit the temptation to burst in there and beat the crap out of Wright is a strong one. Mind you, that would hardly do much for our career prospects.'

'It's an understandable feeling, though. It is asking a lot to expect police officers to remain unaffected by the horrible crimes the like of perverts such as Wright commit.'

'I agree, and it makes you wonder when something happens to them, how energetically officers pursue the culprit. It's a matter of professionalism, I suppose.'

As he was speaking, Adil pressed the short code for Helmsdale CID.

* * *

Nash listened to Adil, before telling him, 'OK, but be extremely careful. Keep your mobile on. I'll put our phone on speaker so that Clara and I can hear what's going on.'

'Should we send backup?' Clara asked.

'Let's see what they find first.'

'OK, Mike, we're at the front door. I've pressed the bell for flat 4A. As yet, there's no response.'

They waited in silence, before Lisa pressed the bell a second time. They could hear it ringing faintly in the far recesses of the building. 'Still nothing,' Adil reported.

On impulse, Lisa reached forward and tried the door handle. The heavy wooden door swung open. 'The front door is unlocked. Shall we go inside?'

'Yes, but remember what I said. Proceed with caution, OK?'

'Yes, Mike.'

Nash and Clara heard the sound effects of the detectives as they crossed the tiled floor and mounted the marble staircase, both symbolic of the affluence of the building's original owners. 'We're outside the flat now.'

They heard hammering on the door, but still there was no answer. 'Try the door,' Nash suggested.

Once again, the door swung open.

'I'm not sure about this, Mike. I can smell something. Hello, police!' Adil called out. 'Police, is anyone at home?' He tried again. 'Police, we're coming in.' There was no response.

'Mike, we're entering the hallway of the flat now. I'm opening the first door leading from the corridor. It's a kitchen, but there's a very distinctive smell. Lisa's about to open the second door.'

'Oh dear God!' Lisa yelled.

'What is it? What's wrong?' Nash asked, in some alarm.

'Lisa, close that door. Let's get the hell out of here,' Adil instructed.

'Will someone tell us what's happening?' the listeners demanded in unison.

They heard Hassan take a deep breath before he answered. 'There's a body on the bed, Mike. A man's body. He's stark naked, on his back, tied up. He's been ripped open. The place is a bloodbath.'

* * *

Ramirez was predictably caustic when Nash had phoned him. 'You couldn't be happy with just one corpse or even two, could you, Nash? Tell me something — is there a special offer on at the undertaker's? Kill two, get one free, perhaps? I suppose I should be grateful the body's in Netherdale. You usually manage to drag me out into the wilds to view the corpses you find.'

Clara stood alongside Nash in the doorway of the bedroom. The pathologist waited while one of his assistants took photographs, prior to them beginning their grisly work. She often thought the necessary process of recording the body as it was found was the most macabre part of the whole procedure. In this case, the results were likely to be particularly gruesome.

'This room is exactly as Sammy described it,' she reminded Nash.

'And I don't think we need anything more to prove it, do we?' He pointed across the room. 'That looks like her gym bag over there.'

'I think I'll go and see how Adil and Lisa are getting on,' Clara said. 'They were both fairly distressed by what they found. Do you want me to send Viv up?'

'Good idea. Of course,' he added, as Mironova turned to leave, 'I could go see them if you prefer, and you can stay here and watch Ramirez juggling body parts.'

The look she gave him would have withered a lesser man.

The pathologist's initial findings were on the terse side of laconic. 'Cause of death, evisceration. Weapon used, extremely sharp, with a long-blade, such as a kitchen or carving knife.'

'That sounds like the one Sammy Rhodes described — in fact, she said the person who freed her actually warned her about how sharp it was.'

'She was right. Time of death, probably between twenty-four and forty-eight hours ago, I'll know better tomorrow at the post-mortem — eight o'clock.'

They were interrupted by Ramirez' assistant. 'The fingerprint reader confirms the dead man as Leonard Wright, known as George Grey,' he told them, before moving away.

Nash watched the man go. 'He's almost as verbose as you,' he told Ramirez, happy to get his own back for the pathologist's barbs. 'Will it be in order for us to take Sammy's gym bag and return it to her?'

'I don't see why not. But wait until the photographer's finished, will you?'

CHAPTER NINE

At the flat, there was little else the detectives could do until CSI had completed their work. That wouldn't even start until the body had been removed. As Nash disposed of his protective suit, he instructed Pearce to find an officer to take over maintaining the log, and arrange some door-knocking. He sent Hassan and Andrews to Helmsdale to write up their reports. 'Clara and I are off to Netherdale to update the superintendent,' he told them.

He put Sammy's gym bag on the back seat of the Range Rover, adding, 'We can drop that off on the way back.'

They paused in the CID office at Netherdale for a word with Tom Pratt. 'Will you order me a copy of Leonard Wright's file?' Nash asked.

When Jackie Fleming heard what they had to say, she commented, 'It seems as if your guess was right. Someone appears to be waging a war against paedophiles. The problem will be that when the media and public learn the identity of these victims, any sympathy they might otherwise have had for the dead men will evaporate. That sort of attitude can only make the job of finding the killer doubly difficult. Potential witnesses could well decide to have a sudden attack of amnesia.'

Nash agreed. 'That could also extend to officers involved in the enquiry. It will be hard to get anyone to adopt a totally unbiased, professional approach.'

He was unaware that he was echoing the thoughts of Andrews and Hassan, but was not surprised when Clara added, 'When I learned of the victim's past, I confess a tiny part of me said, "So what, he had it coming to him."'

'I certainly don't think you'll be alone in that,' Fleming told her. 'The trick will be getting people to acknowledge their prejudice and face up to it.' She shook her head. 'How do you intend to proceed?' she asked Nash.

'Forensics is bound to be another day or two at the flat, so there's nothing we can do there.'

* * *

Their next visit was to Jenny Rhodes, and Nash remained in the car while Clara did the deed. Sammy was at a friend's house, and her mother was delighted they had recovered her bag and phone. 'She'll be so pleased,' she told Clara. 'She's telling all her friends she had a fall during training, hence the bruise, and why she missed the competition. I'm just happy to know that she wasn't really hurt. I hope you've got the man responsible. And if you find the man who rescued her, I'd like to thank him personally.' She smiled.

'I'm afraid it isn't quite as simple as that,' Clara explained. 'Her abductor has been found murdered.'

'Oh, goodness,' Jenny sat down. 'I thought you told me he hadn't really been stabbed and you were only saying that to get Sammy to talk to you.'

'That was correct at the time. But since then we have found the flat where Sammy was held, and the occupant *is* dead.'

Clara watched as Jenny thought for a moment, before she stared at Clara. 'Are you telling me that while my daughter was waiting to be taken away, her rescuer was killing the man?' She began to panic.

Clara took her hand. 'Look, we don't know all the details yet, but we will not, I repeat, *not* be speaking to Sammy again. We will keep her out of it, because this case is going to hit the press, and we don't want anything to reverberate down to you. If you do have any problems, let one of us know at once, and we'll do all we can to help.'

'I understand, thank you.'

'Try not to worry,' Clara said, and headed back to the car.

'How did it go?' Nash asked.

'How do you think?'

* * *

As part of an internal restructuring carried out by the chief constable, the inspector in charge of traffic division, Paul Grant, had been given the additional responsibility for the whole of uniform activities. This was a good choice, welcomed throughout the area force, as Grant was both popular and extremely efficient.

Nash had only been in his office a few minutes when the phone rang. 'Mike, it's Paul Grant here.'

'Oh no,' Nash responded. 'I haven't been speeding, I promise you.'

He heard the laughter in Grant's voice as he replied, 'This has nothing to do with traffic offences committed by you in your Chelsea tractor.'

'OK, so what's the panic?'

'I know how much you've got on your plate at the moment, but I wanted to pick your brains, if you've got a minute?'

'How can I help?'

'We've had a call from the CEO of Good Buys supermarket. He rang to report the company has completed a store-wide stock check, and there is a substantial loss in the wines and spirits section. The largest discrepancy is in the flagship store here in Netherdale, although there are smaller losses in the branches. For the amount involved, he doesn't believe it can be shoplifters. It appears to be a well-organized, systematic chain of thefts.'

'Are you wanting us to handle it? Because I don't think we can. These killings are causing us a lot of headaches. It's slow going.'

'No, not that. I'm looking for inspiration. I just want to know if you have any thoughts as to how to identify the thieves.'

Nash thought for a moment. 'Have you got hold of their external CCTV footage? That might give you a clue as to who the villains are.'

'No, I haven't, but I'll organize it now. Thanks, Mike.'

* * *

Two days later, Paul Grant phoned again.

'Have you had any luck with the CCTV?' Nash asked him.

'Yes and no, Mike. Sorry if that sounds confusing. Good Buys only have external cameras in Netherdale. We've identified a possible suspect vehicle, a Citroen Berlingo van. It's been picked up by the cameras on multiple occasions, but is always parked in such a way as to hide the registration number.'

'Are you sure it's the same one?'

'We're certain. There's a dent on the offside front panel which is unmistakable. We've got an image of the driver, but it's far too grainy. About all we can confirm is it's a male. I wondered if I could borrow one of your techno-constables. I thought Pearce or Hassan might be able to improve the quality sufficiently for us to nail him. I hope you don't mind my asking, but it will be quicker than passing it over to Forensics.'

'I take your point. OK, Paul, I'll send Adil over.'

* * *

It was nearing lunchtime when Nash got an update. 'Adil's managed to get a clear image of the driver, but as we're both strangers in these parts, we weren't able to put a name to the face. Adil suggested he sends the footage to you.'

'Good idea, send it through.'

With Viv Pearce out of the office, it was left to Clara to download the CCTV footage and forward it to the relevant section. As she and Nash watched it, one look at the driver's face was sufficient for her to pause the video, and call across the office, 'Lisa, come and have a look. I think this is an old friend of yours.'

When she joined them, recognition was instantaneous. 'I didn't know that little scrote Lee Machin was out of jail. Call him what you like, he's certainly no friend of mine — or any other law-abiding citizen.'

'Move the tape on, see where he's going,' Nash told Clara. They continued watching and saw Machin walk across the car park, where he met up with another man they couldn't identify. They turned the corner of the store, then disappeared down the side of the building.

'What's he doing down there?' Nash asked.

'I can't see for that big wagon. Perhaps we ought to look at footage from the other camera,' Lisa suggested.

'What other camera?' Clara asked.

Lisa pointed towards to the corner of the building on the screen. 'That one.'

'You're dead right. Well spotted, Lisa. I'll phone Paul Grant and tell him we've got an ID for the driver, and ask him about the other camera footage.' Nash turned towards his office.

'Before you do, why don't I check with DVLA to see if Machin owns a Citroen Berlingo?' Clara suggested.

'If he does, I doubt it will be taxed and insured,' Lisa remarked.

Paul Grant was delighted. Lee Machin, owner of a twelve-year-old Citroen Berlingo, instantly became their prime suspect.

The other information puzzled him when Nash told him, 'We watched a bit more of the footage and saw Machin and another man go down the side of the building with empty trolleys. They returned with them laden with what looked to be wine and spirits boxes. You'll need the other camera to see exactly what went on round that corner after a delivery wagon left.'

'I don't have footage from any other camera attached to the Netherdale store.'

'That's interesting. Either someone forgot to send it through, or perhaps the camera was out of action. If it isn't either of those, I reckon Good Buys have an internal problem.'

'An inside job?'

'Could be.'

* * *

Paul Grant walked into Nash's office, a big grin on his face. 'Morning, Mike, have you heard?'

'And a good morning to you, Paul. Heard what?'

'Your old friend Machin. Had him up before the magistrates this morning along with three accomplices: his brother-in-law, an unsavoury shop owner called Roper, and a now-former security guard at Good Buys.'

'That was good going. How'd you manage that?'

'All down to ANPR. We had an alert out for the van. When it moved late at night, we followed it to Roper's Stores on the Carthill Estate. The shop was closed, and Machin was unloading round the back. My lads called for backup.'

'Why didn't you just arrest him before? You could have got a warrant and searched his house with the evidence on the CCTV footage.'

'I could, but after speaking to you I knew you would have wanted to know what he did with such a large amount of stuff. I got my lads to keep an eye out and sure enough, we got them all. Machin could have had other fences, so I've got some officers checking round other possible shops to see if they've upped the quality of the goods they're selling. I doubt it will come to anything other than scaring the shopkeepers.'

'How did he get the goods?'

'Simple. Text message from the security guard. Once the staff had checked off the delivery, they went in the warehouse, leaving the stock on the dock.'

'Clever, the staff would think they had everything. What about his house search?'

'Enough fancy chocolates and pricey goods to start a shop. So we nicked his wife and daughter as well for aiding and abetting.'

'Well, tell me the best bit. What did Machin get?'

'Remanded and referred to Crown Court.' Paul grinned. 'With his record, he should get a good sentence. The magistrate decided he was the ringleader, so the other three got twelve months each and hefty fines. If you can manage to get out tonight, there'll be a drink for you on the bar.'

'Thanks, Paul. It's good of you to offer, but we're barely seeing our beds at the moment. I'm just pleased we were able to help.'

CHAPTER TEN

The chef at the Fleece Hotel in Helmsdale was furious, and with good reason. Often, when he was in such a temper, his colleagues had to keep their wits about them and be prepared to duck to avoid low-flying kitchen utensils. On this occasion, however, his rage was purely verbal and directed at a source outside the hotel kitchen. He had ordered a selection of vegetables as usual, but their regular supplier hadn't delivered.

As chance would have it — an evil chance, the chef thought — it had been his day off the previous day, when the delivery should have arrived. Because he was absent, nobody noticed that the order hadn't turned up. The chef could have gone to town on them, letting his temper have free rein, but being fair, he knew that the fault was his. No one had noticed the missing delivery because he hadn't warned them to expect it.

That didn't help solve the problem. Although it was only 8 a.m., some of his team should have been busy preparing the lunchtime fare, and following that with the food required for the evening meal. Others were completing the breakfast for two coach-loads of pensioners staying in the hotel. The kitchen had to be run with the precision of a military operation.

Without the essential ingredients and no idea when the missing goods would arrive, the chef was facing a potential disaster. Desperate situations such as this called for desperate solutions. Although the extra cost of purchasing the ingredients from a retailer would decimate their profit, the alternative, a reduced menu, was unthinkable.

The chef summoned his second in command.

Reggie Barnes was a perfect foil for the flamboyant maestro. Quiet, hard-working, shy almost to the point of being a recluse, Barnes got on with the job, usually in total silence. Although he had worked alongside the man for almost two years, the chef knew little about his deputy's personal circumstances, background or interests. Not that he needed to. All he required was a man he could trust to do a good job within the hectic atmosphere of the kitchen.

He handed Barnes a sizeable wad of cash, secured by a large paper clip to a shopping list. 'Get yourself round to Good Buys supermarket chop-chop, Reggie. They'll be open in a few minutes, so don't waste time. Make sure you get everything on that list, and pay special attention to the courgettes. I don't want anything that's even slightly soft. I want to use them in a risotto, and if I get chance, I'll dice that greengrocer's testicles and add them to the dish as well.'

'Yes, chef.' Reggie thrust the notes and list into his pocket. 'I'll be back as quick as I can.'

The chef watched him go. Reggie was a good number two, and seemed to have no ambitions to running his own kitchen. Thinking about it, the chef reckoned it would never work out if he tried. He was too reserved, nervous even, for it to be a success. Being in charge of a kitchen called for the chef to be able to work with a variety of different characters and get the best out of them. Some had to be bullied, others cajoled. Reggie fell into the latter category. Any attempt to shout at him would have an adverse effect. Asking him quietly to do a job was all it took. Unlike most of the others he had under his control, he knew that once he'd given Reggie instructions, he could walk away and forget about it, secure in the knowledge that the task would be performed correctly and within the time demanded.

* * *

Reggie was glad to escape. He knew that the next hour would be unpleasant in the kitchen. When the chef was in a bad mood, everyone around him felt the backlash of his rage, whether they'd earned it or not. Reggie hated loud, angry scenes. He always had done, since . . .

They brought back too many memories, and all of them too painful to dwell on if he could avoid it. Even now, the thought of that time was at the back of his mind, no matter how hard he tried to banish it. In truth, it was with him every day, from the moment he woke until going to sleep. Always there, always lurking, like a phantom in the shadowy recesses of his subconscious.

It was the time his childhood ended and his misery began — misery that lasted until he'd been able to escape. He'd escaped in a physical sense, but as he now knew, there was no escaping the memory. He often wondered how things might have turned out, had his past been shaped differently. What he was really thinking was how his life would have been had his sister lived. But she had died, leaving him in a world he was too young and too ill-equipped to cope with. Occasionally, in the more savage depths of his depression, he even found himself blaming his sister for all he had suffered. He knew this to be unfair, and knew that her suffering had been far worse than his, but at least she was free of the nightmare, whilst his was ongoing. He wondered if others in similar circumstances felt that way.

Reggie was so lost in his own world that he barely noticed his surroundings as he walked through Helmsdale town centre. This might have proved disastrous had the loud, urgent blaring of a car horn not brought him back to reality. He looked up, mildly surprised to find that he was in the middle of the supermarket car park. He glanced round and waved an apologetic hand to the driver of the car that had nearly mown him down. He saw the sign emblazoned on the door panel and smiled. Ted's Taxi was a legend in Helmsdale.

* * *

The supermarket was almost deserted, which was only to be expected at that early hour. Reggie took a trolley and went in, studying the list as he headed for the fruit and vegetable aisles. Selecting the items he needed took some time, for Reggie, who was meticulous, examined each of his choices carefully, rejecting any that showed even a hint of bruising. Eventually, he paused, checking the contents of the trolley against the list in his hand. Only when he was satisfied that he had got sufficient quantities of every item did he turn to head for the only checkout that was open at that time of day.

Reggie had only taken a few steps when he glanced to his left, where a solitary customer was waiting to be served at the deli counter. On the wall beyond the customer was a mirror. From its angle, the mirror reflected the customer's image. Reggie stopped dead in his tracks, unable to believe his eyes. He looked away, peering into his trolley, pretending to check the items as his mind attempted to cope with the shock. After a few seconds, he risked another covert glance. He was right. He hadn't been mistaken. But then, for Reggie, there could be no mistaking that face, despite the scars and the passage of years.

The customer, oblivious of the fact that he was being watched, collected his purchases and turned towards the checkout. As the man passed him, Reggie was able to see him close to, and got all the confirmation he needed.

Reggie leaned on the trolley, his legs trembling, breathing as if he'd been sprinting, his heart pounding wildly. Only when the customer had paid the till operator and collected his shopping did Reggie move. Abandoning his trolley, he followed the man out of the store. He watched the customer load his bags into the boot of a car in the pick-up point and

67

relaxed slightly. If the man was using Ted's Taxi, that meant he wasn't going too far. Ted restricted his driving to within the dale. Not only that, but Ted was an inveterate gossip, and Reggie knew that a few discreetly posed questions would enable him to find out where he'd taken his fare.

As he returned to the Fleece, Reggie whistled happily. Despite the heavy shopping he was carrying, he walked swiftly. The day had started well, better than he could have hoped.

'You took your time,' the chef greeted him, adding sarcastically, 'don't tell me there was a queue at the checkout?'

'No, I got caught short. I think it must have been something I ate.' Reggie accompanied the remark with a cheeky grin.

The chef stared at him in astonishment. He couldn't believe it. Reggie had actually cracked a joke.

* * *

Despite the panic caused by the still unexplained shortcomings of the greengrocer, breakfast and luncheon at the Fleece were served without a hitch. As the chef remarked, once his temper had cooled, 'To the customers, it's all serene, like a duck on the water. They're not able to see that we're paddling furiously under the surface.'

In the more relaxed atmosphere of the early afternoon, before the pre-dinner rush began, Reggie seized the opportunity of his hour-long break to walk into the centre of town. He walked across the cobbled market square towards the taxi rank alongside the town clock.

He was in luck. Ted's Taxi was the first one on the rank. Reggie greeted the owner-driver. 'You were out and about early this morning, Ted. I'd forgotten it isn't only the catering industry that works such anti-social hours. You scared the shit out of me when you blew your horn at Good Buys, but I wouldn't recommend it as a cure for constipation. What got you up at the crack of dawn? Fallen out with the wife again?'

Pretty much everyone in Helmsdale knows everyone else, and Ted was no exception. Reggie's remarks surprised the taxi driver though, for he had always thought of the chef as a polite, quiet young man with little in the way of conversation. Obviously, he had got that last bit wrong.

'I had a booking, one that was too good to turn down. Helmsdale station to meet the first train. Then a trip to the supermarket, where I waited for the fare to do some shopping. That was when I bumped into you — or came very close to it. Of course, all the time he was shopping, my meter was running. Then the final leg of the journey was taking him out to Kirk Bolton to his holiday home. A very nice little earner it turned out to be.'

'Holiday home? He's not a local, then? The thing is, I saw him inside Good Buys. It had to be him, because there was nobody else in the shop. I thought I recognized him, but if he isn't local, I must have got that wrong. Maybe he's a famous actor or something, staying here incognito perhaps.'

'I rather doubt it.' Ted laughed. 'Not unless it's a horror film. He's an ugly-looking customer, and would be even without those dreadful scars on his face. Surly bugger too, although he tips well enough. No, as far as I'm aware he's just a holidaymaker. I dropped him off at Primrose Cottage. Honestly, the weird names people come up with for their houses. There isn't a primrose to be seen. The good thing is, he's booked me for the return journey in a fortnight, so I should get another good tip from that.'

'Makes you wonder what someone on their own would find to do in a place like Kirk Bolton,' Reggie said reflectively. 'Still, it takes all sorts, as the saying goes. See you, Ted.'

He wandered off, and as he went, Ted watched him via the rear-view mirror. He wondered what the chef's interest in his fare had really been. Despite Reggie's seeming indifference, there had been something in his body language that suggested he really needed to know as much as Ted could tell him about the tourist.

Ted's musing was rudely interrupted when someone spoke to him through the open window of his car.

'Are you free?'

The question was delivered so much in the style of a character from *Are You Being Served?* that Ted almost laughed aloud. Concealing a smile, he agreed and flicked the dashboard sign to the engaged position as Reggie returned to the Fleece.

* * *

Reggie's brain was in turmoil at what he'd learned. The excitement of discovering where the man was staying was heightened, thanks to Ted's indiscretion. He not only knew the location, but also how long the man would be there. A fortnight — fourteen days in which to plan and execute a murder. Except that in Reggie's mind it wasn't going to be murder. Far from it — more a judicial execution. Judicial, because Reggie would be the judge, the only member of the jury . . . and most definitely the executioner. The government might have foregone capital punishment long ago, but Reggie hadn't signed up to that.

CHAPTER ELEVEN

Magdalena Klements had worked at the Fleece Hotel for more than two years before Reggie arrived there. At first, Magdalena had been employed purely as a chambermaid, but later, when the management realized her English was good enough, she was promoted and given extra duties as a waitress in the Fat Lamb restaurant. Her new position brought the Slovenian-born woman into contact with the kitchen staff on a more regular basis, and she was required to liaise with all of them, but more particularly with Reggie.

It would be wrong to describe their early meetings as love at first sight on behalf of either of them. To begin with, Magdalena had certainly been impressed by Reggie's polite and quiet manner, and compared this favourably with many of the young men she had encountered. He was friendly, in a gentle sort of way, and conveyed nothing to suggest that he wanted anything more than that. She disliked the forward approach of many men, their sly looks at her figure, her legs, her bottom, and when they thought they could get away with it, a surreptitious glance down her cleavage. Any one of these, coupled with sometimes overtly risqué innuendo, enraged her.

Reggie wasn't a bit like that. Had he known it, nothing could have intrigued or attracted Magdalena more than his understated charm. The fact that he was totally unaware of this simply emphasized his appeal. They became friends. After several months, almost by default, the situation changed subtly, and they began to spend their leisure hours in each other's company. It started almost by accident nearly a year ago. In a slack hour between lunch and dinner, Magdalena happened to mention a film she wanted to see that was showing in Netherdale cinema. 'The problem is,' she told Reggie, 'I have read the reviews and it sounds a very scary film. I would have liked to watch it, but not alone. I think I would be terrified.'

She hadn't intended her remarks as an invitation, nor did Reggie have any ulterior motive behind his reply. 'If you want to see it so badly, I could go with you. What is this terrifying film, anyway?'

'Would you do that, Reggie? I am not sure if you would enjoy it. The film is called *Shutter Island*, and it takes place in a mental institution.'

'That's OK,' Reggie laughed. 'I'll feel quite at home, then.'

He enjoyed the film to some extent, although not as much as his companion. Parts of it were too close to home. What he enjoyed far more was Magdalena's company, a fact which surprised him. As a result, cinema visits became a regular occurrence on their days off. How long their friendship might have remained platonic, had it not been for the staff Christmas party, is anyone's guess.

* * *

The party took the form of a buffet dinner, following which the staff took themselves off en masse to Club Wolfgang, for which their employers had generously provided free passes for that night.

Magdalena and Reggie spent a considerable part of the evening together, a fact that most of their colleagues were far too gone down the road to intoxication to notice. A little after midnight, Reggie had offered to walk her home to the tiny ground-floor flat she rented close to the market place.

On arrival, Magdalena thanked Reggie for escorting her home and wished him a Happy Christmas. Then she'd leaned forward and kissed him. The effect of the kiss was inflammatory. After several minutes, they'd separated, but stood close together, holding hands, staring into each other's eyes as if seeing their partner for the first time. They were both panting slightly, their desire for one another coursing through their veins, intoxicating them far more effectively than the wine they had drunk. Without saying a word, Magdalena had let go of one of Reggie's hands and turned to unlock her front door. She led him through the entrance, and once inside, she'd closed and locked the door behind them. She'd leaned against it, almost as if barring his way should he attempt to escape.

Escape was the last thing on Reggie's mind.

They stood for a moment facing each other, until Reggie at last managed to speak. 'Majda,' he'd asked, 'are you sure about this?'

Magdalena loved the way he pronounced the diminutive form of her name. She reached forward and began to caress him. 'Reggie,' she'd told him, 'Let's go to bed and make love.'

* * *

There was no specific reason for Reggie and Majda to keep their relationship secret — they simply preferred it that way. From the very start, both of them knew that this was far more than a one-night stand fuelled by alcohol. Knowing the affair would be long-term, it seemed a wise precaution to avoid the inevitable gossip at the hotel. Their decision was governed by their own nature, which was to protect their privacy at all costs.

They had been lovers for more than two months before Majda told Reggie her history, and even longer before he revealed his own past.

73

'My family lived in Maribor. When the Kosovo war began, my father decided we should come to England. With a wife and two young daughters to protect, he wasn't prepared to take any risks. My sister Irena was only eight years old, and I was five at the time. He had been offered a job in London, and after the war ended and peace returned, we stayed here. By that time, my father's work was becoming more demanding, and we were settled in our new schools.'

Reggie hugged her. 'I'm so glad you didn't go back to Slovenia. Do the rest of your family still live in London?'

'Yes. My father spends a lot of time commuting to America — he designs computer programs. Irena is a nurse at Great Ormond Street.'

Although Majda had revealed her own background, it was several days later that she realized she knew nothing of Reggie's past. She reasoned that he would tell her when he was ready, and until he was comfortable talking about himself, there was nothing to be gained by asking intrusive questions.

* * *

It wasn't until the evening of Reggie's early morning foray to Good Buys supermarket that Majda learned some of Reggie's childhood. On hearing it, she realized why he had been so unforthcoming.

They had left the hotel, and as they walked hand in hand across town towards her flat, Majda sensed something of her lover's excitement. She had noticed on several occasions during the working day that his mood had changed.

They had barely closed the flat door when he took her in his arms and began to kiss and caress her. There was a new urgency in the way he made love to her, an intensity of passion she had never known in him before. Reggie had always been a gentle, considerate partner in bed, but that night he was more demanding, almost insatiable in his lust for her. Not that Majda objected — on the contrary, his fire ignited a similar flame in her.

Later, she asked him cautiously, almost timidly, what the reason for the change was.

It was a long time before Reggie answered, so long that she was beginning to wonder if she had upset him, or if he felt insulted. In the event, his reply saddened, shocked and appalled her.

'Early this morning, Chef sent me to Good Buys.' He explained about the missing vegetable debacle. 'The place was all but deserted. There was only one other customer in the place as far as I could see. I recognized him immediately. Even though he has suffered some facial injuries, I could never forget his face. Just as I could never forget or forgive the terrible things he did.'

'Who is he? What did he do that was so bad?'

'Someone from my childhood — he tortured, raped and murdered my little sister. She was only twelve years old.'

* * *

Majda stared in open-mouthed astonishment. She was shocked, but listened carefully as Reggie continued, his speech halting, almost as if the words were being dragged from him by some unseen torturer. 'There were four of us — Mum, dad, my sister and me. Five of us, if you include Poppy.'

'Poppy? Who is Poppy?'

'Not who, what. Poppy was our dog, a French poodle, a lovely little thing, full of life and mischief, always on the go. She had bags of energy, tons of curiosity. My sister loved her, and the dog adored her.'

'What happened to Poppy?'

'I'll get to that. I was fourteen years old when it happened, small for my age and skinny. Mum always felt sure other mothers thought I was being mistreated and undernourished.'

'You're not small now, and you're certainly not skinny.'

'No, but that's another part of the story. Like I said, I was fourteen when the trouble started. There was this boy lived a few doors down from us, he was the same age as me. He was creepy, a real weirdo. His parents were a bit odd too.

He was their only child, and everyone thought he was just simple, no worse than that. I remember my mother saying that perhaps it was a blessing they only had the one child, because the next one could have turned out worse.' Reggie paused and smiled, grimly.

'She certainly got that wrong. What nobody realized was quite how badly deranged he was. Perhaps they did, but it didn't sink in. You have to bear in mind that after it happened my parents tried to shield me from the worst of the news.'

The grim smile appeared again. 'They didn't succeed, I'm afraid. Anyway, the boy turned out to be a total psychopath. Those aren't my words. They're the opinion of the psychiatrist who examined him before his trial, and repeated by the judge when he was passing sentence.'

* * *

It was a long while before Reggie spoke again. 'My sister used to take Poppy for a walk every afternoon. There was a big park, only a few minutes' walk from our house. As soon as she got home, she changed out of her school things and took the dog out, usually for half an hour or so. One afternoon when she hadn't returned an hour and a half later, Mum began to get worried. She phoned Dad. He came home from work, and they set off to look for her and the dog.

'Although they hadn't said anything to me, I knew there was something wrong. Anyway, when they came back, Dad rang the police. There was a huge search, but they didn't find any trace of her or the dog. Not for a couple of days. Then one of the neighbours went to put her rubbish out, and there was a terrible stench from inside the bin, and clouds of bluebottles swarming around it. She looked in and found Poppy's body. The sadistic bastard had shoved a wooden stake up the dog's backside.'

Reggie stopped speaking, emotion obviously threatening to get the better of him.

After a while he recovered his composure a little and continued, speaking slowly and quietly. 'Ten days later, they discovered a body in the park. They'd used sniffer dogs to go over the ground during the first couple of days, but they'd found no trace of her. Nor did they discover her when they checked all the neighbouring sheds and outhouses. She must have been dumped in the park after she was killed. But not before the most cruel, sadistic things had been done to her, things I won't even attempt to describe to you.'

Majda wondered if that was to protect her, or himself, if the memories were so vivid.

'I'm surprised they told you things such as that, if they were as bad as you say.'

'They didn't, but kids are cruel. Several of the boys — and girls — at school took special delight in telling me every sordid detail they'd overheard from their parents' conversations. To this day, I'm not sure if all of them are true, or if they made some of it up. Those that were confirmed via the media were bad enough. The only good thing, I suppose, as the local vicar told my parents, was that her nightmare was over. Although I didn't realize it at the time, Mum and Dad had been living their nightmare since she failed to return home. Nor did I know that my own nightmare was only just beginning.'

Majda prompted him. 'Do you feel able to tell me the rest? About your nightmare, I mean?'

'Maybe tomorrow. Believe me, this isn't easy. If it hadn't been for seeing him today, I don't think I could have mentioned any of this to anyone — not even you, Majda. I hardly need to tell you that you're the only person who knows even this much about me. I've never felt close enough to anyone to describe what went on.'

'Why don't I make us some tea?'

Reggie laughed, a little shakily. 'I love you, Majda Klements, do you know that? Who wouldn't love a girl who thinks of tea at a time like this?'

'I know your needs, Reggie. And tea is high up on that list.'

CHAPTER TWELVE

Having got home from work the following day, Reggie and Majda sat in the small lounge-cum-dining area, the silence for once not a comfortable one when Majda asked if he was prepared to continue his story.

After a while, Reggie took a deep breath and resumed his narrative. 'They arrested the boy's father to begin with. I don't know what it was that led them to him. Something to do with the blanket the body was wrapped in. They searched the house and found the cellar. It had been used to keep my sister prisoner. They said she had been gagged the whole time so nobody could hear her screams. However, when they went for a DNA match for semen and other evidence they found on her body, they only got a "familial similarity" — I think that's the term they used. The only other male in the house was the son, and when they tested his DNA they knew they had the killer. The sadist had even taken photos in the cellar whilst he was doing things to her. He was in the process of developing them when they arrested him.'

'If he was only a boy, how did he get her body out of the cellar and across to that park without anyone seeing him?'

'He was fairly big and strong, and she was like me, small and skinny. Getting her up the steps wouldn't have been a problem. The police said he stole his father's car and drove it across to the park late on the night before she was found. Later they found out he'd been "borrowing" the car a few times, usually when his father was drunk.'

'What happened at the trial?'

'It was a foregone conclusion he would be found guilty. The defence tried to argue that he was insane, but the judge wasn't having any of it. When that plea was thrown out, the sentence was life imprisonment.'

'But if he was given a life sentence, how come he's free now? This only happened twenty years ago, so he'll only be thirty-four or -five, won't he?'

'The do-gooders and human rights activists campaigned long and hard against whole-of-life sentences. In the end they had their way, via the European Court. Nobody stands up and argues for the human rights of the victims and their relatives. Nobody seems to worry about what happens to them. They talk glibly about the trial giving closure to the victim's family. What they don't understand is that there is no such thing as closure. The nightmare is with you every day, from the moment you wake up until you go to sleep — if you can sleep, that is.'

Majda remembered several times when Reggie had been restless in the night, muttering indistinguishable words in his sleep. Perhaps they were part of the torment he was describing. A stray thought crossed her mind. 'If you recognized this monster today, how come he didn't know who you are?'

'I said I was little and skinny, remember. My appearance has changed a lot from when I was fourteen years old. There's no way he would have been able to tell I was the boy who lived on his street.'

'Can I ask you one question? You don't have to answer if it's too painful for you.'

Reggie nodded.

'You've been really brave telling me your story, but you've not mentioned your sister's name.'

He smiled. 'No, I haven't, have I?' He reached for his wallet and took out a well-worn photograph. 'Amelia Jane.'

* * *

Majda went to make a fresh pot of tea. She guessed that what Reggie still had to tell her was so bad that he was having difficulty bringing himself to say it.

Eventually, having stared into his cup for some time, he continued.

'The trial and the relentless publicity must have been terrible ordeals for my parents. They tried to shield me from the worst of it, but there was no hiding from the army of reporters, photographers and TV cameras that were camped outside our door for weeks on end. The problem was, I was so lost in my own misery that I didn't appreciate how much worse it was for them.'

'But all that must have ended after the trial, surely? I mean the reporters and the TV stuff.' Majda moved closer and put her hand on his.

'Yes, that went away, eventually. My parents attended every day of the trial. When they came home after sentence had been passed, far from celebrating, they seemed bitter and angry — with the court, the verdict, even each other. In the end, my father walked out and went to the pub. I remember that day vividly, not because of the sentence, but because it was the last time I can recall seeing my father sober.'

He drained his mug of tea. 'His drinking got worse, and the atmosphere at home went with it. Barely a day passed without terrible rows and cruel words. He lost his job — sacked for turning up drunk, which meant we couldn't keep up the mortgage payments. We were about to have the house repossessed when he was knocked over and killed by a bus. The bus driver said he simply stepped out in front of it, giving him no chance to swerve or brake. The death was recorded as accidental, although a lot of people believed he had committed suicide.

'There was no doubt about my mother, though.' Reggie tutted and sighed. 'She was left alone to cope — and couldn't. Six months after my father died, when we'd been moved to a grotty council flat, she went to bed one night in the company of a couple of packets of sleeping tablets and a litre bottle of vodka. I found her the next morning. I was fifteen years old. My grandparents were dead. Mother and father had no siblings. In just over a year I'd lost all of my family.'

* * *

Reggie grimaced. 'Now I was left to the tender mercies of the local Social Services department, who placed me in a care home.' He laughed mirthlessly. 'Care home? That's a misnomer if ever I heard one. An institution for bullying, brutality and sexual abuse would be a far better description for the one I landed in. I was beaten up regularly by one of the older boys, and sexually abused by one of the care workers. After a while, I got an opportunity to stop them. The school I went to had a good gymnasium and I started training with the weights, as well as taking boxing lessons. I think the games master might have suspected something was wrong, because he went to great lengths to ensure I got all the tuition I needed. What really turned out to be a lucky break for me was when he recommended me to a local martial arts instructor who was looking for bright young talent for his karate classes.'

'This is when you began to change from the skinny little boy into the powerfully built man?' Majda guessed.

'That was the start of the process.' He shook his head to rid himself of the nightmare talking about it all had brought to mind. 'I think that's enough for tonight. Let's get some sleep.'

'Sleep?' Majda smiled, tilting her head and fluttering her eyelashes, deliberately.

'OK then, let's go to bed.'

* * *

Later, Reggie knew he had to reveal the rest of his story.

'By the time I was seventeen, I had both the strength and skill to look after myself, even against bigger, stronger opponents. I learned how easy it is to kill someone with a single blow. I knew I was ready to take my revenge on one or two people. Although I couldn't get at my sister's killer, I had some tasty targets close at hand. One night, the care worker decided he wanted some fun. As I got older he left me alone, but I knew he wouldn't stop. I saw him approach one of the young lads and lead him away. He got more than he bargained for.

'My first two punches broke three of his ribs. Then I stuffed a handkerchief in his mouth and proceeded to beat him all over. Not hard enough to kill him, although I could have done so easily, but badly enough to leave bruises all over his face, his arms, legs and body. Bruises that would take a good deal of explaining away. I left him with the warning ringing in his ears that if he tried to report me, I would tell everyone that he'd sodomized me and others on a regular basis for over two years.'

'What happened?'

'A week later, he resigned. I neither know nor care what happened to him after that. The night I sorted him out, I took his keys and went to the office. The boy who used to beat me had left by then, but I found his file and got his new address. I went there and took my revenge. When I left he was barely conscious. I hope he lives to a ripe old age, because I feel sure he'll remember it every day.'

'Did it help?' Majda asked.

Reggie smiled. 'A bit.'

* * *

As soon I was eighteen I had to leave the home. I gave them a forwarding address in Liverpool, one that I'd made up, but I caught a train to Leeds. The last thing I wanted was anyone from my past being able to trace me.'

'Why Liverpool and Leeds?'

'Why not? The night I was making my plans, Liverpool were playing football. It was on the telly. I got off the train in Leeds and caught a local one and ended up in a town called Ilkley. I managed to get a job, but I was restless, and kept moving from place to place. I suppose I was running away still, although I didn't recognize it as such at the time.'

'How did you go on for money?'

'The strange thing was that although there was some doubt over my father's death, he had a life insurance policy, and because the insurance company couldn't prove it wasn't an accident, they had to pay out. Social Services tried to grab it, but they were overruled. It wasn't a fortune, but it was more than enough to tide me over, even though I could only draw a small amount every month.'

'You seem to have stopped running away now, though,' Majda pointed out.

'Even the best runners get tired eventually. For long enough, no matter what I did or where I went, one image remained with me, a constant companion I couldn't ditch, no matter how hard I tried. And I certainly did try. That was the image of the man who had ruined my life, taken my family from me and was now at ease in some prison cell, being protected by reluctant guards from getting what he deserves. That image haunts me day and night.

'Then one day, an item on the TV news brought me great delight. He had been attacked in prison by a gang of convicts. I celebrated that night by getting drunk, and every time I raised my glass I toasted those prisoners, coupled with the hope that he would die a slow and painful death. But that didn't happen, and with the benefit of hindsight, I realize that wouldn't have satisfied my desire for revenge if he had died then. He would have escaped, you see. Nothing less than taking that revenge myself will do, and now I have the chance, I'm not about to pass it up. Someone should deal with *all* these perverts, get rid of them. That's my story. My sad, sorry story.'

He paused, and looked directly at Majda.

'And now, I'm going to kill John Penney.'

CHAPTER THIRTEEN

Reggie waited for Majda's reaction, half fearful of how she would deal with all he had told her. Would she think he was a monster? Understanding was the most he could hope for.

After a few minutes' silence she got out of her chair, walked over to him and put her hand on the back of his neck, pulling his head against her breast.

Neither of them slept well, and as they lay awake in the pre-dawn light, Majda said reflectively, 'It must be carried out in a way that prevents suspicion falling on you.'

Reggie was surprised at her bold statement and listened as she continued, 'It is very difficult to see how that can be done, when you live so close to where he is staying. Whatever happens will require very careful planning. Nothing can be left to chance, and I cannot see a way of you being able to carry it out alone. The police would be bound to suspect you. Once they know who the dead man is, your name will come top of their list of suspects.'

Reggie could hardly believe his luck. Majda had not only accepted his tale, accepted his plan to commit murder, she even seemed prepared to help him. 'There is one bit I left out of my story,' he told her after a moment or two. 'When I left the care home, I left my real identity behind. Reggie Barnes does not exist. I made him up.'

'How could you do that? You would need papers, surely? For work and things?'

'I found someone in Leeds. Up until then, I'd survived by taking cash-in-hand jobs, where the employers were fiddling the taxman, so no questions were asked. What I needed was an identity that would pass muster for National Insurance purposes, so I managed to locate an expert. He charged a hell of a lot for his services, but he assured me the result would be worth it. So far he's been right. He even claimed I'd be able to get a passport or driving licence easily enough, but up to press I haven't dared try.'

'That's brilliant, and it means there's no way the police could connect Reggie Barnes with the brother of a dead girl. Especially as the only description they have of you is a skinny, undersized fourteen-year-old. So now all we have to do is plot the perfect murder. Although I don't think we should consider it as murder. This is merely the execution of a criminal who has escaped the justice he deserves. People like this sick man deserve everything they get.'

Reggie hugged her. 'Majda, you are wonderful. I can't believe how lucky I am.'

'After all you have suffered, perhaps it was time your luck changed. By the way, I'll always call you Reggie, but just what is your name?'

'Philip.'

* * *

Despite her bold statements of support, Majda was torn with guilt and indecision over Reggie's plan to kill Penney. Although she didn't doubt a word of what Reggie had told her about the suffering this evil man had caused, was what Reggie was proposing to do to him much better? Apart from such ethical considerations, what if, in spite of all their careful planning,

Reggie got caught? She knew that she could be classed as an accessory — indeed, she probably was one already. And if he went ahead with the killing and was arrested, she too could end up in prison.

When he announced he had formed a plan, Majda listened with deepening misgivings as he outlined how he intended to deal with Penney. She stared at him in silence after he finished speaking, hardly believing what she had been told.

Eventually, when Reggie prompted her for her opinion, Majda said, 'I think you're mad if you believe for one moment you will get away with this. Just think of all the ways it could go wrong. Please, Reggie, give this foolish idea up. I know how much you and your family have suffered because of this monster, but there must be a better way.'

'If there is, I wish you'd tell me, because I don't know of one.'

In all honesty, Majda couldn't think of anything that would come close to satisfying Reggie's desire for revenge. She shook her head, partly in disbelief at his wild idea, partly because she felt helpless at being unable to persuade him to abandon the plan, but mostly because she could hardly believe that she was conspiring with her lover to help him commit what was nothing more than cold-blooded murder.

You could dress it up however you wanted, Majda thought, justifying it as an act of righteous vengeance against a sadistic and unrepentant killer, looking on it as an execution. But the law would still regard it as murder. They would come down on the perpetrator as hard as they had on the man who had caused him such suffering and distress.

Majda tried her best, arguing long and hard, pleading with Reggie not to go through with his scheme. Her trump card was their relationship — the love she knew she felt for Reggie, and his reciprocal feelings for her. When even that failed to dissuade him, she bowed to the inevitable and accepted defeat.

* * *

The holiday cottage was ideal. Although it was at the end of a terrace, the other two houses were unoccupied. That meant it was completely secluded. Ideal for what he had planned. His contact had found it. He had even gone further and picked out a target. That was how their network operated. It was difficult for Penney, being under regular supervision, but the network members were aware of that. Understanding it was one thing, but they went much further, providing all the background he needed to operate. In return, of course, they wanted a share of the action, but that was understandable, and Penney could hardly argue, considering the lengths they went to for him.

Nearing the scheduled time for his contact to arrive, Penney's excitement grew. What would the victim they would bring him be like? he wondered. Of course, Penney didn't think of her as a victim. To do so would be to admit the depravity of what they planned to do to the girl. He preferred the term 'pleasure'. He glanced at his watch for the fourth, or was it the fifth time? Any minute now, his contact should be here. If he was punctual, that is, and Penney felt sure he would be.

There was a knock at the door. This was it. The moment had arrived.

Penney opened the front door to allow the visitor to gain entry as quickly as possible with his precious cargo. The night was moonless, there was no light showing anywhere. He waited for his partner to appear. Seconds later, even though Penney hadn't been able to pick him out in the darkness, he heard a voice close by. 'John, is that you?'

'It's me, come on in. Have you got what I want?'

'Oh, yes. Here it is.'

* * *

Majda's deep misgivings had in no way abated. They'd intensified as she'd watched Reggie prepare to set out on his mission. There was so much that could go wrong. What if he'd misjudged the man he was going to tackle? What if Penney proved too strong for him and it was Reggie, rather than his intended target, who finished up dead? Worse still, if anything could be worse, what if he failed to reach his destination? Reggie was planning to cycle to the village where Penney was staying. He was going in the dead of night, on a bicycle, clad from head to toe in black. He intended to douse the bike's lights when he got near to Kirk Bolton. Then all it would take would be some careless motorist, possibly one under the influence of drink, and the escapade would end in tragedy.

These and a hundred other worries filled Majda's mind almost from the very second she'd closed the door behind him.

She had no idea how long his mission would take, even if it proved successful. Uncertain when to start worrying because he hadn't returned, she began to fret almost immediately, pacing up and down the small flat, fidgeting, listening for the slightest sound that might signal his return. As the night wore on, her concern deepened, and a dozen questions flitted in a never-ending carousel through her mind, all starting with the phrase 'what if' and all remaining unanswered. Each repetition, each circuit of the carousel, served only to heighten her stress until her nerves were almost at breaking point.

* * *

It was almost dawn before she heard the sound of his key in the lock. She sprang to her feet and rushed over to help him inside with the bicycle and stow it in the space behind her kitchen. As soon as he was inside and Majda had closed the door, she switched the hall light on. Reggie blinked in the sudden brightness. She looked at him. There was no air of triumph about him. On the contrary, his shoulders were slumped as if in defeat, his expression one of agitation and dejection. He certainly didn't bear the excited, almost exalted, look of the man who had been looking forward to exacting his revenge.

'What happened, Reggie? Was he there? Did you get him?'

Almost as she was speaking she saw the bloodstains on his gloves, the darker patches on his clothing. 'Did you do it? Is he dead? Did you kill him?'

It seemed an eternity before Reggie answered. 'Oh yes, he's dead, right enough. Dead, just the way I wanted him to be. He was made to suffer before he died.'

'That was what you went there for, surely? When you say he was made to suffer, does that mean you left him to die?'

'No, Majda, just the opposite. I went to the cottage to kill John Penney — and now he's dead.'

CHAPTER FOURTEEN

Kelly Fielding glanced out of the conservatory window in her Kirk Bolton cottage. Despite the bright sunshine, the room felt cold. She would need a hat, a scarf and her shooting jacket when she walked the dog. She turned to see the spaniel sitting patiently by the door. His request couldn't have been expressed more eloquently if he'd been able to speak. Kelly smiled, 'OK, Boy, I'll put my boots on.'

She would enjoy the fresh air and exercise as much as the dog, especially after being cooped up all the previous day working until late in the evening at a client's premises. Stocktaking is much easier in many companies nowadays, but some of Kelly's clients still preferred a manual check to a computer scan. Life wasn't always easy for an auditor.

The dog stood up, stretched and wagged his tail in anticipation. He watched with interest as his mistress selected her footwear. He associated boots with long walks, with woods, fields and streams. The tempo of the wagging increased, signalling his growing excitement and anticipation.

Kelly was pleased too. Her Springer Spaniel was a highly-regarded gun dog, with a first-class reputation amongst the shooting fraternity in the area. However, as she told the dog, today was merely for walking, not for him to work as a retriever. Kelly pondered telling him the game shooting season was over, but wasn't certain he'd understand this. She liked to give him long walks whenever possible to maintain his fitness level. Today was ideal.

As she closed the cupboard where she kept her footwear, Kelly noticed a pair of her ex-husband's shoes. Those could go to the next jumble sale, she thought. She wondered where Harry was now, and if he was enjoying life with his new partner. Not that she really cared. She had done exceedingly well from the divorce settlement and didn't miss him. Not even for the sex, because as his attention had turned elsewhere his performance in bed had become less and less frequent and certainly far less satisfying. She picked up the dog's lead and let him out before locking the door.

* * *

At the end of the drive they turned right, and from this, the dog knew today wasn't a working day. Once they got to the end of the village street, they passed two cottages. Kelly knew the owner of one of the cottages would be out at work, but she stopped for a brief chat with the other, a retired farm worker, who was tending his vegetable garden. It was too cold to stand around for long, and they soon entered the narrow lane, to emerge alongside the fields bordering the public footpath that led to Kirk Bolton. Kelly reached the woodland, with the dog bounding ahead in search of fresh scents — or pheasants to flush.

They crossed the narrow wooden footbridge that spanned the small tributary of the River Helm. The dog ignored the structure, preferring to splash happily in the shallow water of the stream. Kelly watched indulgently as the animal enjoyed himself, reflecting that the only way to keep a spaniel out of water is to heat it up and add soap. Eventually, he responded to her whistle, and they commenced the return leg of their journey, which took them to the far end of the village from Kelly's house.

The narrow lane boasted a terrace of three holiday cottages, and as they approached the first of these, the dog turned, sniffed the air and then set off towards the building, clearing the waist-high garden fence with all the ease of a steeplechaser.

His behaviour was unusual, to say the least. Once inside the garden, the dog headed for the house door and stopped by the step, head down, barking furiously. Kelly frowned, puzzled by her dog's actions. If this had happened on a shoot, she would have known that he had identified the location of a dead or wounded bird that was to be collected. But this was only a walk, and there were certainly no game birds anywhere nearby.

Kelly opened the garden gate and called her dog back, but he didn't respond. This too was unusual, almost unheard of. He stood looking towards her, then down at the step, then barked again. Obviously, whatever had attracted his attention was something he thought merited her inspection.

Kelly walked up the narrow paved path and as she got close to the step, saw an irregular reddish-brown stain on the stone slab. It looked like blood, and from her dog's reaction, Kelly guessed that someone or something had bled profusely on that doorstep.

Resisting the temptation to drag the dog away, a temptation she later wished she had given in to, Kelly knocked on the door. She waited, and getting no response, knocked again. Still no answer. Perhaps someone had injured themselves severely, and was unable to come to the door? If that was the case, and she didn't at least offer to help, she would never forgive herself.

Kelly tried a third time, but with no success. She wondered about trying the door, and if it was open, going inside, but that would be too much of an intrusion. She glanced to her left, and decided to peer in through the window of the front room. The winter sun was reflecting brightly on the panes, making it difficult to see inside, and the red paint on the window didn't help. Somebody's a messy decorator, she thought. Kelly cupped her hands against the glass, and with this effective screen against the glare, looked a second time.

She recoiled so violently that she almost fell, stumbling over a rose bush that vented its spite via several painful scratches to the back of her legs. Kelly ignored the pain, recalling the horror of what she had seen inside the cottage. Her stomach heaved and she swallowed, once, twice and then a third time, as she fought against the nausea that was threatening to overcome her.

Fortunately, she wasn't of a squeamish nature. She wouldn't have been much use as a handler of gun dogs if she had been, and was more prone to swear than to cry. The sight of blood didn't normally upset her, but the grotesque obscenity of what was beyond the window was too much for even the most hardened character.

She called her dog to heel, in a tone he recognized as being non-negotiable. Together they marched, almost ran, to the end of the lane. It was late morning, and the village shop opposite the lane end had no customers inside. Kelly and the shopkeeper were friends, and when Kelly asked to use the phone in an emergency, her request was granted immediately. She dialled 999, and when the operator asked which service she required, she answered, 'Police,' adding, 'it's far too late for an ambulance.'

* * *

Control room immediately dispatched a patrol car to the scene. It was DC Andrews' day off and DC Pearce was at Netherdale looking though old files on local perverts, trying to find any connection to the bodies. DS Mironova was giving evidence in Crown Court and not expected back until the following day. There was only Mike Nash and Adil in the CID suite when Steve passed on the message.

'OK, Adil and I are heading out. Can you mind the shop, please? Alert Mexican Pete and a CSI team will you?'

'Are you sure you don't want to wait until my lot have checked the place over? If it was someone rehearsing a scene for a horror film and Mexican Pete gets called out on a wild goose chase, you know how ratty he can get.'

Nash had been subjected to one or two of the pathologist's fits of temper over the years. 'Good point, Steve. I'll phone him from my mobile once I have confirmation from the guys you sent. What was the name of the woman who found the alleged body?'

'Mrs Kelly Fielding. She's waiting in the village shop.'

'Right, we'll get going.'

Nash reached the narrow lane and stopped behind the gaudily-painted police car. One of the officers was threading incident tape around the garden fence whilst the other stood guard in front of the doorstep. The second man nodded morosely to Nash. 'Have you been inside?' Nash asked him.

'No fear. Not that room. We looked through the window, that was enough for us — more than enough, to be honest.'

'That bad, is it?'

'And more besides. Put it this way, I hope you haven't eaten lunch, because I wouldn't give much for your chances of holding on to it, once you see what's inside there.'

'Have you checked the rest of the building?'

'Yes, it's all secure. No sign of life.'

Nash winced at the unintentional pun. 'What about the adjoining properties?'

'Both locked up. Doesn't appear to be anyone in either of them. I think all three are holiday cottages.'

'OK, we'll have a quick look through the window, and then go talk to the woman who called us. Have you spoken to her?'

'Yes, we had a quick word when we arrived. Fit as a butcher's dog, she is. A shame she's married.'

Nash concealed a smile and moved across to look in the window. The sight of what was inside effectively removed the last trace of the smile. He nodded to the officer. 'Yes, definitely not for the squeamish.'

He left Adil to supervise the scene and before crossing the road to speak to the witness, Nash used his mobile to call the pathologist.

Ramirez' reaction was as caustic as he could have expected. 'I haven't heard from you for days. I should have known it was too good to last.'

Nash gave him the details.

'And only one body, you say? My, you are slipping, Nash. I'll be along as fast as I can.'

* * *

Kelly was in the back room of the shop, sipping a mug of tea when the shop door opened. The bell announcing a new arrival tinkled merrily, contrasting with Kelly's sombre mood. The day had started so well, but the finding of the body had upset her far more than she was prepared to acknowledge. She glanced through to the shop and assumed the man to be a customer. This couldn't be a detective. He looked far too nice. A shame, really. If he had been a detective, Kelly would have enjoyed being interviewed by him. She looked down at her dog, curled up in the corner, bored by the way his walk had ended. She was surprised when the newcomer was shown into the room and spoke.

'Mrs Fielding? Kelly Fielding?'

Kelly looked round. 'Yes.'

'I'm Detective Inspector Nash.' He held his right hand out, displaying his warrant card with the other. Kelly shook hands as Nash asked, 'Would you care to tell me how you came to find the body?'

Kelly recounted the story of their walk. She described what she had seen without any hysterical embellishments. 'I thought it was paint, not blood.' She shivered.

'That must have been very upsetting,' he sympathized.

She nodded. 'It wasn't exactly what I was expecting when we set out.'

'OK, I'm going to have to leave you for now. I have to attend the crime scene. However, I'll need to take more details, times and so forth. Would it be in order for me and my DC to come to your house when I've finished there? I can't be specific on time, these things can drag on, and I wouldn't want to disturb anything you have planned.'

'No, that will be fine. There's only the two of us.' Kelly gestured to the dog. 'And neither of us are planning on going out.'

She watched Nash leave and went to hand her empty mug to the shopkeeper.

She grinned at Kelly. 'Going home to tidy up before he visits you? I wouldn't waste your time. I've seen him round and about in Helmsdale and recognized him from his photo in the papers. Last time I saw him he had a beautiful woman on his arm, and I'd say he's well and truly spoken for, especially as he was pushing a pram. Judging by the way he was looking at her, I'd guess he's extremely happy with that arrangement.'

Kelly sighed. 'All the best ones have been taken, I think.'

'He is nice, though. You never know your luck. He might have a twin brother.'

Kelly laughed. 'I think that's too much to hope for.'

CHAPTER FIFTEEN

Nash and Adil donned the required protective gear prior to entering the cottage. Not having Clara alongside him felt strange. He had Adil, though, and would be able to see how he reacted as the newest, and youngest, member of the team. It would be interesting to see if he had any ideas.

Clara was due to return tomorrow, and given what he'd seen in that one brief glimpse through the cottage window, Nash reckoned that her timing was excellent. For preference, he'd rather be in the witness box, being grilled by a hostile defence counsel, than having to stare at the horror within the house. It wasn't a sight he'd wish on his worst enemy. As he moved towards the cottage door, Nash wondered how Mrs Fielding would cope with what she'd seen. She'd seemed OK when he'd spoken to her, but perhaps when reaction set in things would change.

He nodded to the two uniformed officers. 'Mexican Pete should be along soon. Tell him we're inside, will you?'

The outer door led into a small hallway, off which was the sitting room. The dining table was situated in front of the window, presumably so holidaymakers could enjoy the pastoral views while they ate. The furniture and fittings were basic, probably bought from the same suppliers as many other holiday cottages, in an area where tourism rivalled agriculture as the main industry.

Nash made a mental note to find out who the owners or letting agents for the property were. Perhaps either the shop-keeper or Mrs Fielding would know. He pointed to the trail of blood leading from the door. 'Watch your step, Adil, stick to the side. Make sure you avoid any footprints and keep your distance from the victim. Otherwise, you might bear the wrath of Professor Ramirez — and that won't be pleasant.'

'I have done this before, sir,' Adil responded.

'Sorry, of course,' Nash replied, happy to note Adil was sticking to the rule of 'no familiarity' when out of the office.

They stared at the body spread-eagled across the dining table. Nash's nose wrinkled in disgust at the sight. The vic-tim had been sliced open, disembowelled almost, the wound appearing to stretch almost from groin to throat. Not only that, but it had penetrated deeply.

'What do you think, Adil?'

'This looks exactly like the one at the flat. It was an act of either insanity, deep hatred — or possibly both.'

Was this the tenant of the cottage? If so, who was he? And what had he done to merit such a violent assault? Nash stared at the stain that covered the surface of the table. One thing for certain, that table was ruined. Nash dismissed the irrelevant and frivolous thought and moved to one side, which gave him a better view. From what he could see, Nash guessed the man's age to be somewhere between thirty and forty. He noted sev-eral scars on the man's face and could guess their significance. Obviously, the victim was no stranger to acts of violence.

Adil wondered if this could be a gangland murder. 'Those scars look like the sort inflicted with a razor, a favour-ite gang weapon,' he said.

'It seems unlikely. Gangs tend to thrive in large towns and cities, not in tiny villages in remote countryside. Not unless he was hunted down.'

Nash's train of thought branched from this, as he recalled there was no sign of a vehicle at the property. How had the man got to Kirk Bolton? Nash knew there were only two buses a week that operated on that route. If the man had travelled on one of them, it seemed likely he was familiar enough with the area to have at least a basic knowledge of the schedules.

The alternatives were he had either come by taxi, or had been driven here in someone's car. Could that have been the killer? Again, it didn't seem likely. Why bring your victim to a holiday cottage if you intend to kill him?

* * *

Nash had got no further with his deliberations when he was interrupted by the arrival of the pathologist.

Professor Ramirez had a fiery reputation that many officers found daunting. Despite his sarcastic outbursts about Nash's necrophilia and his ability to find corpses, coupled with sly allusions to the detective's love life, the two of them had an excellent working relationship.

'What's this? An Easter special, giving up chocolate for Lent, are you? Tempting fate a bit, aren't you, Nash? I thought your type perished if you were exposed to daylight?'

'I have a special dispensation if there's blood about, Professor.'

Ramirez sniffed and glanced across at the corpse. 'There's plenty of that. I don't think someone liked this man very much. Almost as much as they didn't like your friend at the flat.'

'That's just what I was thinking. The problem is trying to decide whether it's personal hatred, insane frenzy or a potential serial killer.'

'Fortunately, that's your department, not mine. I have enough to do coping with the corpses you find for me.'

He glanced back towards the door, where the police photographer plus Ramirez' two assistants were on the point of entering. 'I suggest you two make yourselves scarce for a while,' he told Nash. 'It's going to get very cramped in here, and more than a little unpleasant.'

The assistants were staring at the body. 'What the professor means,' one of them told Nash, 'is that after our friend takes his holiday snaps, it isn't going to be pretty watching us trying to put Humpty Dumpty together again.'

Nash needed no further encouragement to leave. 'Come on, Adil. We'll go and check the rest of the house.'

* * *

Nash headed towards the rear of the property, heaving a sigh of relief as he mentally closed the door on the grim sight in the front room. No matter how often he attended scenes of violent death, he could not remain unaffected by the experience. Not for the first time, he marvelled at how Ramirez and others like him coped with the horror that was a part of their job.

To his left, a narrow flight of steps led to the upper floor of the two-storey building. Nash and Adil climbed the steep stairway, taking care to avoid touching the handrail. Although they were wearing nitrile gloves, even a smudged fingerprint could be sufficient to result in a missed opportunity to identify the culprit.

The first floor consisted of two large bedrooms. In the first, Nash found ample evidence of occupation. A wheeled suitcase stood alongside the window on a folding luggage rack. The lid of the case was unzipped, revealing it to be empty. Nash assumed the contents had been the clothing that was strewn across a chair back and hanging in the fitted wardrobe. The bed had a duvet over it, and one corner of the quilt had been thrown back, as if the resident had just got out of bed. Nash turned his attention to the second room. Like the first, this too had a double bed, but there was no bedding on the mattress, not even pillows. The wardrobe was bare of any clothing, suggesting that this room had not been occupied. However, what there was in the room both puzzled and intrigued Nash. Close to the foot of the bed was a large tripod, on top of which was a very modern and expensive-looking camcorder. Nash stared at this for a moment before turning to look at the bed.

It seemed obvious that the camcorder had either been used, or was to be used, and the bed suggested an obvious subject for what was to be filmed. Additional evidence of this came when Adil pointed to the bedposts. Attached to all four were metal shackles, linked by short lengths of chain to very efficient-looking manacles.

What had gone on in this room? Or what was planned to take place here? Was it some sort of sado-masochistic or hardcore porn home movie? Had the man downstairs been killed as part of some grotesque snuff movie, filmed by the pervert who killed him? Or had he set up the equipment in what appeared to be a torture chamber, only for the planned venture to go sour on him?

Nash made a mental note to ask CSI to prioritize the examination of the camcorder and its contents, before carefully closing the door and returning to the ground floor.

He turned to his left, into the galley-style kitchen. His first act was to check the contents of the fridge-freezer. Both sections of the unit were only part full, and the items were much as Nash guessed someone renting the cottage for a short holiday would bring with them. For the most part they comprised ready meals and convenience foods such as were stocked by almost every supermarket chain. There was no sign of fresh produce, fruit or vegetables. Obviously the shopper wasn't into healthy eating. Nash noted the named price tickets and closed the fridge door.

Adil flipped open the lid of the pedal bin. There were a couple of carrier bags inside bearing the logo of Good Buys. To one side, Nash saw a till receipt. 'Grab that, will you, Adil?'

He passed Nash the strip of paper.

He stared at the date and time, checking the listed items against what he had seen in the freezer. The two matched. He replaced the receipt and looked around.

There was nothing else of interest in either the kitchen or the bathroom and toilet beyond. He was bracing himself to return to the sitting room when his mobile rang.

It was Viv Pearce. 'I've not had much success here and wondered what do you want me to do now? I understand you've a crime scene on the go, and another fairly grim one, by the sound of what Steve Meadows told me.'

'Nobody could accuse Steve of exaggeration, that's for sure.' Nash described the find at the holiday cottage. 'Mexican Pete's about to remove the victim, once they've shovelled all the bits together. I'd like you to come and babysit CSI. That will free the uniforms up. Adil's with me and I want to talk to the woman who found the body.' Nash smiled ruefully as he added, 'That's partly an excuse to get away from this place. It's not just the body, there's something creepy been going on. Don't ask me why I think that, it's just a feeling I've got.'

'OK, Mike, I'll set off straightaway.'

* * *

Nash went back into the front room and was relieved to find that the coroner's assistants had already taken care of the remains. At the end of the garden, he noticed a figure bent double. It was the photographer. Ramirez was still in the front room, carefully placing equipment in his case. Nash averted his eyes from the macabre tools of the pathologist's trade, but that wasn't altogether successful, as it brought the table into his line of vision. Without the corpse to block the view, the amount of blood was a revolting sight.

'What can you tell me, Professor?'

'One of the officers spotted what looks like fresh vomit in the garden. The photographer is snapping it and I'll ask Forensics to take a sample. It wasn't you, was it?'

'I thought you knew me better than that,' Nash retorted.

'Well, someone didn't like what they saw. It might have been the person who rang it in, but I'll leave that to you to find out. I'll email copies of all the snaps to you for your scrapbook. I have lectures tomorrow, so the post-mortem will be early, seven o'clock sharp. Don't be late. I feel sure you won't want to miss any of the fun and you can have your breakfast afterwards. Not that there's much doubt as to the cause of death. Without doing precise calculations, I'd hazard a guess that our victim has been dead since either late last night or the early hours of this morning, but I'll confirm that later. I'm going back to the mortuary now. I'll check the dead man's fingerprints to see if he's known to us.'

As the pathologist was opening his car door, Nash glanced to his right and saw the Forensic team had arrived. He spoke to the team leader, emphasizing the possible importance of the camcorder, the till receipt in the bin and the vomit in the garden.

He approached the uniformed officers and asked if either of them had left their breakfast at the scene. They both disclaimed responsibility. He told them Pearce would be arriving to replace them and take over the scene log, and to ensure they were listed. They both looked relieved to be returning to their normal duties, but whether that was due to boredom, or a desire to put as much distance as possible between them and the macabre crime scene, Nash wasn't sure.

* * *

After Kelly Fielding returned home, her first act was an uncharacteristic one. She went from room to room, checking that everything was secure. When she was content, she decided to take a shower. This too was unusual at that time of the day, but Kelly wanted to try and wash away the memory of what she had seen at the cottage.

Returning downstairs, Kelly was greeted enthusiastically by the spaniel. 'Your clock's fast,' she told him. 'It's nowhere near food time yet.'

The dog gave her a soulful look, but Kelly was used to his play-acting. As she was returning to the kitchen, she noticed a Range Rover pull to a halt at the end of the drive.

She saw the detective and a good-looking Asian man emerge. She went to open the front door.

'Please, come in. I was about to make a drink, if you'd both like one,' she greeted Nash. 'I would normally have had something to eat round about now, but I don't think I can face the thought of food.'

'I know what you mean,' Nash agreed. 'It must have been very upsetting. Coffee would be nice, if it isn't too much trouble.' He turned and indicated Adil. 'This is Detective Constable Hassan.'

As she made coffee, Kelly asked, 'Was it really bad inside there? I only had a momentary glimpse through the window, and that was enough for me — more than enough, in fact.'

'It was pretty grim. It isn't something you get hardened to.'

'I don't know how you both do it. I can't imagine how difficult it must be to see something like that, and then go home and talk to your wife about normal, everyday things.'

Nash smiled. 'Fortunately, my wife knows enough about my job not to ask questions. Poor Adil only has his own company.'

She turned to Adil and smiled sympathetically. 'Oh, you poor thing, having no one to discuss your day with.'

Adil looked embarrassed at the attention.

She passed Nash a mug of coffee, and as he sipped it, he began to ask her about the way she discovered the body.

'I didn't,' she answered with a wry smile. She pointed to the spaniel, curled up on his bed. 'Boy scented the blood. It's what he's trained for as a working gun dog.'

Nash took Kelly through her story again, Adil noting her replies down in his incident book.

'Did you see anyone during your walk?' Nash asked. 'Near that cottage especially?'

'I spoke to one of the villagers. He was planting potatoes in his vegetable garden, but that's on the other side of the village.' Kelly paused as the implication of his question struck her. 'When you asked about anybody near the cottage, does that mean you think the killer might still have been there?' She looked horrified. 'How awful. I never considered that possibility. Was I in danger, do you think?'

Nash hastened to reassure her. 'The pathologist estimated that the victim had been dead for several hours before you found him. I feel certain the killer would have been long gone before you got to the cottage.'

'That's a relief, Inspector Nash.'

'I have one other question. We noticed some vomit in the garden outside the cottage. When you saw that body, did it upset you so much you were sick?'

'No, fortunately I managed to hold on to my breakfast.'

Nash smiled. 'That's good. If you think of anything else, anything you might have forgotten, no matter how trivial or irrelevant it seems, let me or Adil know.' He took out a card for Helmsdale station and passed it to her.

Nash was about to stand up when his mobile rang. He glanced at the screen and apologized to Kelly. 'I'll have to take this.'

She nodded understanding, and watched as he left the room to answer the call.

Within seconds, Nash was angry. 'What?' he exclaimed. 'Are you sure? And there's no possibility of error? No, I believe you. What I can't understand is why we weren't told he was here. No, I appreciate that's nothing to do with you. I was taken by surprise, that's all. Don't worry, I'll be asking questions. Lots of questions — and the answers had better be good. Thank you, Professor.' Nash ended the call and returned to the room.

He stared at Adil, who knew at once Nash's mind was elsewhere.

'I take it there have been developments?' Adil asked.

Nash returned from wherever he'd been mentally. 'We have to go.' He turned to Kelly. 'At some stage I shall have to get you to give a formal statement, Mrs Fielding. If you can call at Helmsdale or Netherdale police stations that would be ideal, then we can get it typed up and signed.'

'Helmsdale would be much more convenient, in case I'm called away.'

'Do you travel a lot? Is that to do with your work?'

'Not as much as I used to. I'm an accountant and a lot of my work can be done from home. Things like stock checks and delivering reports have to be done in person, though.'

'In that case, DC Hassan will be sure to phone and arrange a convenient time.'

She smiled at Adil again. 'I'll look forward to hearing from you.'

CHAPTER SIXTEEN

When Clara Mironova got to Helmsdale Police Station after court the following morning, she was not surprised to see Nash's Range Rover in the car park. However, when the DS got out of her car, she saw vehicles that belonged to Detective Superintendent Fleming as well as those of the rest of the team. It was obvious something serious was going on. She greeted Sergeant Meadows as she entered the building. 'Morning, Steve, is there a panic on?' She gestured towards the upper storey. 'We don't often see Jackie Fleming.'

'Hi, Clara, that's not the half of it. The chief constable's up there too. She came with Superintendent Fleming.'

For Ruth Edwards, their chief constable, to be visiting Helmsdale, the situation must be really bad. Ruth, who long before her appointment as their leader worked for IOPC in London, had at times worked with them. She was usually content to leave investigations in the hands of her small team of detectives, knowing they were among the best around.

'I'd better get up there and report in, or I'll be in trouble,' Clara said, half-jokingly.

The detectives were seated round the large table in the centre of the CID general office. 'Ah, Clara,' the chief constable greeted her. 'How did the case go?'

'Very well, ma'am. We've one less drug dealer to worry about for the next seven years.'

'Good result, and now you're here, we can make a start.'

Mironova took the only remaining seat. 'I take it we have a problem.'

'I think that's putting it mildly,' the chief told her. 'Perhaps we could begin by updating Clara as to what's happened over the last forty-eight hours. Mike, will you start things off, please?'

Nash nodded. 'Yesterday morning we got a phone call from a woman who was walking her dog at Kirk Bolton. The dog followed the scent of blood to a holiday cottage. She thought someone might be injured and knocked on the door. She got no answer, so she peered in through the window and saw a man's body inside.' Nash paused, and Clara noted the grim expression on his face. She guessed what was coming next would be unpleasant.

'The man had been slit open, virtually disembowelled. The table on which he was lying and the area around it were a bloodbath. I attended the post-mortem early this morning, and the injuries are identical, if you can call them that, to Sammy's abductor, Leonard Wright.'

He referenced Sammy Rhodes' kidnapping. 'The girl's description of the weapon her rescuer was carrying fits the bill. I'm not suggesting a direct link between Leonard Wright at the flat and the murder we were called to investigate yesterday, but there are a lot of coincidences that I'm uncomfortable with.'

'We all know you don't believe in coincidences.' The chief gave a hint of a smile. 'Perhaps you should discuss the facts, and leave the coincidences until later.'

'There was one difference, one item, which wasn't apparent until the post-mortem. A piece of wood approximately nine inches long had been rammed up the victim's posterior. What the significance of that is, I've no idea.'

Lisa Andrews felt vaguely sick. 'That's absolutely revolting,' she muttered.

'Everything about this crime is revolting,' Nash agreed.

'When Viv checked with the company that owns the holiday cottages, they told him the name of their tenant was James Weston. However, we already know from the fingerprint match that the dead man is actually John Penney, the paedophile murderer released from prison four years ago.'

'I don't remember the case, although I recognize the name,' Clara said. 'How come he's out of prison?'

'Penney was only fourteen years old when he abducted, raped and murdered a twelve-year-old girl named Amelia Robson. Because of his age, the judge was unable to give him a whole-of-life sentence. Whether Penney took the tenancy or was lured to the cottage and murdered, we can't be sure. If he's been living under the name Weston, which is my guess, then someone found out who and where he was. But how did the killer find out his new identity and whereabouts? That's assuming it wasn't a random killing committed by a psychopath. I think in the circumstances, it's safe to rule that out.'

Jackie Fleming interrupted. 'The most disturbing aspect is that we were not informed that he would be in our area.'

Nash agreed and continued, 'One of the lesser-known facts about Penney's crime is that when he abducted the girl she'd been walking her dog. The animal was later found with a piece of wood rammed up its backside — which mirrors what was done to Penney.'

'Do you think someone is actually carrying out a vendetta against paedophiles?' Ruth Edwards asked.

'Could be. And there is Sammy's tale of how she was rescued. Initially, she was very reluctant to tell us what her abductor actually threatened to do to her, but she did manage to in the end. What struck me is the remarkable similarity between those threats and the crime that Leonard Wright — alias George Grey, call him what you will — carried out years ago. I think to have four paedophiles, three of the most predatory kind, and the same MO, to be operating within a few miles of one another is stretching coincidence to breaking point.'

'Sorry, Mike, four paedophiles?' Ruth Edwards asked.

'I'm including the hanging at Stark Ghyll and the death at Black Fell.'

* * *

Nash took a sip from the water glass at his side, as the others pondered the implications of what he'd told them. After a few minutes, he continued.

'The evidence at the cottage suggests that Penney was in our area for four days. That tallies with the booking. The arrangement was that the keys were left with Ted Smith, the owner-driver of Ted's Taxis, who had been booked to collect the tenant from the railway station and drive him to the house.

'Adil and I found a till receipt from Good Buys supermarket in the kitchen waste bin. It's been kept as possible evidence. The time and date are consistent with him arriving on the first train of the day. One of our priorities should be to interview the taxi driver.'

'Is he a suspect?' Fleming asked.

'Well, he needs eliminating if not,' Nash pointed out. 'One of Mexican Pete's men also found a pool of vomit outside the cottage. Forensics are currently testing it for DNA. It could be the victim's or the killer's. Alternatively, it could be unconnected to the murder, although again, I think that's unlikely.'

'If the crime scene was as horrific as you described,' Clara suggested, 'could the woman who found the body have been sick? The way you told it made my stomach heave. It must have been far worse to actually witness it.'

'I think Mrs Fielding is made of sterner stuff. I'm not saying she's hard, because she was obviously very upset by what she saw, but she didn't give way under the stress of describing what she'd seen — in detail. I asked her if she'd been sick, and she confirmed she hadn't.'

Nash nodded to Ruth Edwards to signify that he had completed his assessment of the situation. Everyone was in need of a break, so Viv and Lisa went to make coffee.

* * *

When they resumed, the chief turned to Superintendent Fleming. 'Jackie, you told me on the way over that you and Mike had gone through the case and formulated some sort of plan of action. Would you care to explain what you decided?'

'I spoke to West Yorkshire CID. They confirmed that John Penney was living under the name of James Weston in Leeds. They were unaware that he was leaving their patch, even though they should have been told, as should we. They had no idea he was going to be in our area. That's something we must take up with the Probation Service. There could have been a leak of information, which obviously has extremely serious implications. One way or another, as Mike suggested, we must find out how Weston was discovered to be John Penney. In order to do that, I've arranged to liaise with West Yorkshire. They'll take charge of searching Penney's house. I told them I'd like a couple of our officers to be present, and that's fine by them.'

Fleming instructed Nash and Clara they were to travel to Leeds. 'The man I've been dealing with, Detective Inspector Peter Hall, will lead the search. I'm due to speak to them again later. I'll tell him you'll arrange a time with him.'

'That only leaves the interview with the taxi driver. You could do that, if you will, Lisa?' Nash requested.

'I'll get onto it, right away.'

Nash's phone rang. 'Excuse me, ma'am. I'd better take this.'

It was the Forensic manager at the cottage. 'We're still working, but one of my men found a tyre print outside.'

'Any idea what vehicle it might belong to?'

'None, it's a bicycle tyre. Thought you might be interested as there's no sign of a bike here. Of course, it could be the local paperboy out on his rounds.'

'Thanks for that. I'll keep it in mind.' He turned to the others and told them.

'It could be nothing, but anything we can get is worth having,' the chief said. 'If that's everything, I'd better end with a word of caution. The news of the murder victim's identity is bound to get out before long. Be prepared for a media blitz when that happens. You may well need a moat and drawbridge around the station when the news breaks.'

'That's everything concerning John Penney, I agree,' Nash told her. 'However, we mustn't lose sight of the other murder cases on our books — the victims I just mentioned near Stark Ghyll. The possible connection to this latest killing is patently obvious. Someone is waging an all-out war on perverts. What we need to find out as quickly as possible is where they are getting information about these men.'

'And as for concentrating officers' minds and keeping them focussed,' the chief added, 'all I can do is to remind them of their moral obligations to the victim of any crime — regardless of the person's past.'

CHAPTER SEVENTEEN

Soon after Fleming and Edwards departed, Lisa reported that she would be unable to interview the proprietor of Ted's Taxis until much later that day. 'It could well be this evening before he's free. It's race day in Netherdale, and he's got bookings to ferry race-goers to and from the course. As the last race isn't until five o'clock, I can't see him being available until seven o'clock or even later. His wife has promised to phone me as soon as he gets home.'

It was later when Nash told Clara, 'I've contacted West Yorkshire CID, and we're due to meet them early tomorrow to conduct the search of Penney's home. We'll also try and interview officers from the Probation Service and see what those inquiries reveal.'

'I had an idea,' Mironova added. 'I wondered if Leonard Wright was ever in the same prison as Penney. If Wright served even part of his sentence in the same place, it's more than possible the two became acquainted. Like calling to like, if you get my meaning. So I spoke to the governor of Felling Prison, but he wasn't aware of any close associations formed there.'

'That could be true,' Nash acknowledged. 'All category 43 prisoners are segregated. Did you find anything useful about the prisoners who attacked Penney?'

'He said there were four men who beat up Penney. Three are still in Felling, but the other man was released four months ago. That could be significant. I've got his details and intend to follow up on him as a priority, providing we're not distracted by more corpses.'

'Get Viv and Adil on that, will you? I've ordered copies of the files on Penney. It includes all the follow-up reports since his release from prison. As soon as they arrive we need to go through them meticulously and check every possible detail. I feel certain that his murder is connected to the crime for which he was convicted.'

'We can do that after we've been to Leeds,' Clara said. 'We might have a clearer picture of what he was like by then.'

'Before we do anything, I have to finish writing up my notes from what happened yesterday so I can send them through to Tom or Maureen.'

Clara couldn't resist having a bit of fun at Nash's expense. 'From the way you described the woman who found the body, I'd say it's a good job you're spoken for. Otherwise you might have been tempted back into your bad old ways.'

'Oh, it wasn't me she liked.' He winked. 'Was it, Adil?'

'Really?' Clara could see another route for her teasing, as Adil looked like a rabbit in headlights.

* * *

When the phone rang, Viv answered it before calling through to Nash. 'It's Mrs Fielding for you, boss.'

'You sure it's not for Adil?' Clara asked, her face a picture of innocence.

Adil glared at her across the office.

'Nash speaking, what can I do for you?'

'You asked me to call if I remembered anything that might be useful.'

'And you have?'

'Well, I don't know how useful it is. I almost didn't ring, because it might be totally unconnected to the murder.'

'Don't worry about that. Our problems come when people fail to report suspicious behaviour.'

'With everything that happened yesterday, I'd all but forgotten the night before. I'd been stocktaking for a client in Halifax. It's extremely time-consuming, and by the time I'd got everything tied down it was very late. I didn't get home until well after midnight.'

'You returned home late. What happened?'

'Actually, it was what happened on my way home that I wanted to tell you about. Like I said, it was well past midnight and I was really tired. It was lucky I'd got my headlights on full beam, because if not there might have been a very nasty accident. About a mile outside the village, I almost knocked a cyclist off his bike. I say "his", but I suppose it could have been a woman. I didn't have chance to notice. The bike had no lights on, the rider was dressed in black from head to toe, and if I hadn't swerved at the last minute, I would have collided with him.'

'I see, but what made you connect this to the murder?'

'The place where it happened is this side of the Bishopton turning. That means the cyclist had to be heading for Kirk Bolton because this road is a dead end. When I got to thinking about it, there are only a couple of people in the village who have bicycles, and one of those is currently on holiday. Above all else, it's a weird time and place to be riding a bike without lights, don't you think?'

Nash considered what she'd told him. It made sense, even if it was a bizarre way for a murderer to travel. 'You certainly did the right thing in reporting it. As you say, it might have an innocent explanation — perhaps their lights had failed.'

* * *

Early the next morning as they drove to Leeds, Nash and Mironova discussed the mystery cyclist Kelly Fielding had almost run down. 'I know it sounds very weird, to think of a killer on a bike, but what other reason could the rider have for going to Kirk Bolton at that time of night? And we have a tyre print at the scene.'

Clara agreed. 'It's not even likely to have been someone on their way home from the pub who doesn't want to use their car. For one thing, if that's anything like a regular occurrence, they would have a bike with lights fitted. And I seem to recall that Kirk Bolton has a perfectly good pub of its own.'

'I certainly think it's worthy of consideration, should we have a suspect in mind. However, as things stand, that seems a very long way off.'

'If this is the work of someone targeting paedophiles, as is beginning to look increasingly likely, do you think they might have others in their sights?'

'That's a very good question, and the short answer is, I don't honestly know. One thought that does keep coming back to me is that if the four murders are connected, how did they locate these men? Leonard Wright and John Penney had new identities. Are they getting inside knowledge, either directly or indirectly? It sounds perfectly logical that the killer is striking at perverts, given the history of the victims. But even if we were certain of it being the motive, we could do little to prevent further attacks until we have some idea of who is behind them.'

'So what do we do? We know there's an underlying feeling within the force that justice is being served,' Clara pointed out.

'Yes, I know, but we can't justify the taking of life, no matter how evil the victim might be. In the eyes of the law, both men have paid for their crimes, and deserve to have their murder investigated with the same rigour as anyone else.'

'I was thinking about it last night, and I wondered if the person behind the murders might have suffered at the hands of a paedophile. Either directly, or had it happen to someone close to them, perhaps? Could it be revenge, like Viv suggested?'

'It's an interesting idea, Clara, but again, there's very little we can do until we have more facts to work with.'

* * *

The detective who greeted them at the Leeds police head-quarters was about Nash's age, Mironova guessed. DI Peter Hall was a round-faced, jolly-looking man, not tall and not exactly fat. 'Compact' was the word that summed him up best, Clara thought. As he introduced the other members of the specialist team that was to search Penney's house, his cheerful demeanour was in marked contrast to the grim nature of their joint operation.

'I had intended to line up a meeting with the probation officer handling Penney's case, but it appears he's on holiday in Majorca. I spoke to his boss, however, and on the face of it, there's an innocent explanation for you not being informed of Penney's move to your area.'

Hall outlined the facts before adding, 'That only leaves us the job of searching his house. I sent one of my sergeants to collect a set of keys. The Probation Service always keeps a spare set in circumstances such as Penney's, in case of prob-lems. I don't think any of them anticipated something as bad as this, however.'

'OK, Peter, as I promised, we've brought copies of our files for both murders. Do you want us to go through those before we start out? It will give you the facts.'

'I think that would be a good idea, Mike. I've a couple of rookies on my team, and it will give them chance to see how officers from another force, with quite different challenges, tackle major incidents such as these.'

Reading between the lines, Mironova guessed that Hall would also use the briefing to size up both her and Nash, which was quite natural, if the two forces were to work together.

On their drive through, they had agreed that Nash should present the facts of the Penney murder, leaving Clara to con-centrate on the Leonard Wright killing. He told the listening officers this beforehand, suggesting they keep any questions until the end.

Their reports contained enough information to keep any such questions to a minimum, and those that were asked proved to be both well thought out and pertinent. Having dealt with them as best they could, given the sparse amount of factual evidence in their possession at that point, the combined team got into the vehicles and set off for the address where Penney had lived.

* * *

After fighting their way through the heavy Leeds traffic, they pulled up at the end of a row of slightly down-at-heel terraced houses, no more than fifteen minutes' drive from the headquarters. Given that most of the journey had been at a snail's pace, Mironova estimated they were less than a couple of miles from the city centre.

'That's the house,' Hall pointed to the second in the row. 'When I knew you were coming over this morning, I put a Forensic team on standby in case we need them, but I thought it best for us to take a look around first before unleashing the boffins.'

Clara reflected on Hall's remarks with envy. The ability to have a team of Forensic officers on standby reflected a much more relaxed attitude to budgetary constraints — or possibly a far higher level of crime — to keep the scientists always available.

Everyone donned shoe covers and gloves before they entered. Hall led the way. The contents of the house proved disappointingly ordinary. Hall's men searched the upper floor, leaving Nash, Mironova and Hall to tackle the ground floor. When their preliminary inspection was complete, they gathered in the small sitting room to compare notes.

The room was sparsely furnished, the settee and chairs of the most basic type. The only concession to luxury was the large, flat-screen TV and accompanying DVD player on a stand in the corner. As the other officers were reporting their findings, or rather lack of them, Nash, who was nearest the set, glanced around. He stared at it for a few minutes, until Hall, who had asked him a question, repeated it. 'Mike, have you anything to add?'

Mironova concealed a smile. Nash, she knew, had been doing what he always did, putting himself in the mind of the criminal. And that, in turn, meant that he had noticed something the others had missed. That included her, so Clara waited to see what he came up with.

'Sorry,' Nash said, 'what was it you said, Peter?'

Hall repeated the question. 'Yes, I do, actually,' Nash replied. 'I was puzzled as to where the DVDs are.'

'DVDs?'

Nash pointed to the player. 'I'm no expert, but that looks like an expensive piece of kit to me. So where are the DVDs? Why purchase something as expensive as that if you've nothing to play on it?'

Hall caught Nash's meaning. 'Damn! I missed that, Mike. So we have to find them, and at the same time ask why they aren't kept alongside the player. Almost everyone I know keeps the discs in the same room as the TV. Why put them elsewhere?'

The most junior of the detectives, who looked as if he'd only recently begun to shave, suggested, 'We know what sort of man Penney was. Doesn't it follow that the sort of DVDs he watched might be the type you don't leave lying around for visitors to inspect? Hardcore pornography, I'd bet.'

Hall regarded him with mocking respect. 'That's fairly close to intelligent for you,' he told the DC. 'I suggest we all take another look around, and this time concentrate on places we might have overlooked, particularly those small enough to conceal DVD sleeves. This time, we'll go upstairs. You lot do down here.'

* * *

The search took considerably longer than their first inspection, but met with no more success until the junior detective stepped out into the back garden. He surveyed the courtyard area, surrounded by a high wall which gave total privacy.

He hurried back to the foot of the stairs. 'Sir,' he called out.

'What have you found?' Hall asked.

'Are we going to check the cellar, sir?'

'What cellar?'

'Both houses on either side have cellars; you can see their fanlights. This one has been blocked up. I thought we should give it the once-over,' the DC suggested diffidently.

'Good thinking,' Hall approved. 'That's two stars for you today,' Hall said, as he and Nash came to join him. 'But how do we get down there?'

Nash walked along the hallway, tapping along the woodwork beneath the stairs. He shook his head. 'It's solid, there's nothing here.'

'Try the kitchen,' Hall said. 'My grandmother had a house similar to this. Look behind the stairs.'

Nash did so, tapping again, this time the sound echoed. 'There's a door here. It's been panelled over.' He continued to tap, adding pressure. The door sprang open.

'Has anyone got a torch?'

'No need. There's a light switch on your right,' Clara said.

Hall smiled before he gestured to the young detective. 'OK, Sunbeam, it was your find. You lead the way.'

He smiled at Nash. 'I don't think he'll find the coalhole of much interest.'

Seconds later: 'Governor, I think you ought to come and have a look down here.'

CHAPTER EIGHTEEN

Having made their way down the stone steps, the four detectives looked round the cellar at what was effectively an extra room. It contained a bed, and a workstation housing a computer and printer. Alongside was a stack of DVD cases.

'Why keep a bed down here?' The young detective asked. 'Did he spend all night on the computer?'

Nash was inspecting the cladding covering the ceiling and walls. 'This place has been sound-proofed,' he said. He turned his attention to the bed as the others were pondering the significance of his remark. He twitched the duvet back and stared at the mattress. 'Those look like bloodstains,' he added grimly.

Mironova walked over to the end wall and inspected something that had caught her eye. Two large iron rings had been cemented into the brickwork. It was quite gloomy there, despite the single, naked light bulb in the ceiling. Clara shone her torch on the rings. 'What do you think these are for?'

There was a long silence, before Nash swallowed. The idea that had come to mind was too horrible to contemplate, coupled with the stains on the bed in particular. 'Shackles,' he muttered.

'What?' Hall exclaimed. 'Did you say shackles?'

'Yes, as in a medieval dungeon — or torture chamber.'

'And those photos on the wall,' the young DC pointed out. 'Do you think they're his victims?'

'OK, that settles it. Let's get out of here and clear the way for Forensics. I want them here pronto, and I don't want to risk any further contamination of evidence.'

As they returned to the ground floor, Clara stopped and looked back towards the cellar. 'I don't understand,' she told the others. 'If Penney was only a kid when he was sentenced and hasn't been out of jail that long, how did he dispose of his later victims? Assuming those are bloodstains down there and that they mean what we think, he couldn't put them in the boot of his car because he doesn't . . . er . . . didn't own one.'

Nash thought for a moment, and then glanced at DI Hall. 'Clara's got a point. I reckon you should ask your boys to do an inch-by-inch search of the whole of this house and the backyard too.' He paused before adding the grim rider, 'At the same time you might want to consider checking the misper files for young girls who've disappeared in the period since Penney was released from prison.'

* * *

Conversation in the car on the return journey to Helmsdale was subdued, with both Nash and Mironova's thoughts on the possible implications of the discoveries in the cellar and the grim possibility that the house might reveal even darker secrets. Hall had thanked them profusely for their contribution to the search, and promised to let them know the results as soon as they were available.

At one point, however, Clara told Nash she'd had an idea as to how the supposed 'paedophile killer' tracked down his targets. 'You asked how he selected his victims, and I wondered if the murderer might be someone connected to the Probation Service, or knew someone who could access their computers.'

'That's an extremely good idea,' Nash responded. 'Definitely worth looking into I reckon.'

* * *

Soon after he arrived at Helmsdale the following morning, Nash phoned Fleming with an update about the events of the previous day. 'I'm waiting for DI Hall to report on what his Forensic people find at Penney's house.' He also told her about Clara's theory regarding the Probation Service, and Jackie promised to look into it.

Hall made good on his promise less than an hour later. 'You were right, Mike. I'm afraid those were bloodstains on that mattress.' The Leeds officer's voice was grim as he added, 'They haven't completed a detailed analysis yet, but they told me the blood is of two different types, neither of them Penney's.' His frustration boiled over. 'Bloody hell, Mike, what sort of evil have we uncovered here, and where's it going to end?'

Nash and Mironova were in the process of telling the others what had taken place in Leeds, when his phone rang again. Nash was getting wary of answering it — each call seemed to bring further bad news. This time it was the leader of the local Forensic team.

'While we were at Leonard Wright's flat, we found something strange. There's an extended warranty document in respect of a laptop. It's in Wright's name, but there's no sign of one. And that's not all. There's something you should know about the cottage murder.'

While he was speaking Nash made notes on his pad, then thanked the man and ended the call. He studied his notes before he turned to Lisa.

'Have you interviewed that taxi driver yet?'

'No, his wife didn't ring back. I spoke to her a few minutes ago, though, and I'm going to see him in half an hour.'

'OK, you go talk to Ted Smith, but don't be too long. I need to report to Jackie.'

The phone rang again. He raised his eyebrows despairingly, much to Mironova's amusement. However, this call was only from Meadows. 'Parcel for Inspector Nash,' Steve announced. 'It's been sent by courier. I'd guess that it's the Penney file you've been waiting for.'

* * *

When Lisa returned from interviewing the proprietor of Ted's Taxis, she went to Nash's office. She was in the process of telling him what she had learned when he received a further phone call from DI Hall in Leeds. If Hall had sounded sombre before, his message this time was even grimmer.

Nash listened in shocked silence, his only response being, 'Thanks for the update, Peter. Keep me posted when you learn anything further, will you?' He added to his notes.

'Sorry for the interruption, Lisa. Go on with your tale.'

When she finished, Nash went into the general office and told the others to listen while he phoned Jackie Fleming. 'Jackie, I've got you on speakerphone so everyone hears what I have to say. It will save me having to repeat myself. If anyone has any ideas, they can chip in.'

'OK, so what have you got?'

'Let me start by telling you what our Forensic officers have come up with. At Wright's flat they believe a laptop has gone missing.'

'Is that important?' Fleming asked.

'Who knows? But more importantly, at the holiday cottage where Penney was murdered, they ran a DNA test on a pool of vomit found in the garden. The results provided a familial match with DNA belonging to Amelia Robson. As her father is dead, and the DNA profile is male, that suggests it must be her brother Philip's.'

'Excuse my ignorance, but who is Amelia Robson?'

'Was, not is,' Nash corrected her. 'Amelia Robson was John Penney's first victim, twenty years ago. He was fourteen when he abducted, raped and murdered her. She was only twelve years old.'

'His first victim? Does that mean you believe there may be more?'

'We're almost certain there could be. You remember I mentioned the bloodstains and DVDs at Penney's Leeds address? DI Hall has rung twice this morning. The first time to confirm that the blood doesn't belong to Penney, and more recently to tell me that he has now had chance to watch those DVDs. He was good enough to spare me the details of the abuse being carried out. He believes he recognizes the two victims, because they are both on their missing persons list, and their photos are on Penney's wall. As we speak, the Forensic boys in Leeds are conducting an examination of every inch of Penney's property, concentrating mainly on the backyard.'

'Look, hold on, I'm going to fetch the chief. She should hear this.' Nash heard the receiver being placed on the desk and the sound of footsteps.

* * *

Moments later, the chief constable spoke. 'I've been updated. How can anyone be so evil?' she muttered.

'It is difficult for normal people to comprehend, I agree, but sadly there are many examples of psychopathic serial killers,' Nash sympathized.

'What can we do to find his murderer?' she asked.

Pearce was unable to contain his emotions. 'Always supposing we want to.'

Ruth Edwards rounded on him. 'I appreciate your feelings, Detective Constable Pearce, but you cannot allow them to interfere with your duty.'

'Sorry, ma'am.'

'There's more. Lisa has been to interview the taxi driver who took Penney there when he arrived. I think you'll find what she has to say extremely interesting. Tell everyone, Lisa.'

'I asked him if anyone had followed his cab. He laughed and said, "At that time of the morning? You must be joking. There was no one else about". Then he said, "Apart from young Reggie from the Fleece. I almost ran him down in Good Buys car park".'

'I don't see the significance,' Fleming muttered.

'You will. Carry on, Lisa.'

'I asked him if anyone had shown any interest in his customer, and he said the only one was Reggie. He'd gone to the rank to chat to Ted at lunchtime that same day. He thinks Reggie was fishing for information.'

Nash continued, 'Thanks, Lisa. I believe that Reggie, full name Reggie Barnes, saw Penney in Good Buys, recognized him and wangled the information as to where he was staying from the taxi driver. Then I believe he went out to Kirk Bolton and exacted revenge for what Penney had done.'

'Why would he do that? What possible motive could he have?' Fleming objected.

'A very strong one, if Reggie Barnes turns out to be Philip Robson, and is Amelia Robson's brother.'

'That's a very strong assumption to make,' Edwards objected. 'But I guess you've had wilder theories that have proved correct before, so I won't argue with it. OK, how do you intend to proceed?'

'I think we should pull Reggie Barnes in for questioning.'

'I agree,' Fleming told Edwards.

'Right, deal with it and keep me posted.' Before finishing the call, Ruth Edwards asked to have a word with Nash in private. He transferred the call to his office phone and left the room, closing his door firmly.

Aware that this action would arouse the curiosity of the other detectives, Ruth began by telling him, 'I want you to pass on the contents of this conversation to the team immediately after I've done.' She paused, 'I think you've a fair idea what I'm about to say, haven't you?'

'My guess would be that it's to keep everyone focussed on catching the killer, despite the unsavoury nature of the victims.'

'Exactly right. It was Viv Pearce's comment that high-lighted the issue. I actually sympathize with him, but I recognize it's a dangerous viewpoint for a police officer to hold. I'm sure I can trust you to get the message across that it's as important to put as much effort into apprehending the person responsible as it would be arresting someone like Penney or Wright.'

'Don't worry, Ruth, I've already mentioned it to them, but I'll reinforce the need for them to remain totally professional and completely impartial. While I've got you on the line, I'd like authorization to spend some money.'

'Oh, yes? And how much of which budget do you intend to exploit?'

'I want to get a DNA test rushed through for Reggie Barnes. If he is the killer of these men, I want him in custody ASAP. With the rate of these murders, he could strike again.'

CHAPTER NINETEEN

It was the mid-afternoon lull at the Fleece Hotel. Majda had joined Reggie in the staff room for a cup of tea. As she sipped her drink, Reggie was busy scanning the pages of yesterday's *Netherdale Gazette*. After a few minutes, he tossed the paper on to one of the battered armchairs that had once graced the residents' lounge.

'There's still no mention of a body being found at Kirk Bolton or anywhere else. I'm beginning to think the whole thing was a dream — or a nightmare. I can't believe nobody's found it yet. And if they have, why is there nothing in the paper?'

'There could be any number of reasons the news hasn't got out yet. For one thing, Kirk Bolton is such a tiny place, what's the likelihood of anyone going to that cottage on any given day?'

Before she could say anything else, the door opened and the manager led two strangers, a man and a woman, into the small room. At first, Majda thought they were guests who had taken a wrong turning, until the man started to speak.

'Reggie Barnes?'

He nodded.

Nash held out his warrant card. 'I'm Inspector Nash. This is my colleague Sergeant Mironova. I would like you to accompany us to the police station. We have a matter we believe you can help us with.'

* * *

When they reached the station, Reggie was happy to supply a DNA sample. He felt certain it would not incriminate him. Steve Meadows assured him it was purely for elimination purposes. As he was led to an interview room, Reggie was unaware an officer had dashed to his patrol car in a hurry to get the sample to Forensics.

One of the lessons Mironova had learned from working alongside Nash was his ability to tailor his interview technique to the relevant offence, and his judgement of the suspect's character. She had seen him take an extremely tough line with hardened criminals, or those whose offence was particularly unpleasant. She had also watched with approval and, on occasion, awe as Mike had lured suspects into traps laid for the unwary. At times, she had seen him being heavily sarcastic — at others, genuinely sympathetic.

* * *

In the preliminary interview with Reggie Barnes, it seemed that Nash had opted for the sympathetic approach. It was obvious Reggie was uncomfortable with the situation.

'Thank you for coming in to talk to us. I'm taping this conversation in case I need to check anything. Do you understand?'

Reggie nodded.

'You need to speak, the tape can't hear nods.' Clara smiled at him.

'Of course.' Reggie grinned.

'Firstly, can you tell me where you were on Wednesday night?'

'At home with Majda.'

'All night? You live together?'

'Er, yes.'

Nash nodded, and looked at the file in front of him. 'Do you know Ted Smith, the taxi driver?'

'Everyone does.' Reggie forced a smile, seemingly unsure where this was leading.

'I believe so.' Nash smiled back. 'I understand you spoke to him on Saturday morning. Why was that?'

Reggie hesitated. 'Oh, that was the day he nearly hit me with the car in the car park.'

'Nearly hit you?'

'Yes. Chef was in a mood about a missing delivery. I was rushing, didn't see the taxi. I went to apologize for getting in his way.'

'Understandable. You weren't trying to find out about his passenger, then?'

'Er, no. Why would I do that?'

'Just a thought.' Nash smiled.

'Tell me, do you know Kirk Bolton village?'

'It's past Bishopton, isn't it?'

'You've not been there?'

Again, Reggie hesitated. 'Not that I recall.'

'I think that's all we need. Have you any questions, sergeant?' Nash looked at Clara, who had been primed that he wanted it kept short. They had only needed Reggie for his DNA.

'I don't think so,' she said.

'Thank you for your time, Mr Barnes. You've been most helpful. You're free to go.'

Clara showed him out and went to Nash's office. 'He's lying!'

'I know. Let's hope we get that test result soon.'

* * *

Nash was in early. He and Clara were studying the Penney files, to find more information about Amelia Robson's murder and her family background. By lunchtime, Nash was seated in his office, drumming his fingers on the desk, willing the phone to ring. When it did, he jumped.

'Morning, sir. I've got those results you wanted urgently.'

'Go on.'

'Full familial match. Reggie Barnes is Amelia Robson's brother.'

Nash thanked the officer and went into the general office to find Clara.

'Another coffee?' she asked.

'No time for that. We've got him. Come on.'

Nash told Steve Meadows. 'I need two officers for an arrest.'

At the Fleece Hotel the manager told them Reggie was on late shift that day. They headed for Majda's flat.

Nash knocked loudly on the door which was opened by Reggie.

'Philip Robson, I am arresting you on suspicion of the murders of John Penney and Leonard Wright. You do not have to say anything, but . . .'

Reggie and Majda listened in shocked silence to the caution Nash delivered. In Majda's case, her bewilderment was heightened on hearing Reggie called by his real name. And who was Leonard Wright? Now she was scared.

Philip was handcuffed and put in the back of a police car for the short journey across Helmsdale. Once there, he was processed and put in a cell. The officers returned to Majda's flat to assist in the search, which soon yielded results.

Majda watched the detectives, her expression sombre as they delved into the laundry basket and removed a hoodie and trousers that bore traces of what looked suspiciously like blood. These went into evidence bags, as did a collection of kitchen knives. The only moment of comedy, or farce, came when the officers attempted to wrap a bicycle in protective polythene sheeting.

Nash and Clara watched this with some amusement, but Majda failed to see the joke. She was worried. The officer mentioned another killing. When was this? Was Reggie responsible? Did she really know the man she loved?

* * *

To begin with, Reggie denied being Robson, denied that he was Amelia's brother, denied recognizing John Penney, and denied having visited the holiday cottage. However, after Nash pointed out the infallibility of the DNA evidence from outside the cottage, and revealed the details of Lisa Andrews' talk with the owner of Ted's Taxis, Reggie's denials seemed to weaken rapidly.

'I think you saw Penney at Good Buys supermarket. I think you deliberately sought out Ted Smith to find out where Penney was staying, and I believe you cycled out to Kirk Bolton in order to take revenge for the rape and murder of your sister. We have information suggesting that someone almost knocked you down outside the village at around the time Penney was murdered. And then there are your blood-stained clothes, currently being tested. We also have your bicycle to see if the tyres match those at the scene.'

Nash paused to allow Reggie to digest all this. To say that he was appalled would be a massive understatement. Eventually, confronted with the extent of the police evidence, Reggie admitted that his real name was Philip Robson, admitted that he had recognized Penney at Good Buys super-market. He admitted he had cycled out to Kirk Bolton that night with the intention of killing Penney.

He denied strenuously having committed the crime.

'Yes, I went there to kill the bastard. Wouldn't you, if you'd gone through what I've had to suffer because of that sick pervert?'

* * *

Reggie began to tell his story, holding nothing back, from the emotional torment of losing his sister, his father's death and finding his mother after she committed suicide. His tale of the abuse at the care home was especially harrowing, but as he ended his account, Reggie maintained one of his previous denials.

'I admit going into the house with the intention of killing him. But when I got there he was already dead, his guts spilled out over that table. It was only when I saw what had been done to him that I realized there was someone whose hatred for Penney was even stronger than mine. The revolting sight of his mangled corpse was what made me sick. And it was only later, when I was back with Majda, that I began to understand that if I'd done what I set out to do, I'd have been just as evil as Penney.'

'Have you ever been up Black Fell?'

'No, I don't have a car, just my bike. It's too far out in the countryside.'

'What about Stark Ghyll?'

'You think I'd try and pedal up there?'

Nash switched track and started to question him about the murder of Leonard Wright. 'I'm not saying I condone the murders of either of these men, even though they were really despicable characters,' Nash told him. 'However, if you admit to the Leonard Wright murder, there is one fact that will weigh very heavily in your favour when it comes to a trial. Rescuing the young girl Wright was holding prisoner was a very good thing to do, and will go down well with a sympathetic jury.'

Watching Robson from her position seated alongside Nash, Mironova was half convinced the arrested man hadn't the foggiest idea what Nash was talking about. When Robson said as much, Clara was close to believing him. She glanced quickly sideways, and saw that Nash was also having doubts. That left Clara puzzled. If Robson didn't know anything about Sammy Rhodes, he couldn't have been Leonard Wright's killer. And if he hadn't murdered Wright, surely he couldn't have murdered Penney in an identical fashion either. No matter how vivid Mironova's imagination was, it didn't stretch to their being two murderers who targeted paedophiles operating in their area within days of one another, both using the same MO.

CHAPTER TWENTY

Once Nash concluded the interview with Philip Robson and the arrested man was taken away to the cells, Mironova voiced her doubts. 'I'm not convinced Robson committed the murders, Mike. From memory, I think Sammy eventually stated her rescuer was around six feet tall, whereas Robson is of average height. Apart from that, Sammy was driven into Netherdale in a car, and as far as we're aware, Robson doesn't own or have access to one. If he had use of a car, surely he wouldn't have cycled all the way to Kirk Bolton and back?'

Nash followed her reasoning and conceded her point. 'You're dead right, Clara. I knew something was bugging me, but couldn't put my finger on it. However, there is still one more possibility — Robson was working in conjunction with someone else.'

'What are you going to do? Let him go?'

'No, we'll let him sweat for the time being. I'll get Steve to transfer him to HQ for the night. We've plenty of time before we need to charge him or release him.'

'You planning on going to HQ in the middle of the night, then?'

Nash looked puzzled.

'Twenty-four-hour rule,' Clara reminded him.

'Oh, damn. I'll ask for an extension. The accomplice theory might still hold good. There's that young woman who was with him at the hotel, for one. She looked very distressed when we arrested Robson. I'm willing to bet they're lovers.'

'It takes one to know one, they say,' Clara grinned. 'Lovers, I mean.'

'As I'm a respectable married man, I'll ignore your snide remark,' Nash said, although he too was smiling. He had to wait until Clara's laughter died away before adding, 'One thing I do reckon, though. I don't think we're even remotely close to the crux of this affair yet.'

As they were talking, Nash's landline rang. He listened to what the caller said and then responded, 'OK, Steve, show him up. I'd like a word with him before he speaks to the detainee. He'll probably want disclosure, but we're not quite ready to go that far.'

He put the receiver down and asked Clara, 'I don't recall Robson asking for a solicitor, do you?'

She shook her head, her surprise evident when Nash told her, 'A man claiming to be his legal representative is here. It'll be interesting to find out who hired him.'

Their suspicions as to the relationship between Robson and Magdalena Klements became certainties when the solicitor confirmed Majda was the person who had asked him to represent Robson. Nash explained about the DNA evidence and agreed to provide details of the Amelia Robson murder case, but told him, 'We cannot give full disclosure at this point in time, because we are still in the early stages of our investigation. However, we felt it prudent to detain Mr Robson in view of the other killings we suspect might be linked to that of John Penney.'

'Other killings?' The solicitor looked shocked. His surprise turned to horror as Nash told him there had been three other murders they suspected had been carried out by the same person. In view of what Nash revealed, he agreed to Nash's suggestion of partial disclosure.

* * *

All the team were in early, and although the discoveries seemed to point to Robson's guilt, Clara commented, 'Even if the DNA from those pieces of clothing confirms that the blood is John Penney's, I still have my doubts.'

Nash agreed. 'I think we need an expert opinion to prove if we're right or wrong. Having seen the charnel house at Kirk Bolton, I feel sure whoever eviscerated Penney would have been soaked from head to toe in his blood. The amount on Robson's clothing doesn't seem anywhere near enough.'

'By "expert opinion", who are you thinking of?'

'I reckon Mexican Pete would only need to take a glance at that hoodie and trousers to tell us if we're right or wrong.'

As they were pondering this, Nash's landline rang again. It was the chief constable on speakerphone, along with Jackie Fleming, who called to congratulate them on the arrest.

'I think it's far too early to open the champagne,' Nash told her. 'Both Clara and I have serious misgivings as to whether we've got the right perpetrator.'

He explained their doubts, but could tell he was failing to convince either of his listeners. Ruth's response confirmed that. 'I think you're worrying over nothing. If the DNA from that clothing matches the victims, I'm going to order the file be sent to CPS. We need this man behind bars. Jackie and I discussed this earlier and she's in complete agreement.'

'Before you do that, I think we need more evidence.'

'How much more proof do you want?'

'For one thing, Philip Robson doesn't match the description Sammy Rhodes gave of her saviour. Sammy told us the person who rescued her was over six feet tall, whereas Robson is much smaller. We need more evidence.'

Ruth agreed, albeit reluctantly. Later, she was to reflect that this was one of her better decisions during her time as chief constable.

* * *

The man stared at the computer screen for a moment. He logged in, using details he'd memorized a long time ago.

There was a message. He read the contents with increasing excitement. This was the news he had been waiting for since he had been approached to join the network. He had helped others to achieve their desire, and all along, he had been promised this reward. Now, it seemed, his promise was about to be fulfilled. He stared for a long time at the image of the young girl, before reading the text below the photo.

Her name is Gina. She is eleven years old, and as you can see, she is extremely pretty. She will be brought to you tonight. A room has been booked for you at the Mitre Hotel in Bishopton. Check into the room and be sure you are inside and ready by ten o'clock. Remember your camera. There will be a knock on the door. She is yours to do with as you will. Reply by 4 p.m. or the deal is off.

He deleted the contents, watching reluctantly as the girl's image disappeared from the screen. He began to type his reply, his fingers shaking. He glanced at the clock display on the corner of his screen. 3:35. He'd only just been in time.

Across the road from the house, in a car with heavily tinted windows, the driver sat hunched over a laptop reading the response and smiled. Seconds later, he closed the laptop, switched on the ignition and drove away. The car's satnav illuminated, showing the destination — the Mitre Hotel, Bishopton.

* * *

At around 8.15 p.m., the receptionist at the Mitre Hotel looked up from the TV screen she was watching, her annoyance apparent as she watched a newcomer shuffle through the door. It really was intolerable for guests to check in at this time of night and spoil her enjoyment of her favourite soap opera. 'You have a room for me,' the new arrival stated. 'Name of Ball, George Ball.'

Once the registration form had been completed, she handed the guest his key. 'Your room is number eighteen, on the second floor. Follow the corridor to the right, where you will find the staircase,' she told him, her irritation evident in her voice as she added, 'There is no elevator.'

She watched him until he was out of sight, before turning back to pick up the threads of the soap. By the time he reached the room, she had forgotten that George Ball existed.

He opened the door, found the light switch and inspected the interior. The room looked ideal for what he had in mind. There were only two floors, and room eighteen was at the end of a short corridor with a door marked 'Emergency Exit', beyond which he noticed a fire escape. Was this how the girl would be brought to him in secrecy? he wondered. The room he would occupy seemed to provide absolute privacy, or as near to it as possible.

He checked the bag he had brought contained all he needed. Tape to gag and bind the girl, and two different drugs, one to ensure his performance was as good as possible, the other to subdue the girl, plus certain appliances that would enhance his enjoyment of the action.

He began to set up his camera and tripod. If not, how would his friends also get to enjoy this?

Next door, inside room seventeen, another guest heard George Ball arrive via the sensitive listening device placed close to the wall of his room. Perfect. Everything was going to plan; time to switch on the fibre optic camera. Confirmation was immediate, the image on the laptop computer stark. Ball was there in the middle of the screen, and as the watcher stared at the monitor, it was obvious that he was preparing for the arrival of his victim. The watcher smiled mirthlessly. 'Boy, is he going to be disappointed!' the watcher muttered.

Switching the monitor off, the occupant of room seventeen reached into a holdall and removed a knife, testing the sharpness of the blade, ignoring the stains. There would be plenty of time to remove the blood, once the mission was complete. There was no point in cleaning it and then having to clean it again. On second thoughts, there was a way of cleaning surplus blood off the blade — and in a way, it would be rather appropriate.

* * *

Next morning, the guest occupying room seventeen checked out before breakfast. The duty manager instructed the cleaner to prepare that room together with three more for new guests, and also to check the others and service them. Later, she reported back that all the vacated rooms had been attended to, with the exception of number eighteen, which had a 'do not disturb' sign on the door.

The manager frowned. 'That room should be empty. The occupant only booked in for one night. Leave it until nearer lunch, and if he hasn't checked out by then we'll have to ask him to leave. There's a honeymoon couple arriving later today and they'll probably want to test the bedsprings out as soon as they get here.'

Lunchtime was approaching with no sign of George Ball. Acting on instructions, the cleaner went to the room and knocked on the door. Receiving no reply, she was about to enter and tell the guest he must leave, but then thought better of it. Using her walkie-talkie, she advised the manager of the situation and told him she'd wait for him to deal with it. Let him confront the guest, he gets paid far more than me, she thought. It was one of the wisest decisions of her life.

* * *

By the time the manager opened the door to room eighteen, the guest who had stayed in number seventeen had returned the hire car to the rental company, before retrieving his own vehicle and driving home. Before doing so, he had taken out his mobile and reported the successful mission.

'*More waste disposal completed.*' He followed his terse announcement, with a question. '*Any success with prime target?*'

This was crucial, because although the previous murders had been executions, carried out to eliminate members of a network, the main objective of their crusade was to conduct a personal vendetta.

The reply was not long in coming. *'Bait taken, my online ID established. Best to ring me'.*

He frowned at the last part of the message. He was pleased to read that they now had the final victim in their sights, but why the need for the call? However, his partner must have a sound reason for making that stipulation. Or had the situation changed? That thought caused him to shiver with trepidation.

CHAPTER TWENTY-ONE

When Clara reached Helmsdale Police Station that morning, she found Nash waiting for the coffee machine to disgorge the first mug of the day. He greeted her cheerfully, which surprised her, giving the circumstances. When she commented on this, he replied, 'I think we've set a record, four murders within four weeks. I was thinking what a pleasant change it made for us not to begin by attending a murder scene, or worse still, a post-mortem.'

Clara, who was used to Nash's frequently quoted advice about invoking Sod's Law, reminded him of this.

'You think I spoke too soon?' he asked.

'Time will tell, Mike.'

It was a few hours before Clara was proved right. Nash was at HQ for a meeting with Ruth Edwards, Jackie Fleming and Professor Ramirez. He'd told Clara before leaving, 'I'm hoping our worthy pathologist will persuade the hierarchy not to proceed against Philip Robson, as we should now refer to Reggie Barnes. I know the DNA belongs to Penney, but I'm certain there should be way more on the killer's clothing than we found.'

Nash allowed Ramirez to put his point across.

'I have inspected Robson's clothing that bears the victim's blood,' he told Ruth and Jackie. 'And I'm sorry to disappoint you, but that is nowhere near sufficient to match the amount the killer would have been covered with. The fatal wounds severed many blood vessels, and with the heart still pumping, the arterial flow would have been like a jet stream. Proof of this is the blood spatter in the room where the murder took place. The ceiling, the walls and window were liberally coated, with the exception of one point, which I believe is behind where the killer was standing. The reason that remained clean is the dispersal would have been intercepted by the perpetrator.'

As Ramirez was talking, Nash's phone rang. He listened and then told them, 'I must leave, and so must Professor Ramirez. The news I've just received might well confirm our suspicions that Philip Robson did not kill John Penney, or any of the other victims.'

'And what news is that?' Ruth demanded.

'There has been another murder — and it sounds like the same killer.'

* * *

The bad news, as so often happened, had come by way of a call from Control. The operator's opening words to Nash, 'Looks like we've got another one, sir,' proved to be a huge understatement.

Five minutes later, as they headed towards the car park, Nash called Helmsdale and issued instructions. 'Clara, take Adil and Viv to the Mitre Hotel and protect the scene. Professor Ramirez will follow me. He's going to summon Forensics for us.'

Having ended the call, Nash told the pathologist, 'There's a body in one of the rooms, and by the description, the same killer has been at work again. The MO sounds too familiar for it to be anyone else. Apparently the manager, who found the body, has barely been out of the toilet since.

He managed to phone the incident in and halfway through the call he had to be sick again.'

When they reached the hotel, Nash met Clara who had instructed Adil to ensure nobody left the building, and to speak to those guests ensconced in the hotel bar-cum-lounge. The uniformed officer who greeted them had already taped across the stairs leading to the upper floor and ensured all the guests upstairs had left their rooms. As the detectives and the pathologist donned protective clothing, he briefed them, adding a warning as to what they would find inside. 'I haven't been inside room eighteen, but my oppo took a look. He's now outside disposing of his breakfast. Actually,' he said after a momentary pause, 'he must be onto yesterday's dinner by now. He's not the worst, though. The manager who found the body is in a dreadful state.'

'I can imagine, but don't fret, we've seen it before — twice,' Nash told him.

* * *

It didn't need the pathologist to confirm that this murder was committed by the same person as the previous ones. A cursory glance round the door was sufficient, and both Clara and Viv were relieved when Nash suggested they need not enter the room.

'Viv, if you work with Adil and take statements from the manager and staff, I'll go in and have a look round.'

Relieved, Viv headed downstairs.

'Are you sure you'll be OK, Mike?' Clara asked.

He smiled ruefully at her question. 'I'll have to be, won't I? Someone's got to do it, and I'm not about to delegate this task to someone else simply because it's unpleasant.'

As Ramirez began his inspection of the corpse, he attracted Nash's attention and pointed to the wound — a broken blade was still in the body. Nash stepped closer, avoiding the copious amounts of blood that had ruined the carpet, and saw the object more clearly. This was something their Forensic team would need to prioritize. The pathologist nodded and promised it would be dealt with quickly.

Nash looked round the rest of the room, keen to avoid concentrating on the obscenity lying on the bed. Apart from the camera and tripod in the centre, at first glance, it appeared to be very much like any other hotel accommodation. As he looked closer, he noticed various items that could be associated with the actions of a sexual pervert.

'If you don't need me, Professor, I'll head downstairs and check on the troops. I'll leave Clara out in the corridor. She doesn't need to see this.' He gestured to the bed. 'If you need me, give her a shout.'

* * *

Viv's interviews with the manager and the receptionist yielded little that at first seemed promising. However, he was able to secure the information the victim had provided by way of identification when he had checked in. He continued to question the staff members.

Upstairs Clara brought an item, now in a clear evidence bag, for Nash to inspect. 'I've just had this handed to me by the professor. According to this driving licence, the dead man's name is George Ball and he lives . . . er . . . lived in Huddersfield.'

Viv took up the tale. 'That tallies with his check-in details. He arrived yesterday evening, sometime between eight o'clock and half past. The receptionist confirmed the time because she was in the middle of watching *Eastenders* and was peeved by the interruption. I don't think disturbing her viewing of a soap opera is motive for murder, though,' he added with an attempt at humour.

Nash took out his mobile and rang Tom Pratt, and asked him to check the details from the driving licence. As they waited for Tom to phone back, he brought Clara up to date with what he'd seen inside the room. 'I'm willing to bet that this guy's name, George Ball is an alias, and that he's another convicted sex offender. There was a syringe filled with some drug on the table by the bed and also some tablets that will need testing, but that wasn't the worst of it. There was also a collection of straps such as you'd use to tie some-one up, plus duct tape, perhaps to silence the victim. The straps have sharp studs on the inside, so they would inflict pain, so my guess is that the deceased was into sado-mas-ochistic sex. I think he intended to film whatever he had planned. I had a careful look, but I couldn't find a mobile phone, laptop or tablet. Whether that means he didn't bring them or the killer took them, only time will tell. Maybe we'll find out more when we search his vehicle. There's a set of car keys on the dresser, but we'll have to wait until the Forensic guys have finished before we move anything.'

'Speaking of which, I think they're here.' Clara gestured over Nash's shoulder to where a phalanx of officers, all wear-ing protective suiting, was heading across reception.

'They look like extras from a sci-fi film,' she muttered.

'*Invasion of the Body Snatchers* perhaps?' Viv said.

They stood aside to allow the scientific team to pass, and then Nash told her, 'Let's get some fresh air.'

Standing in the landscaped garden, Clara eyed her boss, who was also a close friend. She was surprised at his reac-tion. He rarely seemed upset by violent crime, but this, it appeared, had got under his skin.

As if sensing her thoughts, Nash smiled ruefully. 'Sometimes, I think I agree with you. I'm getting too old for this job.'

'Hang on, Mike, you're only in your forties. That's no age. I've only been winding you up, if I've ever implied that.'

'Oh, you have! OK, maybe not *too* old, but possibly I'm beginning to think I've seen enough of the evil that men can do.'

There was no easy answer to that, and within minutes of him having said it, the return call from Tom Pratt added another twist to Nash's statement.

'Sorry for the delay,' Tom told him. 'I'm still waiting for the Huddersfield police to ring back. All I can tell you at this stage is that there's a red flag against George Ball's name on the computer, but what it refers to is anybody's guess at this stage.'

* * *

Viv had taken statements from most members of staff, but the results so far were negative. It seemed that this, too, was likely to prove less than helpful.

'What about the other guests? Has Adil got anything? And where is he?' Nash asked, moments after he returned.

'Still in the bar trying to placate guests who want access to their rooms. There is only one guest who has checked out since the murder, but he hardly seems to fit the bill as a serial killer. According to the description, he's an elderly gentleman who uses a walking stick. He left early, before breakfast was served. I phoned his details through to Tom for him to check them out, just in case.'

They had only been waiting a few minutes when Tom phoned Viv back. He listened to him for a while before thanking him and ending the call. He looked across at his colleagues, who could tell by his expression that he was more than a little surprised by what he'd heard.

'I spoke too soon,' Viv confessed. 'Tom says the name and address the old man gave were both false, and the car he used was a rental.'

'I don't suppose the hotel has CCTV?' Nash asked.

Viv shook his head.

'In that case, I guess we'll have to hope that this mystery man left some clue in the room he occupied. Maybe there will be a fingerprint or some DNA. Get CSI to check it over, will you, Viv? Clara, go and ask Adil to follow up on the rental car.'

It soon appeared their hopes were in vain, when the manager told Viv room seventeen had already been serviced, and that the bedding had been sent to the laundry.

'He had room seventeen?' Viv became alarmed. 'Who cleaned the room?'

'It was Rosita. She had it on her list.'

Viv checked his list of names. 'I don't think I've spoken to her. Can you fetch her, please?'

* * *

Moments later, the manager reappeared with a nervous-looking young woman alongside. 'This is Rosita, she was on her break. She's Spanish but speaks good English.'

Viv smiled, trying to reassure her, and asked about room seventeen. Had there been anything unusual when she serviced it?

She shook her head. 'No, sir. It was a normal service. I changed the bed and cleaned the room and bathroom.'

'OK, thank you.' Viv felt he was getting nowhere.

As Rosita moved to leave, she turned back to face him and said, 'There was only the handle.'

'What? The door handle?'

'No, it was in the bathroom bin. I just thought it was a strange to find a broken knife handle.'

'And where is it now?' Viv tried not to show his excitement, while dreading the thought of searching dustbins.

'On my trolley.'

'Please show me.'

'It's upstairs. I have one for each floor. No elevator,' she added pointedly. 'Do I have permission?' She indicated the stairs.

'Yes, show me,' Viv said.

They ducked under the tape and she led him along the corridor to her service trolley parked outside a guest room. Hanging on one end was a large rubbish bag. 'It's in here.' She moved to reach inside but Viv stopped her.

'Please don't,' he said, as he pulled a pair of nitrile gloves from his pocket. At her direction, he reached into the bag and removed a small bin liner. 'You've been very helpful. One more question. Did you touch the handle?'

'No, I saw it, I but only lifted the bag out and put it in the rubbish.'

'Thank you,' he said, as he set out to find a Forensic officer and report the fact to Nash.

CHAPTER TWENTY-TWO

It was only an hour after their return to Helmsdale that Nash got a phone call from the pathologist. 'The latest victim's identity is not the one he gave when he registered at the hotel. Fingerprints confirm that he is in fact Trevor Mills and, like the previous victims, he is a convicted paedophile living in Huddersfield.'

Ramirez paused for a few seconds, during which Nash heard the rustling of papers. 'Here's the file number.' He read out the string of numbers before adding, 'Given their history, even my team is finding it difficult to show much interest in the victims, and they're certainly not exhibiting the slightest degree of sympathy for what happened to them. I think they regard it as good riddance to bad rubbish. I guess you and your colleagues must be feeling the same.'

'Despite that, I suspect we now have a serial killer on our hands, with at least five to his name.'

'Even that doesn't chill me as much as it would if the victims were innocent. I've emailed the latest crime scene photos to you and scheduled the post-mortem for tomorrow morning. Once I've examined the wounds, I'll be able to confirm if it's the same weapon used in the previous murders and, therefore, the same perpetrator. To be absolutely certain, I'll await the forensic tests on that broken knife blade and handle. Once they've finished with it, I'll be able to compare the blade with the incision marks. I've asked for it to be prioritised and I'll be sure to let you know the minute I have the results.'

Nash confirmed that he would attend the post-mortem and, before ending the call, asked the pathologist, 'Is it possible that these murders could have been carried out by a woman? Would a woman have sufficient strength to inflict the sort of wounds these men suffered?'

Ramirez considered the question for several seconds before replying. 'It's highly unusual for a serial killer to be female, but I see no reason why not, Mike, if she was reasonably fit. However, lifting a victim onto a table would take an element of strength. And only if the blade of the knife was sharp enough, which, given the clean strokes of the stab wounds, I believe to be the case. I take it you have a good reason for this question?'

'No, not really. I keep hitting a brick wall and getting nowhere — other than to crime scenes. Clutching at straws, really, looking for another route.'

He put down the receiver and went into the general office. 'Clara, give Steve Meadows a shout, will you? Ask him to check with the guys conducting surveillance on Majda Klements. We need to know her movements during yesterday and overnight. If, as I suspect, they don't tally with the person who we believe did the hotel killing, it rules both her and Philip Robson out as the murderer.'

The reply came back within minutes. The officers confirmed that Majda had completed her shift at the Fleece Hotel and then, following a brief visit to the supermarket, had returned to her flat and remained there all evening and night.

Nash shook his head. 'As I expected. Clara, sort it out, will you? Have Robson released on bail. We know he was at John Penney's cottage and need to look into that more thoroughly, but we've enough to cope with.'

'Will do.' She picked up her phone and rang the custody sergeant at Netherdale HQ.

Adil then told him, 'I'm afraid the car rental company was unable to give me anything helpful about the man who hired the vehicle we believe was used by our suspect. He gave them the same ID he used to check in at the hotel and paid cash. Same as he did for his room. The only bit of good news is that the vehicle hasn't been touched since he returned it. They've agreed not to let their valet near it until after our boys have gone over it. I've contacted Forensics and they're sending a couple of men to the rental site today.'

'OK, keep me up to date with what they find — even if it's a negative result. In the meantime, Viv, I'd like you to download a PNC file. The subject is Trevor Mills, the real name of the hotel victim. Like the previous ones, he too is a convicted child sex offender. We need the full facts before we get in touch with the local force.'

* * *

Once Pearce had brought the file up on his computer, Nash and Mironova read the details over his shoulder. 'He's from Huddersfield, right enough,' Clara commented, pointing to the screen. 'However, that's about the only accurate thing he put on his registration form. The address he gave at the hotel bears no resemblance to the one we're looking at. Added to which, the crimes listed there seem to match with the equipment we found in his room. Luckily, there was no child for him to attack.'

'Not lucky for him,' Pearce retorted. 'I wouldn't say getting a knife in your guts is lucky for anyone.'

'I'd suggest he was lured to the hotel with the promise of a victim, but what I can't work out is how the killer knows who to contact and how he gets in touch with them. Let's begin by contacting Huddersfield CID and telling them the good news.'

'You think they'll treat it as good news?' Clara asked.

'Wouldn't you, if you learned that you'd one less child molester on your patch to worry about? What we need for them to do, instead of going to the pub to celebrate, is to conduct a microscopic forensic examination of Mills' real address — especially his computer, if they can locate one. Speaking of which, I wonder if Leeds CID have had any joy with Penney's computer.'

'I've just realized,' Clara said. 'It will be a different office for the Probation Service in Huddersfield. Does that rule Leeds Probation out as a possible info leak?'

Nash didn't reply, as his office phone rang.

* * *

When Nash emerged, Clara could tell by his expression that he hadn't received good news. He slumped down on a chair, put his head in his hands and rubbed his face.

'That was DI Hall. He rang to tell me they found nothing suspicious on Penney's computer. There seems to have been very little email traffic, which is where I would have expected to find the bait that brought him to this neck of the woods. What little there was seems to be innocuous. It was mostly to do with online shopping, which, given Penney's notoriety, would have probably been his preferred method.'

Nash shook his head. 'That wasn't the prime reason for Hall's phone call though. It gets worse — far worse.'

Nash took a deep breath before telling them, 'His Forensic team found one email, an order placed with a big DIY store for building materials, namely sand, cement, a shovel and trowels plus a bucket. They already had suspicions about the backyard to Penney's house, which had been concreted over. They dug it up and discovered two bodies. Both corpses were female and the initial estimate is that they were between ten and twelve years old. Although Hall's still awaiting confirmation of their identities, he's convinced they're the two missing girls he identified on the photos and those DVDs we found in the cellar.'

* * *

It was almost eight thirty that evening when Nash was disturbed by the doorbell's musical chimes. He walked down the hallway of Smelt Mill Cottage, wondering who was visiting at such a late hour. Caution bred of previous experience made him glance at the CCTV monitor connected to his sophisticated alarm system.

He recognized the figure standing in the shelter of the porch immediately, her features illuminated by the stark glare of the PIR light. Nash smiled wryly. 'This should be interesting,' he muttered before turning the key.

'Hello, Becks, this is a surprise. Come on in and get warm.'

Becky Pollard, editor of the *Netherdale Gazette*, was not only the former chief constable's goddaughter, but also Nash's former girlfriend. Their relationship had ended when she moved to London in pursuit of her career, but the two remained friends.

Nash took her coat before ushering her into the lounge. 'Alondra's in her studio. Won't be a minute.'

Becky walked into the room, and her eyes widened slightly when she took in the small person lying on the rug, surrounded by toys.

Seconds later, Nash and Alondra entered the lounge. 'I see you've met Lucy,' Nash said, as he scooped the youngster into his arms. He tickled her under the chin, encouraging a smile. 'This little lady won't settle for the night. So I've been given the task of trying to tire her while Mummy works.'

'I'm sorry to drop in unannounced, but I came to ask you a question, Mike. However, in the circumstances, I'm not sure if it would be appropriate.'

'Fire away,' Nash replied. 'There are no secrets in this house.'

'OK, I've been given some info which sounds too fantastic to be true. It's nothing more than hearsay at the moment, but I thought I should come and ask you first, because it will only be a matter of time before the media in general gets hold of the whispers. And if there is any truth in it, the story will be one of the most sensational to hit the headlines for many a day.'

'What does the gossip concern?' Nash asked, although his heart sank with the premonition that the secret he and the other detectives had been at such pains to conceal had been leaked.

'Everybody knows you're investigating a series of murders, probably all committed by the same person. And the rumour is that the victims were all convicted sex offenders of the worst possible kind — child abuse. At present, I'm fairly sure I'm the only one who has got hold of the tale, so I thought it only fair to check the facts before taking it any further. I also wanted to give you advance warning before the rest of the media latch onto it, because you know what will happen once they do. Of course, the rumour might have no substance, but one way or the other, I'd like to know.'

'I can't comment on a current investigation, Becks, as you're well aware,' Nash responded.

'In that case, how about you tell me off the record? I promise to keep it to myself until you call a media conference. That way you'll be ahead of the game, rather than defending yourselves against reporters with an axe to grind, crusading against a cover-up. If this tale is even remotely accurate, I see little chance of you keeping it dark for more than another twenty-four hours, thirty-six at the very outside.'

There was a long silence as Nash considered his options. In reality, he knew he had only one, and that was to take Becky Pollard into his confidence and hope that the strength of their friendship and her ties to their former chief constable would outweigh the desire for a sensational scoop.

'Very well, as long as it remains off the record until we're ready to go public. I'll speak to Ruth Edwards in the morning and suggest she calls a media conference for the day after tomorrow, and as soon as she agrees, I'll let you know. That way, you'll be able to steal a march on all your competitors. How's that for a fair deal?'

'That's more than generous, Mike, and I'll certainly stick to my end of the bargain.'

'Good, so I can confirm that we are currently investigating five suspicious deaths. One of which may or may not be connected, but four most definitely are. They have been played down in the press releases because the victims were convicted paedophiles. I guess that's what you wanted to know.'

'That's fine by me, Mike. I'll await your phone call before I do anything.'

Becky left, and as she drove back towards Netherdale, she reflected on the recent meeting. Nash looked far happier than when she had last seen him, and having met Alondra a few times, she could see why. He deserved to be content after the sadness and disappointment he'd suffered over the time she'd known him, and especially prior to that. She expressed her feelings with an Americanism she felt appropriate. 'Way to go, Mike. Way to go.'

CHAPTER TWENTY-THREE

As always, Tuesday night at the Black Bull Inn in Huddersfield was quiz night. For many, this was merely a convenient excuse for a midweek booze-up. Some, however, took it more seriously and restricted their alcohol intake until question time was over. Only then did they indulge to excess, celebrating their success, or drowning their sorrows if they failed.

One such celebrant was making his way home on foot, warmed by his performance in the quiz — and by the double whisky he'd consumed shortly before leaving the pub. He had almost reached his house when he noticed something unusual at a nearby property. He peered into the darkness, and then realized the significance of the movement he'd caught out of the corner of his eye. It looked as if someone was attempting to break into the house.

The quiz winner didn't like the homeowner. He thought George Ball was a shifty character, and in local parlance, wouldn't trust him as far as he could throw him. But that still didn't give people the right to burgle his house.

After watching for a few seconds longer to determine that his first impression of what was going on was accurate, he carefully slid his mobile phone from his pocket and pressed 999. As the call was answered, he said in a very loud voice, 'I want the police. There's a burglary taking place. Someone's trying to break into my neighbour's house.'

As he finished giving the details, he was relieved to see the shadowy figure had vanished. Then he was struck by another, terrifying thought. What if the burglar was angry at being disturbed, angry enough to attack him? He looked around, fearful, and ran for his home. It was only when a police patrol car pulled to a halt, blue lights flashing and siren blaring out, that the quiz winner relaxed.

'I was coming back from t' Black Bull. I'd been in t' pub quiz and when I came along t' street, there were this bloke trying to get in through t' lounge window.'

'Do you know who owns the house?'

'Aye, it's a reet shifty character, name o' George Ball. Shouldn't wonder if it's all to do wi' drugs, or summat o' t' sort. Anyroad up, that's hardly t' point, is it?'

'We'd better see if there's anyone at home.'

'I reckon tha's wasting tha time. He lives on his tod, and his car ain't 'ere. He allus parks it reet in front o' t' house.'

Sure enough, the officers got no reply when they knocked, which was hardly surprising. Several hours later, they learned the reason, and, along with CID officers, returned to the house previously occupied by the late and definitely unlamented George Ball.

* * *

After attending what was a routine post-mortem, if autopsies can ever be described in such terms, Nash's next task the following morning was to report to the chief constable about Becky Pollard's visit. He'd intended to speak to Jackie Fleming beforehand, but the receptionist at Netherdale headquarters informed him that the superintendent wasn't in. 'It's her weekly physiotherapy session today,' she explained.

'How is her shoulder? It's been a long time since she was shot. Whenever I ask, she says it's fine.'

'She doesn't like anyone to know, and she certainly doesn't discuss it, but I think it continues to cause her a good deal of discomfort even after all this time. She still takes painkillers occasionally, which can't be a good sign. I only know that because I saw her taking them one day and recognized the package of tablets as the same ones I was given after I'd torn some knee ligaments.'

Once he reached the chief's office, Nash explained to Ruth Edwards what had happened the previous night. 'Becky's promised to hold off until we've had chance to organize a press conference, in exchange for which, I suggested we give her a briefing in advance of the others. Once they get a whiff of this story, it'll be open season for the rest of the media. They're beginning to swarm around the Mitre Hotel already. News of a murder in a public place doesn't stay quiet for long. But with a few hours' start, the *Netherdale Gazette* will be first to break the news of the rest. That only seemed fair in the circumstances, besides which, it'll keep them on our side.'

'How the devil did that news get out?'

'How do any so-called secrets get revealed?'

'I hope none of our officers was responsible for the leak. If any of them have been indiscreet, I'll be far from happy.'

'If I had to guess I'd say it probably came indirectly, most likely from one of the mortuary attendants.'

'What do you mean by "indirectly"?'

'Maybe one of them, or even one of our uniformed officers, arrived home distressed and spills the beans. His partner tells her sister, in confidence, and the sister tells her husband, who lets something slip in the pub. Someone who knows Becky Pollard rings her up. That might be totally inaccurate, but it's the way rumours like this get around.'

'Yes, you're probably right, Mike. I'd rather have a local newspaper break the story first than the nationals. Leave it with me and I'll speak to Jackie as soon as she gets in, and get her to arrange the press conference for first thing tomorrow.'

'If you let me know when you've done that, I can tell Becky she can release the news. Before I go,' he added, 'there's something else you need to know.' Nash told her about the surveillance on Majda Klements, and added, 'That rules her out as Philip Robson's accomplice and also points to Robson's innocence, despite his admission that he set out to kill John Penney. It's hard to commit a murder when you're in our custody suite. He's out on bail for the minute, until I've the time to deal with him.'

Ruth Edwards shook her head and sighed. 'So where do we go from here?'

'I think we've been looking in completely the wrong direction. Before we make a final decision, though, I'll be interested to learn what the DNA testing of the broken murder weapon found at the hotel reveals. I have an idea that piece of steel might tell us quite a lot.'

'Whatever the outcome,' Ruth responded, 'I'm glad I haven't sent that file to CPS now.'

* * *

Nash had just returned to Helmsdale and was about to visit the coffee machine when his phone rang. It was Steve Meadows, who told him, 'I've got Detective Sergeant Clark from West Yorkshire Police holding for you. It's something to do with an attempted burglary in Huddersfield.'

Nash was mystified for a moment, before he made the connection. He spent several minutes listening to the officer describing the failed break-in, and then asked, 'Was anything stolen that you know of?'

'I don't think so, because one of the neighbours was returning home from the pub and scared the intruder away.'

Nash then asked another question, one that proved pivotal to their investigation. 'As you're aware, George Ball, aka Trevor Mills, was a convicted paedophile, one of several whose murders took place in our area. We think they're being trapped and lured via the internet — did you find a computer inside the property?'

'Yes, there was a laptop. Do you think that's important?'

'It could be crucial, let me explain our theory . . .'

The call lasted several minutes before agreement as to the way forward was reached. Nash wandered out into the general office, where Detective Constables Pearce and Hassan were staring at their computer screens. 'OK, guys, you'd better enjoy playing sudoku or whatever you're on with while you can. Tomorrow morning, first thing, you've got a journey ahead of you, one that could be vitally important. You're travelling to Huddersfield police station, where you'll meet up with Detective Sergeant Clark and his colleagues. They've recovered a laptop from the house occupied by Trevor Mills, and this will need to be forensically examined. That's going to be down to you, and consider it urgent, which is why you've been deputed ahead of their tech team.'

* * *

Any hope that the laptop would provide useful evidence was destroyed when Pearce and Hassan reported in from Huddersfield. It was late in the day, and Nash was seated with Mironova and Lisa Andrews, reviewing their scanty evidence, when his mobile rang.

'Viv, have you got good news for us?' Nash asked, having put on speakerphone.

'Quite the opposite, Mike. The laptop is clean, no suspicious emails, nothing. We've been through everything. We think it was done to ensure we had no way of tracing any messages. Adil wonders if he might have been using the Dark Web. It's the only alternative. We also think the foiled burglary was an attempt to steal the laptop, which implies the burglar thought there was something on it.'

'What you're saying is the laptop is now of no use to us, right?'

'I'm afraid so, Mike. Not unless Huddersfield have unlimited funds, and ask their tech guys to get into the hard drive.'

'It's their evidence, leave them to it. Just get yourselves back here. At least you tried.'

* * *

Fleming rang to tell Nash about the media conference.

'How did they take the news of the murders and the victims?' Nash asked.

'If we'd have thought it through in advance, we'd have installed a revolving door on the briefing room. At the end of the conference, there was a bigger stampede than you'd see in most Westerns as the reporters tried to exit the building en masse. The paedophile murders will be front page headlines in all the papers tomorrow, and they'll be the lead story on every news bulletin in this country and beyond. You'll have to warn the team to prepare themselves for intense media activity. You'll have a host of journos and TV crews camped on your doorstep for the foreseeable future. What you mustn't let them do is interfere with you conducting the investigation. I've already got a queue of newsmen waiting in reception. They're the ones who had their mobiles on and have sent their copy electronically. They're now looking for backup information — which they're not going to get.'

Nash thanked her and ended the call. He walked to the outer office window and surveyed the car park. Sure enough, there was a small cluster of people hovering near the entrance. He smiled as he saw Viv Pearce trying to access the parking area.

When they were all in the office, Nash summoned the other detectives and explained the situation. 'They're the advance guard. By tomorrow morning there will be two or three times that number all waiting for an inside story. Ignore them, and continue to do so, even when you're sick and tired of saying "no comment", because once you get involved in a conversation, you'll be trapped. It would be advisable to park round the other side of the building and come in via the fire station. I'll have a word with Doug Curran, the fire chief, and let him know we'll be traipsing through his department.'

The link door to the adjoining fire station was installed when the three emergency services had been combined and rehoused. Nash thought for a moment, then added, 'And don't forget to shut the door. If you've forgotten the code, just ask.'

They all nodded their agreement, explaining to Adil the problem which necessitated the need for a keypad, caused a while ago by an access door key hanging on a hook enabling entry to a villain.

'Now, to business. For the rest of today, I want us to clear our desks of other work. Tomorrow, early, I want us each to take a file belonging to one of the murder victims and study it closely to look for anything we might think might be significant. Then I want us to swap the files until we've each read all five of them.'

Nash paused and then added, 'We'll ignore the phone if it rings. Better still, I'll forewarn Steve Meadows to intercept any calls.'

* * *

The following day, after everyone had checked all the files, the team gathered to collate what they had learned. 'OK, let's start with what we know for certain — and what we don't know. Then we can speculate about the rest. We have five victims, three of them murdered in a gruesome manner, which suggests the same perpetrator. Three were convicted paedophiles, and another only escaped conviction because he fled to this country before going on trial. The other was suspected, but his victim committed suicide before the facts came to light. That appears to be the only common factor. Only one of them lived in our locality. The others originate from different towns in separate areas of the country, and in one case from a different country. Those who were convicted served their prison sentences in different jails.'

Nash paused to collect his thoughts, then continued, 'We now know from DI Hall that Penney has committed two further murders since his release, and that there appears to be no suspicious activity on his computer. There certainly seems to be no evidence of grooming, so how did he get in touch with his victims? I, for one, cannot believe that they were random abductions. Penney didn't own a car or hold a driving licence, so how were they lured to his house?

'While you were studying the files, I got a call from the officer in Huddersfield CID who was in charge of the search of Trevor Mills' property, and he reports they found nothing of interest. So how did he turn up at a hotel in Bishopton, equipped to commit another sexual assault, only to end up dead? The obvious conclusion is that both Mills and Penney were both lured to their locations. But how did the killer contact them and pass such detailed information to them? Not only that, but how did he know their true identity, their place of residence and the nature of the crimes for which they were convicted?'

Getting no response from his colleagues, Nash smiled, but with little evidence of humour. 'I guess by your blank expressions that you're totally baffled, and as mystified as I am. Now that you've looked through the files, has anyone got anything useful to contribute?'

Clara nodded. 'I was thinking about Sammy Rhodes and how she was abducted. I don't think it was done by chance. Leonard Wright must have been watching her, known her movements. Her gymnastics training was always on the same day, same time. Even though the school had broken up for the holidays, he probably wouldn't have realized that. It was a fluke she was there that afternoon. If she hadn't had a forthcoming competition, she wouldn't have been. I got confirmation from the garage that her mother's car tyre was deliberately let down. That shows forward planning, but how was it all arranged?'

There was no response other than the shaking of heads, so Nash put forward his own summary of the situation. 'We need to discover how the killer contacted the paedophiles, how he passed information, how he lured them to such locations, and how he did so leaving absolutely no trace. Until we can do that, I can't see a way forward. As it stands, we're no further forward than we were when the bodies were discovered.'

CHAPTER TWENTY-FOUR

At Ramsdale Holiday Village, the occupants of Bramhope Lodge were in deep discussion.

'How's it going?' the man asked his wife. He was standing behind her wheelchair, his hands resting gently on her shoulders.

'Slowly, very slowly,' she replied. 'Have you seen the Sex Offenders Register? It's surprising how many there are.' She clicked a button on her keyboard and scrolled the screen. 'Just look at that lot. They're nationwide, as you know, but I doubt the one we're looking for will be on there. If he is, then I don't know how we'll manage if he lives on the south coast or some Scottish mountain.'

'We can work it out. Who knows, if I say I have to go away on business, that nice lady that's married to the site owner could keep an eye on you.' He laughed as he finished speaking.

The expression on his wife's face told him her opinion before she spoke. 'Very funny!'

He changed the subject. 'You've done well so far.'

'The first ones were easy. Hacking into the Probation Service system gave us all we needed to find their new identities and home addresses. It was also kind of them to note Penney was having a holiday round here.' She laughed.

'Yes, but other than Penney, getting them to come to our area, though, that wasn't easy, was it?' he pointed out.

'I had ways,' she told him with a smile. 'Even though Leonard Wright was already here, he was a problem I didn't foresee.'

'It was unfortunate he already had an arrangement in place that we didn't know about.'

'I should have spotted it on the network.' She shook her head. 'I can't imagine what it was like when you found that poor girl.'

'All I could think was what would happen to you if I got caught.'

'Yes, but you did the job and saved the girl from God knows what.'

'When I dropped her in the alley near the police station, I made her promise not to look as I drove away. She was to count to twenty before she removed her blindfold. I watched in the rear-view mirror and she did just as I asked. I knew she could have taken the reg, and we'd have failed in our mission if she had.'

'Bainbridge telling you he'd met the Slovenian in a bar and got friendly with him was very useful. Did you have to torture him to get the details?'

He laughed. 'You're joking. He was scared witless and wetting himself the moment I put the noose around his neck. When I bargained he could go free if he gave me what I wanted to know, it was like opening a tap. He didn't shut up. It's just a shame he couldn't identify who it is we're looking for.'

'Well, using the VPN he shared with the Slovenian enabled me to penetrate the Dark Web and access the network we needed to infiltrate their ghastly site. He was really helpful with that.'

It seemed like good news, even if parts of it sounded to him as if they were in Ancient Greek. 'I'll deal with as many as I can while you continue your search.'

'Have you seen the photos? All those photos they shared? It could almost be a shopping list. And there are videos on some sort of pay-to-view tab. Those men need castrating.'

'That's as maybe, but come on, you need a rest. Let me help you to bed. Have a lie-down.'

'Not yet. I'm trying to check someone out. Anyone who shows an interest in a message I post, I look to see who they really are and where they live. Only then can I start to set up a meeting for you. Many of these perverts have specific requirements, and I have to be very careful I don't make a mistake and alert the webmaster. That's what's causing the delay. But believe me, I *will* find him.'

'OK, in that case, I'll get your medication and make you a cuppa. When you've finished what you're doing, promise me you'll have a rest.'

'I will.' She smiled at him.

He kissed her on the cheek and headed for the kitchen.

When he returned, he asked, 'How are you contacting them when they reply?'

'I'm using my online persona.'

'And what's that?'

'Didn't you know you're married to Colin, a thirty-three-year-old man who has a preference for girls aged between the ages of eight and eleven?'

'Good God, is that how you're doing it?' He looked shocked.

'Simplest way. They think I'm one of them.'

* * *

When Nash had left the CID suite that night, Pearce was still hard at work on his computer, but his efforts to try and establish a way the victims had been lured to their deaths was proving futile. Eventually, he decided to follow Nash's example and call it a day.

As he went through reception, Viv paused to say goodnight to Steve Meadows. The desk sergeant was awaiting the arrival of transport to Netherdale for a woman who had been arrested for shoplifting. Helmsdale worked office hours unless there was a major operation in progress necessitating use of the cells. As a rule, all prisoners were kept overnight at HQ.

'You're lucky,' Meadows told Pearce, 'by the time I've dealt with this, you'll have finished your dinner and be sitting with your feet up.' He paused and then said, 'Before you dash off, Viv, answer me one question.'

'If I can.'

'When I took over from Jack Binns, he told me that Mike had a bit of a reputation where women are concerned, but I'm finding that hard to believe, because he seems very settled and content with his domestic arrangements. Was Jack pulling my leg?'

'Not at all. Mike did have a few girlfriends — a bit of a ladies' man, you could say. But that all changed after he met Alondra. Do you know the story about how they came to be together?'

Meadows shook his head so Viv explained. 'Her real name is Lottie Davidson, but she prefers to be called Alondra, the name she was brought up with in Spain.'

'Yes, I read about that case, but didn't make the connection. I can't say I blame him, though. I've only seen her a couple of times, but she's drop-dead gorgeous.'

Pearce grinned as he replied, 'I agree, but don't let Mike hear you say that.' As he walked across the car park, he was puzzled slightly by Meadows' last statement. He felt certain something the sergeant had said should have rung bells with him, but he couldn't hear even a faint tinkle. All the way home he kept pondering it, but as is so often the case, the harder he tried to make the connection the more elusive it became. On reaching home he dismissed the idea as fanciful and forgot about it.

Then, at almost three o'clock in the morning, Pearce sat up in bed and announced loudly, 'General David Petraeus.'

Alongside him, his wife Lianne stirred, turned over and mumbled, 'What's wrong, Viv?'

'Nothing. I've just remembered something that might be really important to do with work. I'll just go make a note of it before I forget. Go back to sleep.'

The recollection and the notes he made drove sleep from Pearce's mind for a long time, and it was almost an hour later before he finally dozed off.

Despite his disturbed night, Pearce was first to arrive at Helmsdale next morning, beating even Nash and Steve Meadows, albeit by a slender margin.

* * *

When Nash entered the CID suite at his usual time, the detective constable was seated at the computer, in exactly the same position as when Nash had left the previous night.

'Please don't tell me you've been here all night, Viv,' Nash teased him. 'Or has Lianne seen sense and kicked you out?'

'No, but she wasn't too happy when I woke in the middle of the night because I'd had an idea. Let me explain.'

'I'm not sure I should hear this, it sounds a bit risqué.' Nash laughed.

'Nothing of the sort, this was to do with work and it might be really important.'

'What are you on with now?'

'It all stems from a chance remark Steve Meadows made that sparked a memory. Unfortunately, the spark didn't happen until the early hours of the morning. However, it was nagging at me so badly, I had to come in early to settle the matter one way or the other.'

'OK, so what exactly happened?'

Pearce grinned. 'I sat up in bed and called out very loudly, "General David Petraeus", which, not surprisingly, had Lianne totally confused.'

'I'm with her on that.' Nash replied. 'Who is this General? The name seems vaguely familiar, but I can't place him.'

'Petraeus is, or rather was, an American general who later became director of the CIA. He got mixed up in a scandal and had to "resign".' Pearce emphasized his ironical use of the word with his fingers. 'Investigators discovered that

169

he'd been leaking confidential information to the woman he was sleeping with.'

'OK, Viv, I'll give you full marks for your in-depth knowledge of recent American history, but I'm baffled as to how that is important to us in a rural backwater of North Yorkshire.'

'It isn't, but for one thing — the means of communication used by Petraeus and his mistress. When investigators broke the scandal, they discovered the medium used by the couple for passing the leaked secrets was something known as "dead drop" emails.'

'You've lost me there, Viv, and not for the first time. What exactly is a dead drop email?'

'It's the cyber equivalent of an old espionage technique used by spies.'

'Ah, now I'm with you, like a dead letter drop, but how does it work with emails? Surely the traffic would be fairly simple to pick up.'

'Not necessarily, Mike, not if there wasn't any traffic.'

'You've lost me again. I'm afraid it's the Luddite in me. Keep the explanation simple.'

'I'll try to,' Viv promised. 'Let's take it a stage at a time. It begins with the administrator setting up a new email account on a network. He or she then writes an email containing the secret information, but doesn't send it. Do you know what happens to emails that don't get sent?'

'They go into a folder of some sort.'

'That's correct, a drafts folder. They remain in there until they're either sent or deleted. Having posted a message to the drafts folder, the administrator leaves it there. Along comes his contact, accesses the email account using the same prearranged username and password. He reads the email and then deletes it. There is no trail for the message, because it never gets sent anywhere. The information has been passed without anyone else being any the wiser.'

'OK, I understand all that, but why do you think this might be . . .' Nash's voice trailed off as he grasped the significance of what Pearce had just told him.

'It's only guesswork, but I believe that might be the method used by the paedophiles to arrange their sordid liaisons. Then, and this is even more guesswork, if someone hijacked the system, they could use it to lure the perverts to their death with bogus draft emails. By offering them a temptation they knew the perverts would be unable to resist, they could get them to go to a location they'd chosen in advance. The beauty of that is the place would have to be suitable for the purpose the victim had in mind — and even more suitable for what the killer intended to do. The only slight problem I have with this idea is that these men would have been extremely wary of anything they might suspect was a trap. If, for example, they thought it was a set-up devised by police and they would finish up inside, they'd have run a mile.'

CHAPTER TWENTY-FIVE

It was clear from Nash's response that he'd bought into Pearce's theory.

'They wouldn't have been half as cautious if they believed that the message sender was one of their own, like calling to like, as Clara suggested. Perhaps the administrator set up the network with the intention of procuring suitable victims for the paedophiles, grooming and so forth,' he told Pearce.

'A network of evil, you mean?'

'Yes, but if your idea's right, then at some point, and we can't be sure when, a person with the technical ability must have taken over control of the network. That would enable them to pursue their own, quite different agenda — the destruction of the network and the murder of its members.'

Nash thought for a moment. 'Hang on, what about the original administrator? Surely he would notice the interference on the site.'

'Not unless he was unable to. Incapacitated in some way, perhaps?' Viv supposed.

'Or dead?'

'Could it have been Bainbridge? He was into computer fraud and embezzlement. Perhaps he had the skills?'

'We'll never know, will we?' Nash suggested.

Nash and Pearce looked at one another, stunned by the way their reasoning had developed and the possibilities it opened up for them to further the investigation. There was silence for a few minutes as both detectives pondered the implications.

Then Nash asked the vital question that was simmering in his mind. 'Have you been able to find out how the American investigators discovered the messages if there wasn't any actual email traffic, and if the files never left the drafts folder before they were erased?'

'Not yet, Mike. I hadn't got that far with my research, but with a bit of luck, I might be able to find it online.' Pearce paused for a moment before adding, 'One thing is certain, though, if the FBI and NSA or CIA were involved, the investigators would have access to a lot more in the way of resources, manpower, cyber tools and finance than we can muster.'

'In that case, we'll have to rely on the cyber skills we do have, which means you and Adil, along with any assistance you can gain through liaison with Leeds and Huddersfield CID. Hopefully, they'll have officers with equally good IT training, and if you pool your expertise, you might be able to give us the breakthrough we're desperately in need of.'

Nash thought over everything they'd discussed and then added, 'I suggest we keep this from Clara. She'll probably mark it down as a wild idea, similar to the ones she often accuses me of having, and then she might think it's an infection I've passed on.'

* * *

Professor Ramirez phoned Nash. 'I've received the DNA test report on the broken knife blade and handle found at the Mitre Hotel, and the result is more than fruitful. I've forwarded it via email so you can judge for yourself.'

Nash assembled the team and relayed the contents of the professor's email. 'The knife we found in the room where Trevor Mills was murdered had multiple bloodstains on both the blade and handle. The DNA from the blood matched three people; Leonard Wright, John Penney and Trevor Mills.' He paused to let them digest this, before adding, 'All we have to do now is find out who wielded that knife. One thing we can be sure of, it was neither Philip Robson nor Majda Klements.'

His call to Netherdale was shared by Ruth Edwards and Jackie Fleming. 'Are you certain Robson had no part in any of the murders, with or without an accomplice?' Jackie asked.

'Although he had a deep-seated, and understandable, hatred for Penney, he had no connection to the other four murder victims. Added to that, even if he was pursuing a vendetta, how would he have learned their identities? Robson doesn't even own a mobile phone, let alone a computer, and how familiar would a sous-chef be with the technology required to permeate a Dark Web network?'

'What do you mean by that?' Ruth asked.

Nash explained Pearce's theory about draft messages being read and deleted, adding, 'This was Viv's bright idea, not mine, but I think it's the best workable theory we have. What we must try and do is find a way to access any deleted drafts, and Viv's working on that now, along with Adil.'

'OK, I'll keep my fingers crossed your IT wizards come up with something useful,' the chief said.

'So what do you intend to do, Mike?' Fleming asked.

'We're back to square one, I'm afraid. At present, we've no idea how to move forward with the investigation, which is very frustrating.'

* * *

That afternoon, Nash held a meeting with his colleagues to discuss ways to proceed. 'We need to think of something to help us identify whoever is behind this. What's more, we need to do so before the killer, or killers, strike again. I need you all to put your thinking caps on and try to come up with a solution. I'm open to any suggestions, no matter how far-fetched they might be.'

He cast a sideways glance at Clara and grinned as he added, 'Don't be put off if it appears implausible. I've often been accused of flights of fancy in the past, and they occasionally turn out to be accurate, despite the disbelief of others.'

Despite Clara's innocent expression, the other detectives smiled at this oblique reference to the scepticism she had voiced on several occasions at the credibility of some of Nash's theories.

The situation remained the same with no more killings, during which time other matters had to be dealt with. What Pearce referred to as the 'perverts' execution case' was no nearer to being solved than when the first victim had been found. Nash suspected that several of his colleagues were secretly hoping this impasse would continue, but they refrained from saying so in view of their duty as police officers.

* * *

It was later that afternoon, having given the matter considerable thought, that Clara raised an interesting point, one nobody had thought of or mentioned previously.

She took her idea to Nash, and told him, 'Something about these murders is puzzling me. Given that the crimes committed by the victims all took place miles away, in different areas of the country, and in one case abroad, why are they being lured into our area to be trapped and killed? There is no evidence in their files that any of them operated in our locality, and in a couple of cases, two of the victims had never been to this part of North Yorkshire until their bodies turned up on our doorstep. Why not kill them where they lived?'

Nash thought about this for a long time, before replying, 'That is an extremely good point, Clara, and the answer is, at this precise moment, I have absolutely no idea. Let's ask the others.'

There was a long silence as the detectives pondered Clara's question. Eventually, it was the newest member of the team who thought up a response. 'Perhaps,' DC Hassan said a trifle hesitantly, 'we're missing something that might be important — crucial, possibly.'

His colleagues looked at him, their baffled expressions giving him the impetus to continue.

'What if there was another sex crime, one that was committed in our area, and the relatives or someone close to the victim still lives around here? If they felt aggrieved enough, like Philip Robson did, to want to take action against these sorts of perverts, they might be the one we're looking for. Someone who has lived and/or worked around here for any length of time would be more familiar with the terrain and, therefore, easily able to pinpoint locations suitable for what they had in mind.'

'That is a good idea, Adil, definitely worth following up. With so few solid facts at our disposal, we need to explore every possible alternative. Even if we hit another brick wall with this one, it's got to be worth a try.'

He smiled at Viv and Adil, before telling them, 'The first part is going to be down to you and your technological know-how. Crack on with the research of all such crimes logged on the computer as being from this area or nearby and see if you can strike gold for us.'

* * *

It was two days later when Pearce and Hassan finally surrendered and admitted that their trawl of the computerised records had ended in failure, throwing up no potential cases that seemed to fit their criteria.

Their irritation was evident by Viv Pearce's tone of voice when he told his colleagues, 'We've researched everything we can find, from blokes committing indecent exposure to more serious offences, but there could be several cases we haven't been able to locate.'

He held up one hand to ward off any implicit criticism of their efforts. 'That isn't our fault. The reason we can't be certain we've covered everything is the computer records are by no means complete. Those covering Netherdale and the area immediately surrounding the town go back twenty years, but no further than that, and those for the Helmsdale area cover a similar sort of period. As for anything that might have taken place in Bishopton or thereabouts, you've as much idea as me, because there appear to be no records whatsoever. Why that should be, I have absolutely no idea. As far as Bishopton is concerned, Jack the Ripper could have been running wild there for decades and nobody would be any the wiser.'

Nash told them, 'The decision not to computerize the Bishopton files was made when the police station there closed down, and all cases that occurred in other parts of our area prior to us going online were treated similarly. It was all done because they were deemed to be irrelevant, and wouldn't fit within our budgetary constraints at the time. Sometimes, it's more difficult fighting off economies than it is fighting crime.'

'That is ridiculous and bordering on the obscene,' Clara responded, her tone one of anger. 'What about unsolved cold cases? Any number of serial offenders could be literally getting away with murder, just because some penny-pinching accountant has decided it will earn him brownie points by playing ducks and drakes with police work.'

* * *

'Where do we go from here?' Lisa asked.

There was a long silence before Nash responded. 'As I see it, the only way of covering all eventualities would involve us trawling through the paper files of all cases that haven't hit the computer. That would be a mammoth task, and would go a fair way to offsetting the economy drive that caused the problem. However, I have an idea as to how we can speed up the process with a fair chance of success.'

'Any idea, even one of your wildest ones, would be a bonus,' Clara told him. 'Anything is better than nothing, which is what we've got at the moment.'

'OK, what I have in mind is for us to consult people who might be able to recall something. Think about it, the sort of crimes we're talking about are ones that would be certain to stick in the memory of police officers, whether they were directly involved in the investigation or not.'

'Who have you got in mind to consult?' Viv asked.

'Let me guess,' Clara interposed. 'You're going to ask Tom Pratt and Jack Binns, aren't you? They're the go-to guys whenever you want to know about local history.'

'Not just those two. Even if they can't recall anything, God might help me.'

Clara was the first to catch his allusion, and as Viv and Lisa realized Nash was not about to pray for help, she said, 'That's a good idea. I didn't think of her. She'd be sure to remember a significant case such as the one we're looking for, because sooner or later the file would have landed on her desk.'

Seeing DC Hassan's puzzled expression, Clara explained, 'Our retired chief constable, Gloria O' Donnell, was known throughout the force as "God" because of her rank and her initials, but that was before your time here.'

CHAPTER TWENTY-SIX

Tom Pratt, Nash's first port of call, provided the answer the detectives were looking for, rendering consultation with retired uniform sergeant Jack Binns or the former chief constable unnecessary. Once Nash outlined the type of case they were trying to find a connection to, Tom, who prior to retirement on health grounds had been the region's senior detective, was able to recall a particular case.

'There's only one that fits your criteria. It took place around twenty-two or twenty-three years ago as I recall, somewhere in the Bishopton area. I wasn't directly involved in the investigation, but I did oversee the prosecution. Sadly, even if the Bishopton files had been put on the computer, this one would have been out of the catchment area because it was so long ago.'

Since retiring from active service as chief superintendent, Tom had returned as a civilian support officer, and his knowledge from his previous role enabled him to offer his services when required. 'The hard copies of all Bishopton area cases are now stored in the basement here at Netherdale HQ, so if you want I can dig the relevant one out and bring it over, which will save your lads a bit of time. There might be one or two boxes. I can get one of the lads here to load them in my car, so it would be useful if Viv or Adil was on hand to act as porter.'

'That's no problem, Tom, and thanks a lot. That will be a great help.'

Nash wandered into the general office and told his colleagues, 'I've just had a word with Tom Pratt, and he reckons there's only one case we should look into. He's bringing the file boxes across as soon as he locates them, which should be either later today or tomorrow. There could be a fair amount of paperwork involved, so he reckons he might need a hand with the lifting and shifting.' He smiled sweetly at Pearce and Hassan, adding, 'I've volunteered you two for that task.'

Next morning, Nash eyed the two large boxes Tom Pratt had brought over and told the others, 'I think it will save a lot of time and effort if Clara and I look through these and then brief you as to the contents. That means you'll be able to handle any phone calls, visitors and, of course, the coffee machine. The only stipulation is that regular supplies to my office must be maintained.'

Nash smiled as he saw the look of relief on the faces of his colleagues who had just been freed up from the task of reading a mountain of paperwork. He went into his office along with Clara, who had already picked up her notebook and pencil.

Nash read all the pertinent facts while Clara made copious notes of the relevant details. It was several hours and numerous mugs of coffee later when they were at last ready to brief the team on what they had learned.

* * *

Before Nash began the briefing, Clara told him, 'I think the people who suffered this immense tragedy must be considered as our prime suspects, don't you?'

'I agree, and to be honest, at this moment, they are the only suspects, unless someone else suddenly pops up on the radar.' Nash looked down at Clara's notes, before telling the team, 'Charles Harrison was an accountant, and his wife Linda was a clerical officer for MAFF, which was short for the Ministry of Agriculture, Fisheries and Food, based in Bishopton. They married young, both being only eighteen years old, and two years later had their only child, a daughter named Tracey. With the constraints of her parents' working lives, Tracey spent much of her early years with her grandparents, who were seemingly devoted to the child.

'When Tracey was seven years old, everything went wrong in a truly dreadful manner. Her father went to Bishopton Primary School to collect her, but he was late, having been delayed at work, and when he got to the school, Tracey had vanished. Nothing was seen or heard from the child for two weeks, until a walker found her naked body in woodland alongside a farmer's field near the village of Bishop's Cross, where Tracey and her parents lived. The post-mortem revealed the child had been repeatedly raped and then strangled. Although DNA testing was nowhere near as sophisticated then as it is nowadays, swabs were taken and these threw up an immediate suspect, a man already on the Sex Offenders Register. The culprit was arrested, convicted and sentenced to life imprisonment with a minimum term of twenty-eight years. Three years into his sentence he was stabbed by a fellow inmate and died from his wounds. Whether this brought any solace to the bereaved relatives of Tracey Harrison is open to question. On the other hand, it might have caused bitterness because the guilty man's suffering had ended, while theirs was still an open wound.'

Nash paused there, conscious that the emotional content of the file was affecting his colleagues much as it had done him and Clara. He concluded by telling them, 'Sadly, these files are less than complete. As happens with so many cases, once the conviction had been achieved, the file is stored away, whether online or in the basement, and rarely updated thereafter. We have no knowledge as to what happened to Charles and Linda Harrison after their daughter's murder, so

I think we must make it our first priority to locate them. Viv, would you and Adil get to work on that, please?'

* * *

Lisa Andrews reflected on what the parents had suffered. 'What age would Mr and Mrs Harrison be now?' she asked. 'Wouldn't they be a bit long in the tooth to start a career as serial killers, and if they are responsible, why wait all this time to begin the vendetta?'

'I don't think there's an age limit for murderers,' Clara told her. 'And anyway, they'd only be around forty-seven or forty-eight years old, which isn't exactly ancient. As to the time span before they started their killing spree, there could be all sorts of reasons for that. Maybe a recent event proved to be the spur, either something that happened to them, or elsewhere.'

Although the task Nash had set Pearce and Hassan hadn't seemed a particularly onerous one, it was quite a while before they reported back. The gist of what they had to say represented total failure.

'We tried the electoral roll first, but there was nobody corresponding to their names and ages registered to vote anywhere in the UK. Next we tried the DVLA, because not everyone trusts politicians enough to waste their time voting, but we had no luck there either.' Pearce glanced at Hassan, who took up the story.

'As a last resort, I checked the 2011 and 2021 census records, but there's no trace of them on either. The only possible conclusion we came to is that they might have emigrated, and after such a traumatic incident that seems the likeliest explanation for the lack of detail.'

'Did you think to check other family members?' Clara asked. 'I mean the child's grandparents, plus the mother's and father's siblings, even cousins. They might be able to tell us where to find Charles and Linda.'

'Sorry, we didn't think of that.'

The detective constables scurried back to their computers and recommenced their research.

Nash eyed Clara and said, 'You're on extremely good form today. I hope you haven't been taking any dodgy stimulants.'

Clara snorted with derision. 'Someone has to do the thinking around here, and you're obviously not up to it.'

Pearce and Hassan reported again, and once more it was without success. 'Both Charles and Linda's parents are dead, and as they were both an only child, there are no siblings, which I'm afraid leaves us back at square one.'

'Not exactly,' Nash told them. 'Because, contrary to popular belief around here, I've been doing some thinking, and I've come up with an idea.'

Ignoring Clara's cheeky grin, he continued, 'As we've had absolutely no success digitally, I believe our next step should be to go to Bishop's Cross and begin asking about Charles and Linda Harrison there. Admittedly, what happened took place more than twenty years ago, but with a hugely dramatic event such as that, I feel certain there will be quite a number of people who were living there back in the day, and who are still in the village. They could tell us what became of the Harrisons. Even if we have no luck in the village, we could always try their former employers.'

Having apprised his colleagues of his idea, Nash told them, 'I'll go to Bishop's Cross tomorrow and Clara can accompany me. That way, she can do some thinking for me if I don't feel up to it. One other point before we go. It's something that could be useful. In that file there are photographs of both Charles and Linda Harrison. Viv, would you and Adil please upload them onto your computers and try to age them, so we'd have some idea as what they look like nowadays?'

'We'll give it a go, Mike, but I'm not certain how accurate the result will be,' Viv told him.

* * *

Armed with the updated images, Nash and Mironova set off for Bishop's Cross the following morning. As they were driving towards the village, Clara glanced at the address they were aiming for, which had been culled from the file. 'This property, Elm Tree Cottage, Saxon Way — it sounds idyllic. Anyone who was unaware of the appalling things that happened to the previous inhabitants could be really tempted if it went on the market.'

'I agree, it does sound really attractive, but unfortunately, what you said about trying to sell it could well be doomed to failure. Once they learned about the history of the property, many potential buyers would be put off by the knowledge of what had happened. Admittedly, the brutal crime didn't take place on the premises or nearby, but that sort of reasoning doesn't occur when people think with their heart instead of their brain. It might be classed as pure superstition, but somehow logic doesn't enter the equation when you're confronted with the awful truth.'

As a prophecy, Clara thought later, Nash's statement had to be remarkably accurate.

* * *

Elm Tree Cottage was part of a tiny cul-de-sac on the fringe of the village. As they approached, Clara could see nothing beyond but farmland, the earth a rich dark brown as a result of the ploughing that had recently taken place. Saxon Way was a small offshoot from the country lane. The cul-de-sac comprised of only four properties, all detached two-storey buildings she guessed had been constructed somewhere in the 1960s or early 1970s. Each of them had ample gardens both to the front and rear.

Two of the houses were on the left of the road, the others directly opposite. Elm Tree Cottage was the second property on the right, bordered on the far side by a high hedge that separated Saxon Way from the field beyond.

Their first setback came when Nash pulled the Range Rover to a halt outside the front gate, a rusty, wrought-iron double entrance that looked as if it hadn't been opened for many years. As they stared in dismay at the dilapidated appearance of the property, Clara muttered, 'Oh Lord, what on earth's happened here?'

Whereas the gardens to the front of the other three houses in the cul-de-sac were all well-tended, the one belonging to Elm Tree Cottage was little short of a wilderness. What had once been a front lawn was now a waist-high tangle of rye grass, interspersed with a rich variety of weeds.

The driveway leading to the detached garage had also suffered from extreme neglect, and what might at one time have been an immaculate example of block paving was now in ruins, the effect of unchecked encroachment by weeds. Even the hedge that served as a demarcation from the narrow pavement had not been trimmed for many years. Nor did the house itself look to be in any better condition.

The property was clearly unoccupied, uncared for and unsightly. The cement render on the exterior walls was stained by years of neglect. The gutters serving the drain pipes had long ceased to function, being choked with vegetation that now hung over the lip. One section of the guttering had given way, obviously unable to bear the weight of the weeds growing in proliferation within, and was now drooping at almost a forty-five-degree angle to the horizontal.

Clara noticed one of the panes of the main ground-floor window had been cracked, and wondered what had caused this damage. Shifting her gaze, she saw the letterbox in the middle of the front door had been covered over using strong adhesive tape, thereby preventing the delivery of mail, wanted or otherwise.

'Let's go take a closer look,' Nash suggested. 'Maybe then we'll be able to figure out what's gone on here.'

'I'm glad I put a thick pair of slacks on,' Clara muttered as she stared at the path. 'I don't fancy having to deal with a nettle rash.'

'I don't see any point in knocking, do you?' Nash said. He shielded his eyes with both hands and peered through the grime-encrusted double window alongside the front door.

'There's no furniture inside, and this looks as if it was once used as a living room, but now it's a real mess. There's no carpet, only bare boards, and the wallpaper is hanging off in places, which I guess is the result of damp. In fact, it looks as if there's mould growing near the skirting board. It's obvious nobody has lived in this house for a long, long time, so what's happened to Mr and Mrs Harrison is anybody's guess. Unless,' he added with a touch of macabre humour, 'they're under the patio to the rear of the house.'

Clara shuddered. 'Don't say things like that, even in jest.'

'Let's beat a retreat. It's obvious we're not going to gain anything useful from this house.'

CHAPTER TWENTY-SEVEN

As the detectives turned away from the cottage to walk back to the car, Clara noticed something close to the gate, an object that had been hidden from their view by the mass of vegetation. 'Mike,' — she pointed towards it — 'isn't that a for sale sign?'

Whereas the board had once been erected by an estate agent to advertise the property, it had long ceased to function as a way to attract attention. Stepping cautiously forward, Nash reached down and lifted the board, which still had half the support post attached. The wooden stake had been broken in the middle. As he held it aloft, Nash stared at the barely legible estate agent's details. This was far from easy, as prolonged exposure to the elements had faded the script almost beyond recognition.

'If all else fails, we could try and contact this estate agent,' Nash told her before releasing his grip on the post, allowing it to fall to the ground. 'The name isn't familiar, which leads me to think they might not be a local outfit. Before we do that, I suggest we go and knock on some doors and see what the neighbours can tell us.'

Nash didn't add 'if anything', which Clara later thought he shouldn't have omitted.

Their only success from the three remaining properties came from the house diametrically opposite Elm Tree Cottage. The young woman who answered the door couldn't have been much more than twenty-five years old, Clara guessed, which drastically reduced the chance of her being able to tell them anything useful.

She eyed the couple on the doorstep with suspicion until Nash produced his warrant card, signalling Clara to do likewise. He explained their purpose, which was to try and contact the people who had occupied Elm Tree Cottage.

'I assume you mean the Harrisons. I've no idea what happened to them. Me and my husband only moved here a few months ago. He's at work, but I don't think he knows any more than I do. We were told about the terrible thing that happened, of course, but no more than that. So I'm sorry, I don't think we can help.'

'Do you think any of the people who live in the other two houses on the cul-de-sac might know more?' Nash asked.

'I doubt it. One is a holiday let, like that Airbnb lark.' She sniffed disdainfully and gestured to the final house. 'That one belongs to some bloke with more money than sense. He's from that London, which probably explains it. He comes up here every so often, poncing about in his flash Porsche sports car along with his lady friend — she looks a right tart.'

* * *

Having met with no success, the detectives walked back to Nash's car. 'About the only thing we've learned so far,' Clara told him, 'is that the young woman we've been talking to detests London and Londoners, which isn't exactly useful, so what do we do next?'

'I think we ought to go to the pub.'

Clara stared at him in disbelief. 'Has our failure in this mission turned you into an alcoholic?'

Nash chuckled. 'No, but I've always found the best place in a village to hear all the local gossip is the pub. If we fail there, we can try at the village shop, and if we've no luck at either place, as a last resort, we could contact that estate agent whose sign we found.'

The first indication that their next attempt to discover information might be unsuccessful came before they entered the pub.

As Nash pulled onto the forecourt of the Bay Tree Inn, Clara noticed a sign on the front wall of the entrance porch. 'That doesn't look promising,' she told Nash, pointing to the board, on which was written, *Under new management.*

'One of the traits I've noticed you exhibit from time to time is a sort of unflagging pessimism,' Nash responded. 'Although in this case it could well be justified. At this early hour the bar isn't going to be full of gossiping locals, but seeing we're here, we might as well give it a shot. Even if the manager's a newbie, the bar staff could be old stagers.'

Within minutes, it seemed Clara's reservations were justified. There was only one person in the room, which given the fact that it was barely opening time was understandable. When Nash showed the man his warrant card and explained the reason for their visit, the response confirmed that their visit had been in vain.

'I'm only the locum manager. I'm looking after the place for three months until the new tenants take over. The pub belongs to a national brewery,' he explained, 'and I reckon it was a toss-up whether they continued the tenancy or put the place up for sale. That might still happen if the new tenants can't make a go of it. I'm sorry I can't be of more help, but I know very little about this village or its inhabitants, past or present.'

* * *

With only one possible source of information remaining, any hope that the village shop would provide the answer they were seeking was soon dashed. The blinds covering the entrance and windows alongside were pulled down, and there was a notice affixed to the glass panel of the door, which read, *Closed. It's our turn for a holiday.*

'I think we've done everything we can in the village, short of knocking on every door,' Clara said gloomily. 'So what next?'

'I think we should head back to the office and try to locate the estate agents and see what we can get from them. Apart from that, I'm suffering extreme caffeine withdrawal symptoms.'

'That's all very well, but I couldn't even make out what their name was,' Clara objected. 'The letters on that for sale board were indecipherable.'

'Their name is Yardley's, so as we're driving back you can contact Viv or Adil and get them to do an online search.'

'How on earth did you work the name out? Is it some special sort of talent you've hidden from us, the ability to read invisible letters?'

'No, it's more down to my love of cricket.' Seeing Clara's bemused expression, Nash told her, 'Something about the configuration of the letters suggested a name such as that. Norman Yardley was a famous Yorkshire and England cricketer, and the shape of those letters looked as if this was the possible title of the agency.' He grinned. 'Apart from that, I looked on the other side of the sign — it wasn't as badly weathered.' He laughed at Clara's expression as she shook her head.

'To be fair,' Clara said as they pulled into the car park at Helmsdale, 'once we found that sign, and if you deciphered it correctly, the estate agent has to be our best bet. They would have to know where and how to contact the people on whose behalf they were selling the property.'

'You could be right,' Nash agreed. 'But you're making a big assumption in that statement, so it's by no means a foregone conclusion.'

'And what's that?'

'You're assuming the agent is selling the house on behalf of Mr and Mrs Harrison. That's not necessarily the case. It's quite possible the house has been sold once, maybe twice or three times, during the past twenty odd years. Yardley's could be working on behalf of Mr and Mrs Zebediah Tring from Ashby-de-la-Zouch, who are the most recent owners. Added to which, there's another strong possible alternative behind that for sale notice.'

Clara smiled at Nash's comical suggestion for the name and address of a new owner, but was puzzled by the latter part of his statement, and asked what his possible alternative was.

'It could be that the house was repossessed because the owners, whether it was the Harrisons or someone else, failed to keep up with their mortgage payments. Yardley's could be acting on behalf of the mortgage lender, either a bank or building society. Actually,' Nash added after a moment's thought, 'that is the least likely explanation, because the lender would want to cut their losses, and if the property remained unsold for any length of time, they would have it auctioned off.'

* * *

If Nash and Mironova thought their luck would change when they contacted the estate agency, that hope was dashed immediately they entered the CID suite.

Clara saw Viv, Adil and Lisa glance at them, then look away. She realized the trio were trying to decide who should be the one to deliver the bad news. In the event, it was Viv Pearce who shouldered the responsibility.

'We've had no luck with the estate agency. Yardley's are no longer in business. The company went into administration. They were based in Leeds, so I took a chance and phoned an old school mate who works for another outfit there. He told me the business was already failing, and they pulled the plug rather than make things worse.'

Viv glanced down at his notes and told them, 'I decided to call the administrators who handled the insolvency.

They're a national firm of solicitors, so I spoke to one of the partners in their Leeds office, but he couldn't or wouldn't give me any useful information. He said all they did was supervise the winding up of the business. What happened to individual clients and their unsold property was not something they were directly concerned with. I got the impression he might have known more than he was prepared to say, but I could be wrong.'

As Clara was recounting their fruitless trip to Bishop's Cross, Nash wandered across the room and stood near the wall, staring at the calendar. He stayed there for some minutes, until Lisa asked him if something was wrong.

'Not really,' he replied. 'I was just checking the date. We've had so much bad luck today, I felt sure it must be Friday the thirteenth.'

* * *

Later, over a mug of coffee in his office, Clara asked Nash what he thought of Viv's comment about the solicitor. 'I don't think it's suspicious,' he told her. 'If you think about it, an unsold property hasn't attracted any commission, so it would hardly have entered into the profit and loss account for the purposes of the insolvency figures. The only costs they would have incurred would have been that for sale sign, plus whatever they did to advertise the property.'

'So where do we go from here?'

'I think my answer to that would be the same as earlier, when you accused me of lapsing into alcohol addiction. I think we should go to the pub. Or rather,' he corrected himself, 'we should go back, but this time, go in the evening when there are bound to be a few locals in the bar. The manager might not know anything useful, but someone who has lived in Bishop's Cross for twenty years or more would be bound to have some idea as to what happened to the Harrisons, given the traumatic nature of the tragedy in their lives.'

'Do you have anyone in mind to accompany you on this onerous task, or are you thinking of flying solo? It might not be difficult getting someone to go to the pub, especially as they'll be able to claim it on expenses.'

'Actually, I wasn't thinking of going — I thought you might like to ask your husband to take you. Like you said, the outing would be on expenses. I know you're from Belarus originally, but David's from round here, and being a Yorkshireman, he's bound to appreciate a free pint or two.'

'OK, I'll see if I can persuade him. I'll even volunteer to do the driving, that way he can get sozzled.'

A few minutes later, Clara wandered back into Nash's office and told him, 'It's all fixed, David and I are going to the Bay Tree this evening.' She grinned as she added, 'Strangely enough, he didn't take much persuading. Either that, or he hid his reluctance remarkably well.'

CHAPTER TWENTY-EIGHT

It was shortly after eight o'clock when Clara and David wandered into the Bay Tree. As David went to the bar to order a pint of Theakston's for himself and a glass of lemonade for Clara, she glanced around the room. There seemed to be quite a number of people there, which seemed unusual for midweek. The reason for this became clear a few minutes later, when there was a sudden influx of newcomers.

'Welcome to the Bay Tree,' the manager told them in a voice loud enough to be heard above the hum of conversation. 'First pair on the oche in fifteen minutes. Before that, what can I get you all to drink?'

It was clearly darts night, and the new arrivals were members of the opposition, another local village pub. As the players were being served, Clara suggested to David they should go and sit away from the hubbub in the far corner of the room, where there was a table free. The only occupant in the vicinity being an old man who was sitting on the bench alongside the fireplace, staring somewhat morosely at his half-empty pint glass.

Once they were seated, Clara leaned across to her husband and whispered in his ear, in what must have seemed to onlookers as affectionate sweet nothings. 'Don't rush, darling, but try and down your pint by the time the old man's finished his.'

David blinked with surprise. 'Why?' he whispered back.

'Because when you stand up to go for a refill, I want you to offer to buy him one as well. That way, hopefully I'll be able to get him talking.'

He smiled at her and said, 'You've told me on several occasions how devious you think Mike Nash is, but I reckon you've been taking lessons from him.'

* * *

Sure enough, a short while later the old man accepted David's offer, and his remark to Clara as they awaited their drinks gave her the cue she had been hoping for. 'You're new here, aren't you?' the old man asked.

'Actually, we live in Netherdale, so we're just visiting. Bishop's Cross looks such a lovely village. Have you lived here long?'

'Aye, getting on fer fifty years, I reckon.'

'Not only is it very pretty, but I assume you'll have no crime around here, not the serious stuff we've to put up with in Netherdale, anyway.'

'Aye, you're reet, there ain't much, at least not recent, like.' Clara saw his expression change as he spoke. Obviously her question had sparked a memory, an unwelcome one at that. Perhaps what he'd recalled was what she wanted to know about.

'Sorry, I should have introduced myself. I'm Clara Sutton, and my husband over there is David.'

'Pleased t' meet you. I'm Enoch Marsden. That's Enoch, as in t' Old Testament prophet.'

'Why did you say there wasn't much serious crime recently? Did something bad happen in the past?'

Marsden's face got even grimmer, and it was a few seconds before he could bring himself to reply. 'There were one thing happened, abaht twenty year back. It were terrible, and I

195

reckon t' village and them as lived 'ere never got over it proper. Sometimes it seems t' me as a load of folk get lucky and go through life wi' nowt bad happening to 'em, while others get dumped on again and again.'

'I take it you're just referring to one specific incident? If so, how come it affected the village so much?'

As Clara asked the question, David returned with their drinks, so it was a few moments before the old man replied. 'Aye, it were just one thing as happened, but it were that awful, I reckon it gave folk nightmares for years and years.' He took a sup from his pint. 'There were a little lass, a reet bonny, sweet girl she were, and she got kidnapped, raped and murdered. Poor little bairn, she were nobbut eight or so year old.'

He took a hefty swig of his pint before continuing, 'If ever there were a case for bringing back hanging, I reckon that were t' one. Given the chance, I'd have strung the bastard wot did it up missen. Anyroad, the coppers nabbed him and that DNA stuff proved it were him as did it, so he got sent down, and then he got his just desserts.'

Clara knew what happened next, but seeing David's enquiring glance, Enoch told them, 'It were after 'e'd bin inside for two year or so, 'e got into it wi' another inmate. Anyroad, this guy stuck him wi' a knife and cut 'is throat. I hope they didn't punish bloke as did him in, cos I reckon 'e deserved a medal.'

Clara looked sympathetic. 'How awful that must have been for the poor girl's parents. I don't know how they could remain here after such a dreadful tragedy, when everything around them would be a painful memory of their loss.'

'You're dead reet, lass, they couldn't stand the place. So much so they upped and went off abroad. After what happened t' their little one, they were determined t' try and help kids who might be in danger o' something similar happening t' them. They were keen as mustard t' try and prevent the suffering they'd been through. Sadly, that just made things worse.'

'I don't know how anything could be worse than what they'd suffered.'

'They went t' work wi' one of them charities like you see on t' telly, helping kids in Africa, them as live in poverty an' 'ave t' drink mucky water. Can't remember exactly where they went, but it were t' end for them.'

'How do you mean?'

'They both got struck down by one o' them virus things, a reet deadly one. Can't remember t' name offhand, but it meant four years after their little lass were killed, they were both dead. I did 'ear tell that because o' t' way they died, they couldn't even be brought back t' be buried 'ere.'

Clara glanced at David, who knew this was his cue to change the topic of conversation. Clara had the information she needed. It was time to lighten things up.

'I see the pub has a darts team, but is there a cricket club here in Bishop's Cross?' David asked.

'There is reet enough, a rare good un too. We were top o' t' Netherdale League last season.' The old man stopped suddenly and slapped his hand on his thigh. 'That's it, I knew it 'ad summat t' do wi' cricket.'

'What had?' Clara asked.

'That virus, the one as killed Charlie Harrison and his missus. It were called t' E-Bowler virus.'

Half an hour later, as they were walking across the pub car park, Clara asked David, 'Have you suddenly taken an interest in cricket? Because it's news to me if you have. If that's the case, would you mind keeping it to yourself, please? It's bad enough being in the office and having to put up with Mike, Viv and Adil talking about inswingers, outswingers, leg breaks and cover drives, without getting more of it at home.'

David chuckled, but reassured her. 'It was all I could think of to switch the conversation away from the terrible story Enoch had told us.'

* * *

Next morning, Clara updated her colleagues with what the villager had revealed, ending by telling them, 'So it looks as if we've hit another brick wall, and that puts us back to square one again. That's unless another local family have suffered in a similar fashion, one we don't know about yet. However, finding out if there is such a case would probably mean having to trawl through ream upon ream of paperwork to discover their identity. Even if we did, it might be another dead end. Every time we've had a potential suspect in our sights, it turns out to be a red herring. I'm beginning to think like Mike, that we're stuck in *Groundhog Day*, and the date must be Friday the thirteenth.'

The mood of depression that hung over the CID suite wasn't lifted until the following day. As Clara entered the office she greeted Lisa and noticed Nash was on the phone. Once he ended the call, he summoned her into his office.

'I was talking to Viv. You remember he and Adil are giving evidence today at Netherdale?'

'Don't remind me. I didn't enjoy it last week.'

Nash continued, 'I wanted to ensure they both return here as soon as they're available. The thing is, I've had an idea that I want them to follow up on. It's going to take hours of work, even with their IT skills. Oh, and before you go sounding off about me having wild ideas every verse end, this one is all your fault.'

'How come it's my fault?' Clara demanded.

'Because my idea stemmed from the one you had. I was thinking it over last night, and I wondered if your suggestion was accurate in every respect, but with one omission.'

'Would you care to explain, preferably in simple terms, and in English not Spanish, because so far you've got me completely baffled — not the first time that's happened, may I add.'

Nash grinned, but told her, 'Yours, and Viv's, idea was that the perverts were murdered by someone seeking vengeance, which I think is something we can all agree on. You developed the idea by suggesting that the vengeful person could be a parent or someone close to the victim of a crime that took place in this area.'

Clara nodded.

'OK, going on from what we discovered about Mr and Mrs Harrison, and how they were unable to remain in Bishop's Cross, what if the same happened to someone else?'

Nash saw Clara was beginning to come to terms with what he was saying, and continued, 'What I want Viv and Adil to do is start working in reverse, trying to trace someone who moved *into* our area. Someone who felt unable to continue living somewhere that had so many terrible memories for them, and hoped a change of scenery would make life less painful.'

Clara thought through everything Nash had said and gave the idea her cautious approval, with one major reservation. 'How on earth are we going to identify them, especially if they want to keep a low profile?'

'I'm hoping our IT whizz-kids will come up with a way to do it, because without it, or a huge slice of luck, I don't think we stand a chance.'

CHAPTER TWENTY-NINE

As Nash, Clara and Lisa awaited the return of their colleagues, they speculated on how the two detective constables, categorized by Nash as 'our tame whizz-kids', might go about trying to discover information regarding the background of potential suspects.

'It isn't as if we're only thinking about close relatives of victims,' Clara said, summarizing the possible difficulties, 'because the killer could be a distant family member, or might not even be directly related to the victim. He could be a close family friend, or related only by marriage. They wouldn't necessarily share the same surname. Come to think of it, a stepbrother or stepsister could also possibly carry a different last name.'

'Haven't I mentioned your unflagging pessimism before, Clara?' Nash reproved her mildly. 'You're getting to sound like Viv.'

'Really?' She snorted. 'Recognizing in advance all the potential difficulties lessens the chance of bitter disappointment. Such as when one of your wild ideas proves to be totally wide of the mark.'

Ignoring this exchange, Lisa Andrews concentrated on a particular aspect of Clara's assessment of the situation that puzzled her. 'Are we sure the killer is a man?'

'It goes back to something the only eyewitness to our killer's activity said,' Nash replied. 'I'm referring to Sammy Rhodes, the young girl who was abducted until the killer rescued her.'

'That's right,' Clara added, 'and we know the killer swore Sammy to silence. Maybe he asked her to lie on his behalf as a gesture of gratitude for her release. You were at the interview, Lisa. She was terrified and confessed that she hadn't been telling the truth, and that the man who rescued her was also much taller than she'd made out in her original statement and spoke with a Yorkshire accent.'

* * *

They were no nearer to thinking up a possible way to trace potential suspects when Viv and Adil returned in the middle of the afternoon. As they entered the CID suite, Clara noticed that both men were smiling broadly, and asked if the case was the reason they were so cheerful.

'Not exactly,' Viv Pearce told her. 'It was more what happened afterwards, when we'd just left the courtroom.'

'Why, what happened?' Lisa asked.

'Adil was talking to the prosecution's chief witness, thanking him for his contribution to us getting a conviction, and I was standing nearby. Alongside me were two solicitors, who had obviously been dealing with another case, some kind of procedure regarding a person who had died intestate. I overheard what they said, which meant I missed Adil's conversation with the witness. Adil's just told me what the man said, which was why we were laughing. Go on, Adil, tell them what the guy you were speaking to overheard — or rather, what he thought he'd heard.'

Hassan took up the story. 'Although the verdict was the right one, our star witness didn't look particularly happy. I asked him what was troubling him, and he nodded towards the two men standing by Viv. He told me, "Those two are supposed to be solicitors, yes? But I think they're a bloody disgrace. Referring to their client as an arsehole is highly unprofessional, in my opinion. No matter how much money he's got, I feel really sorry for Benny Fisher, the way those two talked about him.'"

'OK, so what was funny about that?' Lisa asked.

'Viv heard what the solicitors actually said — go on, tell them.'

They looked at Pearce. 'The first guy said, "I think that's been a very successful morning's work, don't you?" To which his colleague replied, "I certainly do, and the outcome means that our sole beneficiary is going to be a very wealthy man." However, the witness misheard "that our sole beneficiary" as "that arsehole Benny Fisher".'

It was a while before the laughter died down and Nash was able to pass on the gist of the conversation they had missed during their absence.

* * *

Later, Nash asked if they'd had chance to give any thought as to a way to track or identify potential suspects for the murders on their books.

'We have, Mike,' Viv replied, 'but to be honest, so far we've been unable to think how to go about it. It's beginning to look like the opening of an episode of *Mission Impossible*. Short of cross-checking relatives of victims of any similar crime registered to vote throughout the whole county and cross-referencing their names with entries on the Police National Computer, we can't think of any other way to do it. That would probably mean we'd both be drawing our old age pensions and still only be halfway through the list.'

'That's not all, though, Mike,' Adil told him. 'Even if we were able to get through the whole list, we could easily miss the person we're looking for. If they haven't bothered registering, they won't appear on the electoral roll, and if they happen to be living in temporary accommodation, they won't automatically be on the local authority's council tax register.'

'What sort of temporary accommodation are you thinking of?' Clara asked. 'I thought even tenants were liable for council tax.'

'That would only apply if they were living in a permanent structure. Alternatively, if they were camping, living in a caravan or a mobile home, they'd be completely off grid, except possibly from the DVLA.'

This blow to their hopes was yet another setback, and the impact of it was only mollified slightly by Clara's earlier and accurate summary of the potential difficulties. The despondency, allied to frustration, continued to affect the team until, quite by chance, a glimmer of hope appeared. However, even that was nothing more than a glimmer.

* * *

With no further clues as to who might be responsible for what Viv Pearce facetiously referred to as 'the pervert popping', the detectives were at a loss as to how to break the deadlock. Pearce had even gone so far as to suggest that fate was taking a hand, with the intention of preventing them from interfering with the course of natural justice. 'Maybe because they've got what they deserved, the gods don't want their executioner to be punished.'

That statement earned Pearce a mild reprimand from Nash, who, whilst reminding him that their job was purely and simply to apprehend anyone who had committed a crime, added, 'We are not the ones who will sit in judgement. The merits or otherwise of the perpetrators will be decided elsewhere. Once we have identified and detained those responsible and collated evidence that points to their guilt, the rest is up to the courts. Don't confuse natural justice with the laws of the land, because the two don't always tally. In some instances, far from it.'

On Friday of the week Nash had delivered this homily, Clara told him, 'I appreciate we're lucky to be getting any time off, but I've swapped my weekend off with Adil. I was supposed to be on call, but because David's going away for the next three weeks we want to spend this weekend together.'

She smiled as she added, 'Strangely enough, Adil seemed quite happy with the arrangement, and I wondered why, until he explained that his new girlfriend is working on Saturday and Sunday. So as the cricket season hasn't started yet, he'd be bored silly with nobody to talk to and nothing worth watching on telly.'

'Adil's got a new girlfriend, has he? That's good to hear. Where does she work, or don't you know?'

'Yes, she's an assistant at the local chemist in Netherdale. I had hopes for him with Kelly Fielding, but he doesn't seem to be interested.'

'Clara, go home,' Nash said as he shook his head. 'Have a good weekend.'

* * *

When Clara arrived home, she found her husband had beaten her to it. David was standing alongside the dining table, staring ruefully at the mound of paperwork on the surface. After they'd exchanged a loving greeting, Clara asked what all the files were there for.

'Those are the personnel records of a group of new clients who I'll be meeting for the first time on Monday. I know this weekend was supposed to be just for us, but I'm afraid at some point I'll have to spend a few hours going through this lot and making notes, so I can familiarize myself with any specific needs each individual has before we come in contact.'

David Sutton, who had been a senior army officer serving with the SAS, now led a support group he had organized in conjunction with the army. It was formed specifically to assist current and retired army personnel with physical or mental problems stemming from their service.

A large percentage of his work was the delicate handling of men and women who were suffering from PTSD.

'Don't worry about it, David,' Clara reassured him. 'Your work is hugely important, and you can't allow a few hours of separation to impede it. Actually, why don't you study those files tomorrow morning? I can spend the time doing some shopping, and with a bit of luck, I might be able to squeeze in a visit to the hairdresser. I might be able to bag an appointment if I ring Sally first thing. That way, I'll be out of your hair for two or three hours, maybe longer.'

David groaned. 'You've been talking to Mike Nash again, haven't you?'

'Yes, we were chatting just before I left the office, but how did you know?'

'Because your "out of your hair" pun is about as bad as any of Mike's. Why the visit to the hairdresser anyway? Your hair looks fine to me.'

'I only want a trim. I meant to go a couple of weeks back, but we were just too busy at work. It's getting a bit too long for comfort.' Clara paused before adding, 'Unless, of course, you want me to have it dyed purple or green.'

'Don't you dare,' Sutton exclaimed, before seeing her smile. 'You're a wicked tease, Clara Sutton, but I love you just the way you are, so don't even think of changing your blonde beauty.'

* * *

Aware of David's need for deep concentration, Clara left their apartment early. A quick phone call to her hairdresser had enabled her to book an appointment. Having completed her shopping, she headed for the salon. Although she was aware that she would arrive there well before her appointed time, Clara knew she could sit in one of their comfortable chairs, and, if she was lucky, might be given a drink while she waited.

Sure enough, her hairdresser greeted Clara warmly and supplied her with a mug of coffee. As she began sipping it, Clara rummaged on the table in front of her, choosing which of the magazines to read. As was often the case, they were mostly back copies, but they helped to pass the time as clients waited. She turned the pages idly, until an article, complete with a photograph of the subject, caught and held her attention.

Clara began to read the story about a well-known chef who had achieved a prestigious Michelin rating but had now, it seemed, decided to quit and announced his intention to retire. This was an unusual decision for someone who, by his appearance, had yet to celebrate his fortieth birthday, but as Clara read more of the man's background, she felt a tug of sympathy as she learned what this minor celebrity had suffered.

Sometimes, she reflected, fame and fortune are meaningless when compared to the heartbreak such as had affected this man. To suffer one, let alone two major traumatic events within a short space of time must have left him broken almost beyond repair.

To lose his only child, the victim of a sexual predator, was bad enough, but then, only a month later, to be faced with the possible loss of his wife, victim of a horrendous car crash, was even worse. The details of the life-changing injuries she had suffered made Clara wonder if it would have been more merciful had she died at the crash site rather than being rescued.

The cause of the crash, and the reason for the horrific wounds to her body were explained in graphic detail. She had been found to be over three times the legal drink limit for driving. That explained why her car left the road, collided with a tree and overturned. From what Clara read, the car she was driving had been her husband's one indulgence, a vintage sports car. These, Clara knew, were built long before the introduction of safety devices such as seat belts and airbags.

The woman had been thrown through the windscreen by the force of the impact, and as the car rolled over, it landed on top of her and crushed her legs beyond repair. Amputation was the only solution, leaving her in wheelchair for the rest of her life, and with severe facial scars caused by the windscreen.

Subsequently, the chef's five-star West Country hotel had been sold. His mission statement, which formed the ending of the magazine article, was that his intention was to return to his Yorkshire roots, where he could care for his wife and they could mourn together.

Clara found the reporter's final comment very interesting.

During my time interviewing Julian Parker, I understood his anguish when he said, 'I hope and pray that the evil monster who took our beloved daughter gets what he, and those like him, deserves.' Julian had then added, 'Be it by the police or some other form of justice.' I felt that given the chance, he would administer that justice himself.

CHAPTER THIRTY

Clara was absorbed in reading the magazine article, which in many ways fitted the profile of the person they were looking for, but for the fact that these events had occurred many hundreds of miles away.

She failed to notice Sally, her hairdresser, was standing behind her. Sally peered over Clara's shoulder and gasped slightly as she saw the photograph.

Clara looked up. 'Sorry, Sally, I was so busy reading I didn't see you. Are you ready for me?'

Sally didn't reply, and Clara saw her attention was fixed on the image of the retired chef. 'Is something wrong?' she asked.

'No, not really, Clara, it's just that I think I've seen that man on more than one occasion here in Netherdale. I could swear it was him.' She pointed to the photo as she spoke, adding, 'Either him or his twin.'

'Are you sure, Sally?'

'Well, it did look very much like him, but a little older.'

'Where did you see him?'

'Just round and about, you know — supermarket, that sort of thing. Oh, and I once saw him coming out of that disability shop in the market place.'

Although Clara's interest was now piqued, she shrugged. 'This man gave up his job some years ago, so he could be anywhere now. He might even be living next door,' she said dismissively.

They laughed at this, but before leaving the salon after her coiffure, Clara asked if she could borrow the magazine for a few days. 'I promise I'll return it as soon as I've finished with it.'

'That's OK, Clara, you can keep it. We've plenty more in the back room to go at.'

* * *

When Clara reached the CID suite on Monday morning, Nash was already in his office. He was on the phone and in response to her waved greeting, made an unmistakable signal. Clara grinned and headed for the kitchen to fill the coffee machine.

She was watching the liquid trickle through into the carafe when Nash joined her. 'Sorry, I didn't get chance to do that earlier. My mobile rang just as I was taking my coat off.'

He noticed Clara's contented expression and commented on it. 'I take it you've had a good weekend off. Is that smug expression the result of two days in bed with David?'

'Nothing of the kind,' Clara reacted angrily. 'Trust you to think of something lewd as an explanation. Honestly, you've a mind like a sewer.'

Having scolded him, Clara went on to explain, 'I went to the hairdresser's on Saturday and I got there early, so while I waited I picked up one of the magazines, the type that focus on human interest stories. I spotted an article which might turn out to be a goldmine for us, but alternatively, could be a dead end.'

'Bring the coffee through and tell me.'

They went into Nash's office and Clara gave him the details. 'The person featured, the circumstances and their back story, fit all the parameters for someone seeking vengeance for a foul deed that ruined their life. I think the profile is almost exactly the one you outlined, so I've brought the magazine in, and I'd like you to take a look and see what you think. I'm sure you'd take great pleasure in telling me if I'm barking up the wrong tree.'

'I won't do that, Clara, because at least you've hit upon a potential suspect, which is one more than we had a few minutes ago. I'll take a gander.'

Nash perused the article before delivering his opinion. 'I certainly don't think you were barking up the wrong tree, Clara. Everything I've read here fits with the sort of emotional distress that could cause a previously law-abiding citizen to go off the rails. What we need before we get too excited by this is a comprehensive check on this man and his wife. Coupled with that, we should try and find out where they are living nowadays. For all we know they might have planned to return to Yorkshire but then left the UK altogether. Given what happened to them, I wouldn't be one bit surprised, and I certainly wouldn't blame them. Alternatively, they might have returned to where they were brought up. We weren't given any clue in this article where that might have been, and Yorkshire's a big place. All this is idle speculation until we can get Viv and Adil to research this couple and see if it's a hit or a miss.'

Before the rest of the team had arrived, Nash spoke to Viv. 'I want you on your computer immediately. I have some research for you to carry out on the PNC.'

By the time all the team was in the office, Viv handed Nash a few sheets of paper. 'I only got the basic facts. You do know this is a cold case?'

Nash nodded. 'I'll explain in a minute.'

* * *

Once Nash had the information he had requested from Viv, he returned to the general office. 'Listen up, all of you. Over the weekend, Clara read a very interesting magazine article.

I'll let you all have a look at it in a while, but first, here's a précis of what it contains.'

He glanced down at the magazine he was holding. 'This article refers to a talented and well-known chef by the name of Julian Parker. He had been working at a popular hotel in the West Country. He was, in fact, part owner of the establishment, which appeared on one of those TV cookery programmes. The subsequent publicity, plus his Michelin three-star-rating, resulted in him becoming a minor celebrity. But then his life, and that of his wife, was turned upside down as the result of two horrific and tragic incidents.'

Nash paused before getting to the gist of the matter. 'Julian and his wife, Olivia, who was a computer programmer and software designer, had one child, a nine-year-old daughter by the name of Delia. They were a very successful couple, but three years ago, Delia vanished.

'Viv has researched the case on the PNC. These are the facts. Two weeks later, her naked body was found in a patch of woodland close to the hotel where her father worked. Delia had been violently raped over and over again, and had been restrained while the sickening abuse was carried out. She was alive, but only just. Had her parents not been so well off financially, matters would have ended then and there. The life-support machine would have been turned off. But her parents paid for her to be moved home and treated privately, where she remained in a coma until she eventually passed away.'

Nash paused, aware of what he was about to reveal was disturbing.

'When she was found, despite close examination of her body, there was no trace of DNA, nothing that could identify her attacker. The case remains unsolved to this day.'

Nash took a sip from his, by now, cold coffee. 'As if that wasn't tragic enough, less than three weeks after Delia's body was found, when she was still comatose, her mother suffered a life-changing road accident. Her husband's one indulgence was his passion for vintage cars. He owned an MG MGA sports car. That model was manufactured prior to nineteen sixty-two — long before the advent of safety features. Olivia Parker was driving home late one night in her husband's car when she went off the road, hitting a tree, careering down an embankment before rolling over twice. Olivia had been flung through the windscreen, suffering multiple cuts to her face and arms.'

'That's terrible,' Lisa said. 'That poor woman.'

'That's not the worst of it, when the car rolled over, the engine landed across her lower body, causing massive internal injuries and crushing both legs. As a double amputee, she was confined to a wheelchair for life and has to live with her scars.'

Nash paused again, and it was clear the emotional impact of the story was taking its toll on him. 'Olivia tested over three times the legal limit for alcohol, but that seemed immaterial as it was considered unlikely she'd survive, let alone drive a car again. It was thought the reason for her drinking was to drown her sorrows. Given her capacity for working from home, and Julian's rigorous daily schedule, Olivia spent much of that time caring for Delia, which brought her even closer to their daughter.'

It was clear all the detectives were appalled by what Nash had told them, but Pearce interrupted at this stage, asking, 'If all this happened in the West Country, how come you and Clara are so interested in it?'

'The article goes on to reveal that Julian Parker gave up his illustrious career, selling his fifty per cent shareholding in the hotel at the same time, and intended to return to Yorkshire.'

Nash glanced down at the magazine. 'He's quoted as saying, "I hope and pray that the evil monster who took our beloved daughter gets what he, and those like him, deserves. Be it by the police or some other form of justice". The reporter then added, "I felt that given the chance he would administer that justice himself".'

'That seems to me to be a mission statement, and it fits with all we know, or suspect, about the mindset of the person who is seeking out and slaughtering paedophiles. There are other factors too, one of which is that the physical description of Julian Parker fits with that provided, albeit grudgingly, by Sammy Rhodes. The second factor, which to my mind is even more pertinent, is that his wife, albeit physically crippled, just happens to be a highly-proficient computer specialist and software designer. Who better to hack into and infiltrate the network of evil on the Dark Web we suspect those perverts were using?' Nash lowered the magazine.

'One other key fact is a possible sighting of Parker in Netherdale. Clara's hairdresser spotted Parker's photo in the magazine Clara was reading and swore she has seen him in the town more than once.'

'Oh, I'm sorry,' Clara interrupted. 'There was one other thing Sally mentioned. She claims to have seen this man coming out of the disability shop in Netherdale. Surely that fits the family dynamic.'

Nash looked at the rest of the team, who seemed in agreement.

He nodded at Clara. 'Good point. Finally, although this is pure speculation on my part, the surname Parker is by no means uncommon in this neck of the woods. So there is a possibility that Olivia and/or Julian were born, or brought up, around these parts and might gravitate back here after the traumas they had suffered.'

Nash handed the magazine back to Clara, at the same time instructing Pearce and Hassan, 'OK, guys, go to it and see what you can find out. I want a full background profile on Olivia and Julian Parker, plus all their relatives, together with any information you might be able to unearth as to their current whereabouts.'

CHAPTER THIRTY-ONE

Although Pearce and Hassan set to work immediately, it wasn't until late afternoon that they were ready to deliver their findings. Viv Pearce started the briefing by telling his colleagues everything they'd been able to discover about the chef. 'Julian Parker was born in the town of Otley, midway between Leeds, Ilkley and Harrogate.'

Nash, who had been raised around there, smiled at Pearce's attention to detail, but applauded his thoroughness.

He listened carefully as Viv continued, 'From what I can gather, Julian spent a happy childhood there, and by the time he left catering college at the age of twenty-one, his future career seemed to have been mapped out for him. He was already, according to an article in the *Yorkshire Evening Post*, being spoken of as an up-and-coming talent in the world of catering. He had gained a position as sous-chef in a top-class restaurant in Leeds, which was a highly prestigious post for someone so young.

'Julian had only been working there for about eighteen months when he met Olivia Dawson. Six months later they were married. Julian was later head-hunted by one of the country's leading chefs to work in his West End restaurant and the couple moved to London.'

'How did you find all this out?' Nash asked, his curiosity roused.

Pearce grinned. 'I spent several hours trawling through social media and managed to access Julian's Facebook profile.'

'Oh, I get you, but something like Facebook is a closed book to me.'

As the other team members groaned at Nash's dreadful pun, Pearce turned to the next page of his notes and continued, 'Four years down the line, he had become head chef at the London restaurant, but he decided it was time to move on. This time it was to a top-class hotel in a small village just outside Taunton. With the help of a large investment from his wife, Olivia, who had sold the rights to a program to be used for gaming, Julian became a fifty per cent shareholder in the hotel. By this time, their daughter Delia, named in honour of Julian's cookery idol Delia Smith, was eighteen months old.'

'It must have been terribly difficult for Julian, holding down a job like that, with such long and anti-social hours. Plus caring for an infant simultaneously,' Lisa Andrews commented.

'I agree, but most of the care seems to have been undertaken by Olivia. Fortunately, given her occupation as a self-employed computer program designer, she worked from home. According to the entries on Facebook, she was quite happy to share the burden of childcare. That,' Pearce ended, 'is everything I've been able to learn about Julian, until the twin disasters that ruined his life. Adil's got all the gen about Olivia, so I'll hand over to him.'

'Before Adil starts, I think we should have a coffee break,' Nash suggested. 'That will also give us time to assimilate everything you've told us, Viv.'

* * *

A while later, suitably refreshed, the team settled back to hear what Hassan had been able to find out about Olivia Parker.

His opening sentence was sensational, to put it mildly, and it was sufficient to convince the team that they were finally on the right track. 'Olivia Dawson was born and grew up in Netherdale.'

There was a short silence, broken only by the rustle of movement as Adil's colleagues moved restlessly in their seats. 'Olivia was six years old when her parents divorced, leaving her mother, Mary Dawson, to raise Olivia and her two older siblings, Michael and Diane, on her own. Olivia attended Netherdale Primary and from there went on to Netherdale Secondary School, where she excelled in scientific studies — in particular, mathematics. Her ability was such that she was accepted for a course on computer studies at Leeds University, which she passed, attaining an honours degree, and later a doctorate. It was as she embarked on her first year of the postgraduate course that she met and married Julian Parker.'

Adil glanced down at his notes. 'By the time they married, Olivia had already designed and sold two computer programs designed for the rapidly-growing gaming market. These proved so lucrative that she was able to repay the huge student loans and tuition fees owing to the university. Olivia was apparently very shrewd, and this showed by the deal she did on those programs, because she insisted there should be a usage royalty element in the contract, which enabled her to continue receiving payment for years after the sale. That explains how she was able to put up the money for Julian's purchase of the West Country hotel. She continued to reap success, but that's all I can find about Olivia until the twin tragedies that we know about.'

'What about Olivia Parker's siblings — Michael and Diane, I think you said their names were?' Clara asked.

'Diane Dawson went to Cambridge University, which I assume is where she met Jack Tennant, a fellow student, and after they married, the couple went to live in New Zealand, where I believe they are to this day. As for Michael, that's another very sad story. He was a keen walker and he went on a hiking tour of the Scottish Highlands. When he failed to return to the pub where he was staying, the landlord called Mountain Rescue out. There was a lot of dense fog around the upper reaches of the hills at the time, and the assumption is that Michael got lost in the mist and wandered off the hiking trail. It was almost thirty-six hours before they located him, but sadly, they were too late, because he died of hypothermia.'

'What about Olivia and Julian's parents? Are they still alive?' Lisa asked.

'No,' Viv and Adil answered in chorus, 'they're all deceased.'

As his colleagues were absorbing this fresh tranche of information, Nash asked the so-far-unanswered question. 'Have either of you been able to find out where Olivia and Julian Parker are nowadays?'

The answers were both instantaneous and disappointing. 'We've tried checking on DVLA, the electoral rolls, plus every local authority in the area's council tax register, but we've drawn a complete blank with all of them,' Pearce replied.

'Which means that either Clara's hairdresser got it wrong, and the person she saw was not Julian Parker, just a lookalike., Alternatively, if she did get it right, the couple must be living completely off grid.'

Nash paused, having given voice to this thought, and then added, 'If they are living in this area off grid, I think we can discount a rental property, unless it's a bungalow, or a specially adapted mobile home, because without significant alteration, access to any of them would be far too difficult for someone with the level of disability Olivia Parker now suffers from. Which leaves us with another conundrum — what type of property might they be using? I think we ought to give serious consideration to this, because although I admit there is a possibility that Clara's hairdresser was wrong, Olivia Parker's strong local connections would tend to suggest otherwise. Meanwhile,' — Nash glanced at Clara — 'I think we

217

ought to take the details of everything we've discovered so far and present them to Jackie Fleming and the chief constable. They might also have some input that could prove useful. Who knows,' he added with a little humour, 'they might even come up with a bright idea as to how we take this case forward. I'll phone Netherdale now and see when they'll be available.'

Clara nodded at Lisa, who said, 'That will save Jackie Fleming phoning him constantly asking for non-existent updates.'

* * *

Next morning, Nash and Mironova went through to HQ to present their findings, and to share the theory based on Clara's reading of the magazine article.

Superintendent Fleming was sceptical, pointing out the complete lack of physical evidence to back up their idea. 'OK, I suppose it is feasible. But you seem to be basing this on the fact that a similar-looking man came out of a disability shop. I'm far from convinced we should divert resources to this, when in all probability it will end up as a wild goose chase, and a waste of money and manpower. Look at it this way. For all we know from what you've provided, this couple could have decided to forsake Britain altogether and are now living in Miami, Melbourne, Mallorca or Milan.'

The chief constable, however, was far more receptive to the theory. 'I agree with almost everything Jackie has just said, even her poor attempt at alliteration,' she told the detectives. 'But I certainly don't believe we should let this go without at least making an effort to identify these people as the culprits for five murders we know of, and possibly even more. Alternatively, our investigation could rule them out completely and allow us to concentrate our efforts elsewhere.'

She looked across her desk at Nash and Mironova as she added, 'Have you been able to come up with any possible locations where Julian and Olivia Parker might be living, or using as a base for their operations, should they be the guilty parties? There can't be that many possible candidates, given the extent of the woman's disability?'

'We haven't, not so far,' Nash said. 'But we only started looking at them as a possibility yesterday, and it was nothing more than a remote theory, until we learned of their family connections to this area.'

'I had an idea while you were talking about them living off grid,' Ruth Edwards told them, 'and I'm not certain whether it will be helpful or not. I was wondering if they might have gone to one of those holiday parks with cabins or chalets. That's assuming they can stay for long periods, those places being intended for holiday use, I mean.'

'I think that's worth looking into,' Nash responded, and with a sideways glance at Jackie Fleming, added, 'and it wouldn't use up too many resources checking them out, as there can't be many such sites in our area.'

Jackie, it seemed, had now bought into their theory. 'I've had an idea too. I'm not sure how those places operate, but how about an Airbnb house, or bungalow? Even a ground-floor apartment, providing they have disabled access.'

'I think both of those are well worth following up on,' Nash agreed. 'When we get back to Helmsdale, I'll get everyone on it trying to identify possible locations, either in holiday parks or rental homes.'

'Before you go, Mike,' Jackie Fleming stopped him. 'I've had another idea that might be worthy of consideration. If we're to go ahead with the chief's plan, ought we not also get the media involved? And possibly issue all our officers, either plain clothes or uniforms, with copies of the photograph from that magazine? If they have no idea what Julian Parker looks like, he could be standing next to them in the queue at a supermarket checkout and they'd be none the wiser.'

'That's an excellent suggestion, Jackie,' the chief constable agreed, 'but not the media. We have no evidence to link these people with the killings — in fact, we have nothing.

And if they are responsible, one glimpse of a newspaper and they would be gone.'

'Yes, I wasn't thinking. But I will get Tom Pratt and Maureen Riley cracking with printing and distributing the photo to uniform division and the bulletin boards.'

As Nash turned to leave, Ruth Edwards told him, 'By the way, Mike, I've got some news I think you'll find amusing. I met the CEO of Good Buys supermarkets last Friday, and he told me something interesting. I intended to pass it on, but I'd forgotten about it until Jackie mentioned supermarkets just now. He said that as part of the group's plans for expanding their network of stores, they've made a start on one aspect already. Their plan is to provide a larger chain of small convenience stores, and they've already purchased one property that came on the market unexpectedly. That shop is the one that used to be known as Roper Stores on the Carthill estate. I believe the term for that result is poetic justice.'

'I think that was a really good outcome,' Clara said, as she and Nash were travelling back to Helmsdale, 'better than we could all have hoped for.'

'I agree, and between them, Ruth and Jackie came up with a couple of excellent suggestions that should help our search. Let's hope their ideas, coupled with your theory, provide a positive outcome, and we can at last put this highly distressing case to rest.'

For a while, it appeared that Nash's statement was little more than wishful thinking, and that their hopes were purely false optimism, but then, two days after the meeting, everything changed dramatically.

CHAPTER THIRTY-TWO

The room was in semi-darkness, the only source of illumination coming from the desk top monitor being studied by the only occupant. Her fingers moved deftly across the keyboard, clearly the action of someone totally familiar with such devices. She had now been working on this over several weeks, delving further into the network until she was satisfied. Having constructed the all-important message, she read it through carefully, ensuring every detail was correct. She needed to be certain it would provoke the response she hoped for. Any slight deviation from the norm might cause the recipient to become suspicious, and that had to be avoided at all costs. Having satisfied herself that everything was as it should be, her mouse hovered over the word 'Send', before she took a deep breath and pressed it. Now, all she could do was wait — and hope.

It was three weeks since the last paedophile murder — another one dealt with, but there was still the main one left to find. The others had been easy; convicted for their crimes and given new identities on their release from prison created no problems for someone with her talent. Hacking into the Probation Service mainframe had supplied all the details she required. But this time, she knew an unsolved crime gave no leads to the person responsible.

What she did have, however, was access to the network, where she had repeatedly posted a message she hoped would eventually attract him. Every time there was a response, using her skill, she checked the sender's real identity, digging deeper into their background.

It took some time before the true identity of the latest responder was complete. She stared in disbelief at what her search revealed.

Pushing at the desk with both hands, she sent her wheelchair freewheeling across the room. She turned away from the screen, an action that was as much mental as physical as she tried to distance herself from the horror of what she had learned.

She felt nausea growing, and had to fight hard to refrain from being physically sick. What she had just read on the screen, was, in her mind, without doubt the most revolting example of betrayal possible.

It was a long time before she was able to control her emotions sufficiently enough to react to the knowledge. It was no use trying to persuade herself that there was an error — that the facts she had obtained were a distortion of the truth — because she knew for certain they were real.

At this moment, she was alone. He rarely left her side, unless necessity demanded. That would be when supplies were needed or when there was a target in view. But now he had to be told. What his reaction to the news would be scared her. She knew they would have to plan, as they did with the others. How she would stop him from dashing out to deal with the person featured on her screen, she didn't know.

Eventually, and with a heavy heart, she picked up her mobile, her fingers trembling as she tried to compose a text. She read it back before sending it, then waited for a reply.

As the recipient read the simple one-line sentence, the demand was clear. *ID confirmed, get back here ASAP.*

Seconds later, the mobile screen read, *On my way, there in fifteen.*

* * *

Their meeting was a tense one, prolonged as both parties tried to come to terms with the new situation. Now they had all the information they needed, and their prime target was at last in sight. Much of the delay came from their mutual reluctance to accept what, to them, was unacceptable.

Time after time, the computer expert had to answer the question from her partner, 'Are you sure this is correct? Is there no possibility of error? Did you check, double-check and then check again?'

In other circumstances, giving her undoubted technical ability, she might have taken umbrage at this implicit slight on her skill, but this was far too serious for such trivialities. Eventually, when they were both certain beyond measure there was no possibility of the information being incorrect, they were able to move on, to concentrate their thoughts on the task ahead.

They had waited years for this moment, and despite their previous successes, marked by the disposal of some evil and perverted creatures, everything they had achieved thus far was as nothing compared to their final operation, their coup-de-grâce.

Their killing of a group of perverts had been conducted dispassionately, but their next one would be highly personal. The facts they had learned would enable them to wreak vengeance on the man who had ruined their lives, despoiling and taking from them the only person who mattered.

Never, they reflected, had the old saying 'Keep your friends close, but your enemies closer' ever been more appropriate than in their situation. Betrayal of trust hurts deeply when it is committed by someone near to you, much more so when the snake in the grass is someone you believe to be a friend.

The way they would go about it reflected the way they had always worked, their circumstances heightening the need to apply their particular talents. Ability with all things technological was coupled now with the privations that restricted her mobility.

That had left her partner to deal with things she was no longer able to accomplish. For some while, she had ranted about her perceived lack of contribution to their mission, which they both saw as a sort of Holy Grail.

In return, she was told in no uncertain terms that this line of thinking was totally inappropriate, and this was pointed out in the planning of every stage of the operation.

'Your input is critical, more so than ever, so don't talk such arrant nonsense,' she was told. 'It's one thing to dispose of those evil beings, that's the simplest part of the whole procedure. Your task is much more important, and is something I could never have hoped to achieve. It's no use sending this evil monster to a well-earned death unless he's made aware of the reason for his execution. Equally important, if not more so, is ensuring the whole world is made aware what a disgusting and loathsome excuse for humanity he is.'

She nodded in agreement.

'We must present our case in such a way that people will regard us as rightful seekers of justice, worthy of a medal rather than punishment for what we have done. All that will to be down to you. So let's start concentrating on ways and means to achieve our ultimate goal.'

There was one fact that, in all their discussions, the computer expert steadfastly refused to share with her partner in crime. This was a development she would have to handle alone. She'd been aware for three years that this time would come. To reveal it now would risk them abandoning their quest for justice, and there was no way she would even consider allowing that to happen.

When they had achieved their final goal, things would be different. Then, and only then, she would be able to share the news that she was dying. Within months, possibly even weeks, as a legacy from her horrific accident, she would be dead. The doctors had warned her that the internal injuries would shorten her life expectancy. The medication she had been prescribed at the time, and now purchased online, was no longer dulling the pain. From her research, she knew her days were numbered.

That knowledge lent extra urgency to their mission. Whether she would live long enough to see it through was open to question.

* * *

In the general office at Helmsdale, all the computers were occupied. It seemed everyone wanted to source a potential hideaway for the couple.

'Got another one,' Viv called out.

'Make a note and keep going,' Clara told him. 'There seems to be loads of them.'

At her desk, Lisa was concentrating hard, as were all the team. Now they had something to get their teeth into, they weren't giving up.

Unwilling to disturb anyone, Nash realized he would have to be the barista and headed for the kitchen.

When he returned carrying a tray of coffee, Lisa called to him, 'Mike, come and look at this.' She grinned.

He handed out the mugs and came to look over Lisa's shoulder. 'What have you found?'

On screen was a picture of a wooden chalet, surrounded by woodland. It had a ramp to the door and the external veranda. Lisa moved the cursor, and other images appeared showing a large open-plan kitchen and lounge, two good-sized bedrooms and a large bathroom equipped for a disabled person's use. The final image showed the location on which it was sited — at the furthest, and probably quietest, area of the holiday park.

'That looks interesting.'

The others came to take a look, all telling Nash it presented a better option than anything they had found.

'How did you find that?' Clara asked.

'I used a booking site, like you do when you're looking for a hotel to go on holiday. I kept setting different parameters until it eventually showed this one. I then went to the park's website to get more details.'

Lisa looked up to see Viv shaking his head. 'Sorry to spoil it for you, Lisa, but have you seen that wording there?' He pointed at the screen.

'Damn, I didn't see that.'

The terms and conditions running along the bottom of the screen clearly stated that the maximum occupation was twenty-eight days.

'Has anyone got anything yet that looks as good a potential as this?' Nash asked.

There was no response.

'OK, I'll get Steve to send a uniform round to the site office with the photograph and ask the question.'

* * *

In the office of Ramsdale Holiday Village, the owner's wife was seated at the reception desk. She was minding the shop, as her husband was supervising repair work to one of the lodges on the furthermost extremity of the park. To while away her time, she was reading, or to be more exact scanning, the most recent edition of the *Netherdale Gazette*. Her reading was interrupted when she heard the door opening, and looked up to see two uniformed police officers entering the building. One of them approached the desk and asked to speak to the owner.

'I'm afraid he's not here at the moment, but I can get him if it's urgent. Alternatively, is it something I can help you with? I'm his wife, and also his secretary.'

'It's nothing urgent.' He smiled. 'We're trying to trace a man who we hope can assist us with our enquiries.'

The woman looked horrified.

'It's nothing major,' he said, attempting to mollify her. 'He will probably be travelling with his wife, who we know to be severely disabled, which would limit the number of places they can stay.'

As he was speaking, the officer placed the photograph of Julian Parker on the desk. The woman stared at it for a few seconds and then gasped with surprise. 'Oh. That's Mr Berry. Such a lovely man, always pays his rent on time. Shame about his poor wife, though.'

'How long have they been staying here?' The officer tried to keep the conversation on a casual level.

'I'm not sure.' She looked flustered. 'My husband would be able to help with that.' She forced a laugh and shook her head. 'But of course, we've only just opened for the season.' She tutted. 'Silly me.'

Having obtained the details and location of the lodge, the officers left. 'Secretary?' one of them said. 'I wouldn't let her work for me. She doesn't know what she's doing — or she's hiding something.'

What nobody knew was that had the officers arrived at Ramsdale Holiday Village half an hour earlier, Julian Parker would still have been on-site. They would have found him beside his wife, reading a handwritten note from Olivia, effectively a love letter.

As he'd driven away from the lodge that had been his and Olivia's home, Julian's heart was heavy, because he knew he was now completely alone. Olivia's note was in his pocket — the tears would come later. Only one task remained, the greatest of all they had set out to achieve, and he would have to accomplish it without support — either that, or die in the attempt.

CHAPTER THIRTY-THREE

A few minutes after the officer placed the photo on the desk, Mike Nash and the team at Helmsdale received the news they had been waiting and hoping for. Julian Parker and his wife had been traced, and in fact had been living slap bang in the middle of their area while all the murders had been carried out.

They needed to speak to the couple, and soon, to eliminate them or establish if they were responsible. Any doubt as to the identity of the persons wreaking vengeance on the worst kind of perverts would be either confirmed or denied.

Nash and Clara drove to the holiday village with Viv and Adil following.

They passed the patrol car Nash had requested remain at the entrance to the site and approached Bramhope Lodge, identified by the park owner's wife as the one where Julian and Olivia were staying.

'It seems quiet,' Clara said, as she looked across the site. 'I suppose most occupants will be out for the day. There aren't many cars around.'

'That's as well. We don't want a crowd gathering for what could turn out to be nothing.'

'Is that what you think?'

'We'll soon find out,' Nash replied, as he headed for the door.

When there was no response to his repeated knocking, he reached forward and tried the door handle, which turned easily. They entered the building.

* * *

When Pearce and Hassan arrived, Nash was standing outside with Clara and told the DCs, 'There's a body inside. It appears to be Olivia Parker. She's in the bedroom, and it looks as though she's been laid respectfully on the bed. There's a child's teddy bear alongside her and a single rose.'

'Clara, will you ring Steve Meadows, please? We need Mexican Pete and a CSI team here pronto. I'm not taking any chances. Viv, there's a massive computer system set-up in there; get your shoes covered and go in and have a look at it, will you? See if there's anything that will help us find Parker.'

Viv did as instructed, adding his gloves. The computer screen lit up at his touch, with several tabs open. He clicked the first one and stared at the document — it was a suicide note.

My name is Olivia and I am married to Julian Parker. Three years ago our wonderful daughter Delia, aged nine years, was abducted, brutally raped and left for dead. It took fourteen weeks for her to die, and during that time I was out of my mind with worry. After we had brought her home to be nursed, I drank too much, crashed the car and have suffered my own punishment for doing so.

I have coped with the pain, both mental and physical, from the internal injuries, by using my skills to rid the area of these perverted monsters while I search for our daughter's murderer. If I could have wielded the knife myself, I would have done so.

I have searched the network they use and have now found the person responsible.

I have left two tabs open on this computer so that you, the police, can deal with the rest. There you will find all the details you need.

A word of warning — be careful how you extract the information.

I have installed a virus which is set to destroy this evil network twenty-four hours after the first tab has been opened.

Now I have succeeded in my task, I can stop the pain. I only have a matter of weeks left to live and to save any more heartache for my husband, I have chosen to go now, peacefully.

Julian has loved and cared for me these past years and I believe I have cared for him by uncovering the website and revealing the name of the man responsible for our despair.

Julian knows nothing of the severity of my condition or of my intention. I only want to spare him further pain by ending this myself. I am sure he will understand.

What Julian does know is that I love him as much as we both loved our daughter. I have reminded him of this in the personal letter I have left for him.

My last wish is that he kills the monster.

Olivia Parker

Viv clicked on the next tab. It showed a website advertising services for perverts and paedophiles, inviting membership. Those interested were to apply with a headshot and a pseudonym, along with a list of preferences.

Viv was disgusted, but knew the information held on the site could prove very beneficial to the police as a whole. He would have to work fast.

The next tab was different. It showed a man, listing his achievements and a list of girls' names, along with explicit photographs. Among them Viv read the name 'Delia', which was highlighted, obviously by Olivia Parker.

Viv went outside and told Nash about the suicide note. 'She mentions leaving a letter for her husband, but I can't see one. I assume he must have found her after she killed herself. He has to be the one who laid the rose on her, who else could it be?'

Viv then revealed the computer contents. 'It's time-sensitive,' he added. 'Not only were they destroying the paedophiles physically, but she has literally set the site to self-destruct — soon.'

'OK, wait for Forensics and make sure they know not to touch anything. You get what you can from the computer.'

Viv held up his car keys, and indicated a small flash drive attached. 'Already done. I always carry this. You never know when it might be needed. I've copied the site and taken photos on my phone, just in case.'

Nash nodded. 'That was quick thinking. Thanks, Viv.'

He turned to Adil. 'You're with Clara and me. We're going to talk to the site owner's wife, and if she can tell us what I hope to hear, we'll need your technical expertise.'

Hassan frowned, puzzled by this. 'What are you hoping she'll tell us?'

'I'm hoping the park has CCTV cameras, so we can gauge what's been happening at Bramhope Lodge, and possibly even give some clue as to whether Julian Parker has been here recently. If that's so, with luck, we might even be able to pick up the number plate of the car he's driving.'

'They do. I noticed cameras as we arrived. Let's just hope they're operational and not just there for show.'

* * *

The woman's reply to Nash's opening question provided confirmation, if any was needed, that they were on the right lines. 'Can you tell us more about the couple who currently occupy Bramhope Lodge?'

'They're registered as Mr and Mrs Berry.' She hesitated. 'More than that, I can't say.'

'Do you have a home address listed, or details of a debit or credit card they used to pay with?'

Before she could stop herself, the woman said, 'No, they've paid cash, every month.'

By her expression, Nash knew she wished they would leave. Something was bothering her, so he pressed on. 'Every month?'

'Sorry, my mistake, it was empty. Erm, that's when we were closed, er, out of season.' She was starting to panic. 'I really think you ought to speak to my husband.'

'I don't think that's necessary. What about future bookings? I expect your lodges are very popular.'

She seemed to relax. 'Oh, yes, we have several enquiries and bookings for this spring and summer.'

'In that case, just give us those details for Bramhope Lodge.'

Having looked on the computer, she smiled before she told the detectives, 'A Mr and Mrs Ramsay.'

'And after them?'

'Mr and Mrs Oliver.'

'And?' Nash asked.

'Mr and Mrs Kerridge.'

Nash kept his face straight — this woman clearly had no interest in cooking shows. No doubt the site owners had broken some rule or licence regulation. But despite this, they had confirmation that the man they were seeking was using the aliases of celebrity chefs to protect his real identity.

The office door flew open and her husband dashed in. 'What's going on? There are police everywhere.'

'And you are?' Nash asked.

'I'm the owner.'

'Good. Now, I'd like you to give my colleague here access to your CCTV footage. This is a matter of urgency.'

'But what's this about?'

'Police business,' was all Nash would reveal.

As Hassan was viewing the camera images, Clara told Nash, 'That was a bit cheeky, don't you think? Using the names of fellow chefs as cover.'

Nash agreed. 'I wonder what Mary Berry, Gordon Ramsay, Jamie Oliver and Tom Kerridge would say if they were told about it?'

'I dread to think about the language in Gordon Ramsay's case,' Clara replied.

'Alternatively, they might find it highly amusing.'

* * *

It didn't take Adil long to uncover all the information the CCTV could provide. Using this, and having Tom Pratt access the DVLA computer, they had confirmation Julian Parker was driving a Ford Tourneo. By the time Ramirez and the CSI team arrived at the holiday park, the registration details had been added to the ANPR system, with a warning to observe, but not to attempt to stop, the vehicle.

As they were doing that, headquarters Control staff, together with civilian support officers, were checking cameras. It was the latter activity which provided the first positive information. The results were puzzling, and as the news was fed back to the detectives, they tried to make sense of it.

Tom Pratt conveyed the details. 'The vehicle was picked up on Daleside Avenue. It was last spotted on the outskirts of town, travelling towards the Winfield estate. Paul Grant has dispatched a couple of unmarked cars to cruise along that stretch of road and see if they can pick up anything more recent.'

At the holiday park, Nash put in a call to the ARU team and asked them to be on standby. 'I get the feeling you might be needed soon, but we're waiting for an update,' he told their leader. 'If I'm right, this could be time-critical.'

Only minutes later, he received a call.

'Right,' he told the detectives, 'Julian Parker's Ford has just pulled up outside a cottage at the foot of Riven Scar, below Black Fell Foss. Tom Pratt checked and it's a holiday home, belongs to someone called Clive Morton who lives in the West Country.'

'I recognize that name,' Adil said. 'He was co-owner of the restaurant with Parker.'

'We need to head there immediately. Clara,' — he threw her his car keys — 'you drive.'

As they were travelling, Nash phoned the ARU chief and reported their position, then he phoned Ruth Edwards to make her aware.

Clara asked Nash if he thought Clive Morton might be Julian Parker's principal target.

'I certainly do, because while we were waiting for Mexican Pete and his body-snatchers to arrive, Viv checked Olivia Parker's computer. She had brought up Clive Morton's name, along with some extremely unsavoury facts in which Julian and Olivia's daughter Delia's name was listed. I firmly believe they have discovered it was Morton who killed Delia. Now Julian knows, he intends to make him pay for it.'

'Aren't you tempted to let him get on with it and arrest him once he's done the deed?'

'Very tempted, but that's not what we're paid for.'

* * *

Within half an hour, they had the cottage surrounded. Led by two ARU officers, Nash and Mironova approached the front door, while their colleagues looked on nervously. As they got to the entrance, Pearce and Hassan had launched their drones, and before the officers knocked on the door, they provided what turned out to be a critical update.

'Mike, get round the back,' Pearce said, urgently. 'The drones show the garden and the River Helm. It's in full spate after the heavy rain. Three people are standing on the river bank. It looks as if this Morton character is being confronted by Parker. Morton's holding a child in front of him, using her as a shield. Parker has a pistol in one hand and a knife in the other.'

Caution was vital, but so was speed. The officers raced round the building.

Nash noticed the person held by Morton was a young girl, still not in her teens, he guessed. She was clearly in distress, her wrists bound, her mouth covered in tape.

Nash had just begun to speak, issuing the formal caution, when there was a flurry of movement. Parker stepped forward out of the firing line of the ARU officers, the knife raised.

His downward stroke with the knife sliced through the tape binding the captive girl's wrists. At the same time, he raised the pistol. Before he could fire, Morton swung his prisoner out over the river bank, clearly intending to drop her in the water.

Parker moved again, to the far side of Morton, trying to free the girl. For a second, he was in the sights of the ARU officers, one of whom shouted a warning. When a gun fired, it was not Parker but Morton who was hit. He released his hold on the girl.

Her muted squeal of distress as she plunged into the water caused Nash to run, casting off his jacket and shoes.

He dived into the river and swam towards where the girl was being swept away. He grasped one of her ankles and pulled her towards him, feeling for and removing the tape covering her mouth. Before he could swim towards the shore with his burden, the fast-flowing river carried them rapidly downstream.

Above them, Morton fell to the ground, and before the armed officers could fire again, Parker turned and dived off the bank into the river and was soon lost to view.

Clara called on Viv and Adil to concentrate their drones on the river below the cottage. The order was unnecessary — both men had been watching the activity on their monitors.

For what seemed an age, they scoured the stretch of water without anything to report.

Nash was buffeted from side to side by the velocity of the current, but maintained a tight grip on the girl. He tried to get near the bank, but felt a sharp pain in his leg and, moments later, another in his shoulder as he hit the underwater rocks. Then his head collided with something hard, and he felt consciousness beginning to drain away. He concentrated his ebbing strength on reaching the riverbank. He felt the girl being snatched away. Then consciousness left him.

All Mironova and the ARU officers could do was wait and hope.

More than ten minutes passed, which to Clara seemed like an hour, before Viv Pearce spotted something. Hidden by the undergrowth alongside the river, he could make out a possible heat source. He prayed it wasn't just local wildlife.

As quickly as safety would allow, the detectives and other officers scrambled along the bank until they reached the spot.

There, they found two bodies.

CHAPTER THIRTY-FOUR

Clara remembered the rest of that day as a mixture of fluctuating emotions coupled with an unending stream of phone calls. Having summoned the ambulance service, she then contacted headquarters, to report developments to the chief constable.

Trying to maintain her composure, Clara told her, 'Mike has suffered significant injuries. I —' she stammered, 'I can't get any info from the paramedics. They're blue-lighting him to Netherdale General. And they've taken a young girl, name unknown, who Mike rescued. They're both unconscious.' Clara bit back a sob, before adding, 'We believe Julian Parker has drowned, and Clive Morton, who we suspect to be the ringleader of the Dark Web network of evil, is dead.'

'Was this down to our ARU team?'

'No, he received a gunshot wound, but that was only a graze. It was Julian Parker's knife. He severed Morton's jugular vein just before he dived into the river.'

The chief constable's response was pragmatic, bordering on the callous. 'It sounds as if he'll be no loss, and neither will the Parker man. Keep me posted. I'll get Jackie, then we'll head to the General. I'll ring Alondra.'

'No, please, I'll do that, Ruth. I have her number on my phone.' She ended the call.

The chief constable's brow creased with concern as she tried to assimilate all she had been told. And Clara had called her 'Ruth', which wasn't proper procedure at all, but in these circumstances, quite understandable.

Clara's next task was one of the most difficult she had ever undertaken. As she told Alondra what happened, she emphasized Mike's extreme courage. 'He dived straight into the river to rescue the child, despite it being in full torrent.'

* * *

Regaining consciousness brought pain. Nash wanted to open his eyes, but had a splitting headache. In addition to that, his shoulder felt as if it was being wrenched by some invisible force, and his left leg felt heavier than the right one. Someone was holding his hand. Eventually, curiosity overcame the pain, and he blinked, forcing his eyes open. He was in a large room, painted white, and big though it was, the space seemed crowded as he tried to focus.

One by one, he recognized the inhabitants. Alondra was by his bedside, along with Clara, plus a gentleman in a white coat with a stethoscope dangling from his neck, and a woman in a blue uniform.

From the doctor, he learned that he had been knocked unconscious while attempting to rescue a child from the river. In the process, he had acquired a dislocated shoulder, a severe laceration to his scalp, several cracked ribs and a broken leg, which was now in plaster.

'The girl — I lost the girl!' he stammered.

'No, no, you saved her,' Clara reassured him. 'She's safe, Mike.'

The medics left the room and Nash squeezed Alondra's hand. He tried to smile, but his head hurt.

'I'll leave you for a moment,' Clara said, and headed for the door.

'Where's Lucy?' Nash said, panicked.

'It's OK, Mike, she's in the village with Jonas. I had no option. I phoned the school; Daniel's on his way. The headmaster is arranging transport. I didn't know what I was going to find when I got here. The officer who brought me didn't have any details.'

'You had an escort?'

'No, I had a chauffeur, speeding through Netherdale with the blue lights on.' She shivered. 'Apparently the chief constable had instructed him to get me here as quickly as possible. I don't think she realized how much worse that made the situation for me.' She stared at him, tears running down her face. 'Mike, I thought you were dead.'

Nash gently reached out, wiped the tears away and cupped her chin. 'Alondra, darling, I love you and I'm not going anywhere.'

She smiled. 'Yes, you are — home. And when they discharge you, you'll be in my care, and perhaps I can convince you of the error of your ways.'

At that moment, the door flew open and Daniel careered into the room, accompanied by Clara. 'Pa, what have you done?'

'I'm OK, son, I'm OK.'

Clara smiled at the family reunion. 'Sorry, but I have to leave and start work trying to climb the paperwork mountain.' As she turned to go, she fleetingly rested her hand on Alondra's shoulder, then on Daniel's. 'Look after the hero, and whatever happens, don't let him use nasty four-letter words such as "work".'

* * *

Once she had gone, Nash looked apprehensively at his wife and son, clearly anticipating a rebuke for what they must have regarded as a rash act, taking such an unnecessary risk. He was surprised, however, by Alondra's opening remark, backed by Daniel's contribution.

'Clara's right,' Alondra told him. 'You are a true hero, Mike, and I'm so proud of what you did. It is obvious that, but for your action, the poor girl would have drowned.'

'I agree, Pa. It must have taken real guts to jump in the river like that. I saw the Helm when I was on the way here, and all that rain has caused it to become a raging torrent. I've always been proud of you, but this takes my admiration to another level.'

'You know I should shout at you for what you did,' Alondra said. 'You take the most terrible risks, and I think you sometimes forget about us, your family.' Again, tears streamed down her face.

Nash looked at her. 'I think you've said something like that before.'

'Yes, and I will keep on saying it until you stop trying to kill yourself.' She squeezed his hand, then she smiled and stroked his face. 'I'm sorry, but it was such a shock when I got the call from Clara. I know it's your job to help people and catch criminals, but can't you let someone younger take the risks?'

'You're really beginning to sound like Clara. I'm not that old!'

Eventually, at the insistence of the sister in charge, his family had to leave. Once they'd gone, he revisited what he could remember of the riverbank scene. The painkillers and sedatives began to take effect, and he drifted off to sleep before he could continue his thought processes.

* * *

The following day he had a succession of visitors. From Clara, he learned what had happened after his rescue attempt. In the process he was told the young girl's details, plus the fact that she had been unharmed, either by Morton or by her river ordeal. She told him Morton was dead and was able to report on some extremely unpleasant findings from within his house, the sort referred to loosely as 'snuff porn'.

Clara also told him what had happened to Parker. 'There's been a search of the river, which is ongoing, but the belief is that Julian Parker was swept away and drowned.'

Later, Ruth Edwards arrived and discussed the case, assuring him the entire force from Netherdale and Helmsdale sent their regards. Before she left, she told Nash he was on sick leave for the foreseeable future, at least until his leg healed.

'And don't try and convince me you can work from your desk. Remember your office is on the first floor — and before you ask, I will not authorize funding for an elevator. After your discharge from hospital, you will remain at home, get fit and well, and . . . and . . . and play with your daughter.'

A while later, a couple with a young girl were shown into his room. The girl smiled at him. 'Mr Nash, I'm Beth. I've come to say thank you for saving me.'

'You're very welcome. I'm just glad you're OK,' Nash told her. 'It was quite a swim we had.'

The girl giggled and smiled.

Her mother took up the conversation. 'The doctors told us she swallowed a lot of water, but physically she's fine. We wanted to thank you before we go home,' the mother said, tears welling in her eyes as she turned and left the room with the girl.

Her father remained to explain. 'Beth was abducted as she walked home from school two days ago. She's unharmed, thanks to you, and we don't know how we can thank you enough for saving our daughter. She will need some counselling for a while, to help her recover from that pervert's actions, but at least he hadn't touched her.' He reached out and shook Nash's hand, nodded, turned and left.

Late afternoon brought an unexpected visitor. There was a gentle knock on the door, and a voice Nash had no difficulty recognizing called out, 'Are you decent?'

The former chief constable Gloria O'Donnell walked into the room clutching a bunch of grapes. 'I see you still don't follow the rules,' she said pointedly, as she took a seat alongside his bed. 'What on earth possessed you, Mike?'

'I didn't think.'

'No, you never did.' She smiled. 'How are you?'

'Been better.'

'You think so? I suppose we have to be grateful that this time you weren't shot.'

'Don't remind me of that.' Nash knew she recalled the incident several years ago when his life had been at risk. 'Honestly, I'll be OK once I'm out of here. If it wasn't for the head injury, I'd have been home.'

'Well, at least this time you have a wife to look after you.'

Nash smiled. 'And believe me, I know how lucky I am.'

'I brought this.' She handed him the latest edition of the *Netherdale Gazette*, the banner headline HERO OF THE HOUR emblazoned across the top.

'Becky?' Nash asked.

'Oh yes. My goddaughter is having a field day with this. She beat the nationals with the story and is delighted. She sends her best wishes, by the way.'

'Tell her I'm glad to be of service.' He sighed and attempted to shake his head, but gave up.

They chatted for a while about her retirement, and the promised travels she had taken with her husband, before she said she must leave. 'You need your rest, so get well soon, and give my regards to Alondra.' She patted his hand and headed for the door.

'Thank you for coming,' Nash said, as his eyelids began to droop once more. Before sleep overcame him, he remembered something Clara had said that didn't seem to fit with what little he could recall of the dramatic event. She'd told him they believed Julian Parker had been swept away and drowned. But although he couldn't be certain, he seemed to remember someone gripping him firmly by the arms and dragging him out of the water onto the bank. And how did the girl get there?

Next morning, moving with extreme caution, he peered at his upper arms and saw bruising, about the size of a man's hand. He decided not to mention this to anyone.

* * *

Sergeant Steve Meadows was in reception at Helmsdale Police Station when the phone rang. He listened to what the caller had to say, making notes as he went along, before responding, 'I'll have someone out there as soon as possible.'

Having ended the call, Meadows sprinted upstairs to the CID suite. With Pearce on his day off and Hassan on holiday, Mike Nash, recently returned to duty, was there, along with DS Mironova and DC Andrews. They were the only detectives in residence, and Nash's duties were curtailed by the chief constable's limitations.

'For a while, I want you on office duties only,' she had told him firmly. 'Unless it's a double murder. Then I *might* excuse you going out and about.'

Steve entered the general office and told them, 'I've just had a call from Professor Carol Kirby, an archaeologist. She's in charge of a dig taking place near Gorton Village, where they believe there's a Stone Age settlement. This morning, one of her team uncovered some human remains, in the form of a skeleton.'

'Can't uniform deal with that, Steve?' Clara asked. 'I believe it's not uncommon to find such things when archaeologists are at work.'

'I'm afraid it's not quite as straightforward as that, Clara.'

'Why not?' Lisa asked.

'Professor Kirby is convinced the remains are modern, despite it being skeletal, and certainly nothing to do with the settlement, or a Stone Age burial site.'

He took a deep breath before continuing, 'The reason she believes the remains are more recent is there's what appears to be bullet hole in the skull.'

EPILOGUE

The following March, as Easter approached, it was the start of the tourist season on the Greek islands. In a taverna on one of the smaller islands, the recently appointed chef took a break from readying his kitchen. He was sitting outdoors, coffee to hand, reading a newspaper online. It was not a local publication, but the *Netherdale Gazette*. The lead article, along with an accompanying photo, had caught and held his attention.

The photograph showed a smiling man in police officer's dress uniform with a handsome woman alongside him, holding a small infant by the hand. Also in the picture was a smartly dressed teenage boy.

The caption over the article read,

*DI MIKE NASH RECEIVES POLICE
MEDAL FOR BRAVERY*

As he closed his laptop down, Julian Parker murmured, 'Good for you, Mike, you deserve it — in spades.'

THE END

ACKNOWLEDGEMENTS

With any book there is always an element of research. On this occasion, I did not consult with any relevant authority on the topic covered. I did my own research. I can say that only by referencing the atrocities I discovered was I able to convey the actions of the men involved in this hideous abuse.

There are, however, several people who do require acknowledgement, namely my go-to 'tech-guy', Jamie Clements, whose assistance into the workings of the Dark Web and networks was invaluable.

My reader, Wendy McPhee, who told me the first draft was below standard, enabling me to write, what I now consider to be, a much better plot.

All the helpful and encouraging staff at Joffe deserve my thanks — Laura, Kate, and my editors Jodi and Matthew, the cover designer, the production team and the marketing department, far too many to name.

And of course there's Val, the in-house editor, the person that is behind me all the time. She edits, she argues the point until the book is fit for purpose, and without her there would be no more Nash.

THE JOFFE BOOKS STORY

We began in 2014 when Jasper agreed to publish his mum's much-rejected romance novel and it became a bestseller.

Since then we've grown into the largest independent publisher in the UK. We're extremely proud to publish some of the very best writers in the world, including Joy Ellis, Faith Martin, Caro Ramsay, Helen Forrester, Simon Brett and Robert Goddard. Everyone at Joffe Books loves reading and we never forget that it all begins with the magic of an author telling a story.

We are proud to publish talented first-time authors, as well as established writers whose books we love introducing to a new generation of readers.

We won Trade Publisher of the Year at the Independent Publishing Awards in 2023 and Best Publisher Award in 2024 at the People's Book Prize. We have been shortlisted for Independent Publisher of the Year at the British Book Awards for the last five years, and were shortlisted for the Diversity and Inclusivity Award at the 2022 Independent Publishing Awards. In 2023 we were shortlisted for Publisher of the Year at the RNA Industry Awards, and in 2024 we were shortlisted at the CWA Daggers for the Best Crime and Mystery Publisher.

We built this company with your help, and we love to hear from you, so please email us about absolutely anything bookish at feedback@joffebooks.com.

If you want to receive free books every Friday and hear about all our new releases, join our mailing list here: www.joffebooks.com/freebooks.

And when you tell your friends about us, just remember: it's pronounced Joffe as in coffee or toffee!

www.ingramcontent.com/pod-product-compliance
Ingram Content Group UK Ltd.
Pitfield, Milton Keynes, MK11 3LW, UK
UKHW020026050825

7227UKWH00004B/242